The
Camera's
Eye

Judith Kirscht

New Libri Press

This is a work of fiction. Nothing is in it that has not been imagined.

Copyright © 2017 by Judith Kirscht

Cover Copyright © 2017 by New Libri Press

ISBN: 978-1-61469-063-4

Published in 2017 by New Libri Press
Seattle, WA 98103
www.newlibri.com

New Libri Press is a small independent press dedicated to publishing new authors and independent authors in both eBook and traditional formats.

The
Camera's
Eye

Acknowledgments

I am grateful, as always, for the help of my fellow writers of the Skagit Valley Writers League: Serena DuBois, Helen Gregory-Nopson, and Patricia Cowgill. For her patience in putting up with and encouraging a writer, I thank my housemate, Joyce Kleinholz. For their advice on my continued marketing efforts, I'm grateful to my tech guru, Kate Williams and publicist, Alice Acheson. Finally, for their continued faith in my authorship, I thank both Michael Muller and Stasa Fritz of New Libri Press.

Chapter 1

The crash sat Veronica Lorimer up in her bed. A second one, followed by a revving engine and spurt of gravel from spinning tires, sent her toward the stairs, pulling on a robe as she went. Half way down, she stopped, staring. Cold rushed in through a gaping black hole where the window had been, and a pair of rocks lay on the rug in a pool of shards, glistening in the porch light.

"Lotti?" Her call was a hoarse whisper as shock opened a vast space around her, and her head spun. *Who? Why?* People threw rocks to make other people leave—Muslims, Blacks, Asians—anyone different. Not gray-haired white ladies who looked like English teachers.

"Charlotte!" Her voice expressed her impatience this time, but there was no response from the back bedroom where Lotti slept with her hearing aids out.

She stared out into the blackness until her eyeballs burned, but could make out nothing but the wall of trees silhouetted against the night sky. She clenched her teeth to stop the shivering as the November air penetrated her robe. Evergreens dripped from the night's rain, pocking the silence. Just a small, sleeping island in the Puget Sound.

Her gaze swept the room searching for some reason and landed on her camera—Constance the Nikon—sitting on the coffee table. Was that it? For years Constance had captured whatever caught her eye with no thought of consequences. Some secret laid bare? Veronica mentally scanned the photos laid out on her work table for her next book. What had she exposed? Veronica slammed her mind shut as the faces of her children rose, dimmed by the wall of silence they'd imposed. No. Surely not after all this time. Not rock throwing.

What then? Driven by the wrongness, the need to make sense, she pulled on the rain boots that stood next to the front door and crunched through broken glass through the kitchen to the glassed-in porch that was her studio.

She turned on the light, then turned it off again. Grabbing the flashlight off the sill, she yanked open the back door—and shrieked as a snarling body streaked past her.

"Trix!" she gasped. "Great Scott! Are you trying to kill me, too?" She picked up the tiger cat and held him to her face. "Did we leave you out? Well, I'm sorry about that, but you're too old for such shenanigans." She warmed her against her chest. "And God knows, so am I." With her free hand, she swept the clearing behind the house with her light. Nothing but grass turned green now with fall rains, the deserted stubble of November garden beds and the surrounding protective wall of evergreens that now seemed to hide intruders. Charlotte was right; they needed floodlights. She closed the door and turned the light on again, depositing Trix on the corner of her drawing table, cocking her head at noises Veronica couldn't hear.

She shivered again and pulled her robe around her more tightly. *Damn it, Charlotte, where are you?* She headed for the stairs but stopped in spite of herself at the photos that stared up at her from the worktable. *It's you! It must be.* Again the never far submerged images of her children rose, accusing. She shook them off. For ten years she'd carried their hostility in her bones; it had become old with the wearing. Surely not an explanation for this sudden outburst of rage. Something else.

She began examining her photos, one by one. A pair at the ferry rail became lovers escaping from their spouses. A barn, covered in moss and crumbling into the earth, revealed too many footprints around it. A meth lab? A pair of children at play on the beach were transformed into kidnap victims. Only the reflection of Mt. Baker in the Sound refused to turn sinister. Unless that speck of a boat—*don't* be *absurd.* Drifting into paranoia wouldn't help.

Who said it was this bunch of pictures, anyway? Why not any of the photos in her published books? Once her pictures were published they separated themselves from her on-going life the way those in the family album captured the finished past. But her conviction that the rock thrower—or throwers—had spotted her with the camera refused to fade.

What about pictures she'd discarded or even those not taken? She emptied her basket of discards onto the floor, spread them out and sank onto the couch to stare at them. A picture of a fishing boat brought back her walk along the bay. Was that a missing husband setting crab pots? An escapee from some long-ago crime? The bed-and-breakfast out on Summers Point—did the red car in the yard mark the location of a wife fleeing from a violent lover? The photos took her along the beach, past abandoned coolers, tennis shoes, and buoys among the driftwood, telling tales of who-knew-what disasters.

Then there was the decaying queen of a house whose image she could never get right. A dozen times at least she'd driven into the lane at the tip of the island to walk its perimeter looking for the right shot. Always it had been deserted. Was someone there? She picked up a photo she'd discarded because its light was flat and examined it more closely. A window next to the porch was broken—recently? She sat back, thinking of the boy who wandered the woods on a nearby island, breaking into houses. The daily television news stories had touched her, for her own son had wandered that way, rootless and lost, after her husband, Simon, died. Her body went numb as the futile hours of searching came back. But David had vanished. Had her son, too, become a vagrant, stealing food from vacant houses to survive? She often awoke in the night with such dreams. Wherever he was, he was no boy now, but her heart ached for all such boys, cut loose in the world too soon. This one had been caught once, but managed to get free. Since then he'd proved to be a master of escape.

She stared at the picture, knowing that such a boy might well heave a rock at the world that had abandoned him. Was that door open a crack?

"Roni? What on earth? My God, what happened?" Charlotte's voice from the stairs brought her head up.

"Careful!" Veronica headed back through the kitchen to intercept her. "Don't come through there barefoot."

"Those are rocks!" Charlotte stood, tall, angular and barefoot at the bottom of the stairs. "Someone threw rocks through our window?"

"They did. About a half hour ago."

"You've been up—why didn't you call me, for heaven's sake?"

Veronica raised her hand to cut her off. "I did. I was coming to get you, but ..." she stopped as she remembered the cause of her detour. She didn't want to hear another complaint about Constance's recklessness.

But Charlotte had fallen silent, staring at the shards of broken glass. Then she sat down on the steps. "Bruno Gutterman."

"What?"

"Bruno." She closed her eyes, then opened them. "Ten years. He's out of prison."

Veronica opened her mouth and closed it again. Why had it never occurred to her that Charlotte might be the target? Charlotte, after a career prosecuting criminals was, after all, the likelier. Except that she had practiced under her maiden name. "How could he find you, even assuming he wanted to? I know he threatened to get even, but throwing rocks? That's greasy kid stuff, Charlotte."

"Or angry mob stuff," her friend muttered.

"What angry mob?" Her mind brought up the week's television images of fist-shaking demagogues decrying the social chaos brought on by homosexuals and immigrants. "Here on the island? Nothing's happened here."

Charlotte looked at her a moment, then leapt to her feet. "It's freezing. I'm going to get dressed. Have you called the police?"

"No. Lotti? What are you thinking?"

Charlotte stopped and wrapped her arms around herself before she spoke. "I'm thinking about your book launching last week."

"What?" Veronica's mind scanned the bookstore crowd—polite interest, friendly encouragement, glances of passing customers. "Why? What did you see?"

"A pair of women around the corner behind the first set of bookshelves, looking through your book. Very tight-lipped."

"Ah?" Veronica considered without much surprise. Her pictures often brought that sort of disapproval; they were not all intended to quiet the spirit. "Not the sort to pitch rocks, surely."

But Charlotte had vanished up the stairs, leaving the acrid smell of possibility in her wake and awakening again the memory of her children's bitter accusations. Her friend had always been far charier of the way others saw them; her work had exposed her to the nastier side of humanity, and she lived with the echo of curses and threats: "You just wait…" "I'll get you …" "Remember me, I'm coming back …" But in their five years on this island, no one had treated them as anything but the pair of aging widows they were. She searched her memory, bringing up the faces of neighbors and shopkeepers to sense anything amiss. Nothing.

She went back to the porch, where the pictures confronted her like so many turned rocks. The quiet little island where they'd retreated suddenly teemed with secret crimes and hatreds. She'd always put Constance between herself and the images she caught. Constance's eye caught the emotions emitted by each scene, object or person; their source, once captured, faded into obscurity. Now she looked at the old house again and thought of the boy. If she called the police, and he was living in that house, his life as a boy would be over. The papers had said they would treat him as an adult when they caught him again. But Charlotte's question had stuck to her bones. The rock was police business.

She looked at her watch. Seven o'clock. If she didn't call, Charlotte would. Well, the clearing was gray with dawn now; it wasn't the middle of the night, anymore. They wouldn't come with sirens. She went to the phone.

"Grafton Island Sheriff's Office," a tired voice answered.

"Someone has thrown rocks through our front window!" Veronica exclaimed.

"Name and address …?" The voice faded into a yawn.

She rattled off the information, then had to repeat it, spelling out their last names.

"Anything taken?"

"Taken? What does …" She broke off to snort. "What burglar would wake the house by smashing a window, for heaven's sake?" She stopped to control her mounting frustration. "Look, send someone out, will you?"

"When I have a deputy in the area, ma'am." His voice soothed, like placating a child. Faced with the man's patronizing, the chill of the attack returned. She shook it off and went upstairs to find warm clothes.

By the time the officer arrived a half hour later, Veronica and Charlotte were both booted and jacketed, armored against the cold flowing through the gaping hole.

"I'm Deputy Hansen. Hear you've had some trouble here." He was clean-faced and young. His eyes moved from the mess on the floor to the pair of them, then he scratched his head as though embarrassed. "You live out here alone? Just the two of you?"

"Without husbands, you mean? What's your point?" Charlotte had retrieved her prosecuting attorney voice.

"Just looking at the facts, Ma'am." He dug out his notebook and wrote. "You're—ahh—partners, then?" he mumbled, still looking at the page.

"What? We're friends." Veronica folded her arms across her ample chest and gave him the full value of her height, which exceeded his by two inches. Trix appeared and circled his ankles, arching her back. "And what does that have to do with anything?"

"Don't know, Ma'am." He put his notebook back in his pocket, not meeting her eyes. "Just thinking how it might look to others—if you know what I mean."

"No, I don't," Charlotte objected. "Suppose you tell me."

"Well, I expect there are some that might take exception." He met her gaze then dropped his to the mess on the floor. "Nothing missing, you said."

They stared at his discomfiture without answering.

"Well, I'll report this, ladies. You call us if you see any strangers about the place."

Charlotte's eyes narrowed dangerously. "That's all? No more questions?"

He looked surprised.

"No questions about enemies, other incidents, and such?" Charlotte jammed her fists into her parka pockets.

"Oh. Well, I didn't think ..." He laughed, embarrassed again—or still. "You just don't look the sort—I mean—and it's pretty clear ..."

"Clear? What's clear?" Charlotte challenged.

The deputy stared, his mouth open, as though fishing for words.

"Never mind." Charlotte relented. "I'm a retired attorney—prosecuting attorney." She viewed his shock with pleasure. "And I do have a few leftover enemies, so if you would check, please."

"Yes, Ma'am." He opened his notebook again.

"Bruno Gutterman. He murdered his wife's lover—his right, he insisted. And would return to get even. To teach me my place, I believe he said." She waited while he wrote the name. "And you might check on one Joseph Marchand, who I sent away for beating his wife."

The man's brows went up. "That's all?"

"Mm. That's what he thought."

"No, no," he hastened with a nervous laugh. "I mean anyone else?"

"I'll think about it and give you a call," Charlotte promised.

Veronica watched him scribble down the names. He'd turn to her, next. What was she going to say? Maybe nothing. With his attitude, he'd probably see the sinister possibilities in her pictures as old-lady hysteria. She wasn't in the mood.

"This is Veronica Lorimer, the photographer," Charlotte continued, voiding Veronica's decision to stay silent. Her friend pointed to the coffee table where Veronica's latest book, *The Way We Are*, lay next to the guilty camera. "She launched that at Island Books last week. You may have seen the write-up in yesterday's paper."

The officer's eyes widened as he stared at the cover, then went still. "So that's you." His voice had acquired an edge, and when he looked up his eyes no longer questioned. His whole bearing was that of a man who'd had his opinion confirmed.

Charlotte's eyes narrowed. "You know the book." It was not a question.

"I've seen it." He gave his attention to his notebook without looking at her. "Some of the pictures ..." His voice faded out as he wrote.

"Some of the pictures, what?" Charlotte persisted.

"Caused talk." He snapped the notebook shut. "Well. That's it then." He looked from one to the other of them. "Well, good day, ladies." He swung away.

"What sort of talk?" Charlotte's voice was calm but insistent.

He opened the door then turned to meet Charlotte's cold gaze. "Upset. I'd say definitely upset." He turned away again.

"You wouldn't happen to be a member of Grace Bible Church, would you?" Charlotte's voice pursued him.

"I am, in fact." He turned, surprised. "Odd you should ask."

"Isn't it."

He gave an uncertain smile and left.

When the door had closed after him, Charlotte turned away, slapping her hands against her sides. "So. Your book has offended the good people of Grace Bible Church."

"Where on earth did you come up with that?"

"Their billboard, remember? I pointed it out to you. The sermon—'Homosexuality and Sin.'"

Veronica closed her eyes and let her breath out in a hiss as her children's condemnations echoed from the past. The ogre had risen again. She nodded, finally, in agreement. "His whole attitude changed when he saw it." She considered the iconic Sound scene of water dotted with wooded bits of land disappearing into the distance. The scene was familiar to Grafton Island residents, except that Constance had focused on the black wall of clouds about to eclipse the sun. The photo made the front page of the weekly *Grafton Island Press*.

"That isn't the picture that 'caused talk,' as he put it."

"At Grace Bible Church." Veronica finished. She picked up the book and flipped through, stopping at a picture of a preacher, the cross-crowned steeple rising behind him, his mouth twisted in rage, then flipped to another of the signs proclaiming God's will trampled underfoot by an anonymous mob, and finally to a photo of a gay marriage set against the rising sun.

"Right," Charlotte said over her shoulder. "Any of those will do."

"Well at least it's just one church out of … how many on the island? Four, at least. Not the whole island by a long shot." But the words didn't reassure. She was the target. Her stomach clenched.

"True, but that stuff spreads. The nation is sick with it."

"Are you saying my book is kindling, Lotti?" And why was she acting as though she hadn't suspected the same? Pretending she'd ever tried to stop Constance from showing whatever she thought needed saying.

"Your book is great, Roni—a true picture of our times. But …" She swept her arm across the glass littered scene and didn't finish.

"So I really need to find the culprit. We can't let this go on." She headed back to her photos as though they would reveal more answers.

"Maybe it won't," Charlotte said, following her. "Maybe we're overreacting. Somebody got a bunch of anger out of his system, and it's over." She looked down at the photo of the old house on the point. "Where's this?"

"Coleman Point. You know those stories we've been reading about that boy over on Drummond Island who breaks into empty houses? Norris Stoner, that's his name."

"Yes. You were thinking it might be him?"

"Well, at least it has nothing to do with Grace Bible Church."

"And why would he throw a rock through our window?" Charlotte wasn't to be so easily diverted. "He only breaks into empty houses."

"He was just the first who came to mind. That's all. That and the sense that it was some boy with a huge grudge against the world."

"Like David?" Charlotte's voice was gentle but persistent.

"Like David." She sighed. "And this has nothing to do with him. I know that. It just brings it all back, that's all." Resolutely, she turned her attention to the other pictures. "The problem is that now I don't know what Constance saw in any of these. Someone—whoever pitched those rocks—left me with another pair of eyes. See that car half-hidden in the trees?" She picked up the photo from her discard pile. "Is he an errant husband?"

"Mm." Charlotte looked at the picture, accepting the diversion. "There was a time I'd be able to name you several possibilities."

"Right. And all I saw was a car ruining my picture. This whole thing has left me your eyes. Seeing crimes in every eye. How do you stand it?" She gathered up the pictures and thumped them into a stack. "We need breakfast."

"Too damned cold. Just make coffee—and toast. I'll call the glass company." Charlotte turned toward the phone. Once a marathon runner, she walked stiffly now. Arthritis, yes, but her body said she was as worried as she was angry. She would have named it "stress" and run it off back then—they both would have. Now, the mixture of fear and anger just filled the air and turned the smell of the surrounding evergreens ominous.

"They won't be here until noon," she reported, returning to the kitchen. She fell to silent pacing while Veronica stood, equally silent, watching the coffee pot. "We need a dog."

"You really must be worried." The battle between the responsibility of a pet and freedom was a longstanding issue between them, but she never blamed Charlotte for needing escape more than she did. Photography had always given her a freedom that Charlotte, tied to case, court, and an invalid husband could only dream of. She poured the coffee and buttered the toast.

Charlotte shrugged. "It's probably that boy or some nut from the church crowd, but whoever it is, I'd like to scare them off." She took a decisive bite of toast.

Veronica nodded. "Well, you know I'll never object to a dog."

"Not a puppy." Charlotte's tone was final.

Veronica laughed. "Not a puppy."

Charlotte fell silent again. She was, Veronica knew, still opening up case after case in her mind the way she'd been examining every photo. A dog wouldn't fix that. "We need to find out who did it."

Charlotte looked up from studying her mug. "A pair of old biddies playing detective, you mean? You've been reading too much Agatha Christie."

Veronica gave a laugh. "Maybe. But I need to be doing something."

"It's no game, Roni. And given that deputy's attitude, we have no protection."

"And when have we ever had protection, my friend?" She took the last bite of toast. "Our deceased husbands would say we have that one thing in common—not giving a damn for anyone's warnings. They'd probably be amazed this hadn't happened to us long ago."

Charlotte grinned. "For sure." She rinsed her plate at the sink. "Okay, you're on. Where do we start?"

"That old house. The boy. Just to eliminate that possibility." Veronica picked up her camera. "And because I have no idea how to deal with the church." She looked at the floor. "Leave this mess, for now." She headed for the door.

Charlotte stopped her on the porch. "You'd make a lousy sleuth."

"What?"

"Footprints, my dear."

They found prints in the rain-soaked ground, but obliterated by other feet—Deputy Hansen's, no doubt. There were fresh tire tracks in the gravel of the drive and pock marks where the vehicle had hit the accelerator. The tracks had been blurred by others, undoubtedly the cruiser's. They gave a collective sigh and headed for the car.

Chapter 2

The house on Coleman Point, with its peeling paint and loose shutters, looked no different than it had when she'd snapped its picture. It sat in a small, sunny meadow that had once been a garden, surrounded by deep woods. They climbed the steps to the sagging porch. The shards of broken glass around the window were dusty, but the door opened at their touch, and a moment later Veronica gasped. She hadn't truly expected to find him, but there he was—a boy asleep under a pile of blankets in the corner of the empty room.

He was little more than a child, growing the first scattered whiskers of manhood. His dark hair was tangled and dirty, his long form still waiting for the heft of muscles. This was the boy newscasters said was "terrorizing" the islands? Veronica snapped his picture, then turned and motioned to Charlotte.

Once outside, they walked to the edge of the clearing before they spoke.

"We have to report him to the sheriff." Charlotte pulled out her cell phone.

"He's no adult," Veronica objected.

"Look Roni, I know you're thinking of David, but ..."

"Of course," she conceded. "And hundreds of other missing boys. This one the media has turned into a Jesse James."

Charlotte fell silent, and Veronica was grateful to her for not mentioning that her son would no longer be a boy. "Who's going to rescue this one? He's been in detention—you're not suggesting prison as salvation, are you?"

"And if he's pitching rocks through our window?"

"Let's go find out." Veronica headed back up the broken remnants of a flagstone walk.

"For Heaven's sake, Roni ..." Charlotte muttered, following her.

Veronica shook the boy's shoulder.

He awoke with a start and jumped to his feet. Charlotte stood before the closed door, barring his way. He turned toward the shattered window, but Veronica had hold of his belt, and she outweighed him by twenty pounds at least. "Stop. You're going to talk to us."

He yanked away, but Charlotte was on his other side now, pushing him back until he sat on the staircase behind him. "Do we have to tie you up?"

Together, Veronica discovered, they made a considerable presence.

"Who are you?" he croaked.

"We might ask you the same question," Charlotte retorted.

"I ain't nobody! Leave me alone." He tried to look fierce but only succeeded in looking defiant.

"We think you're somebody. Somebody who threw a rock through our window last night." Charlotte again spoke in her prosecuting attorney voice.

"I never." He pushed with his heels. "Wasn't me."

"You're the boy the police are looking for all over the islands. Norris Stoner." Charlotte's voice was calm and professional. "You break into houses."

"Just for food. That's all. And not if anyone's there. I'm not that dumb."

"How do you know we weren't home? You don't know who we are."

"Yes, I do. I recognize you now. You're the pair of old dykes they talk about. You live back in the woods off Bowman's Trail. You hide in the woods—like me." His face twisted in a sneer.

Charlotte's mouth opened and closed again. They exchanged a long look.

"And who, exactly, are 'they'?" Veronica asked.

He shrugged. "Just folks. Heard them talking at my mom's."

"Your mom lives around here?" Charlotte was the detective collecting information, now.

"On Drummond, now. She went off with her boyfriend. I don't belong with her, anyway. I belong here. In these woods." His tone was defiant. "Like you!" he spat.

They stared at him in silence. *We aren't hiding*, Veronica wanted to protest, but some part of his words rang true. They were both happy to be done with it all—Charlotte with human nastiness, Veronica with the emotional turmoil of her children who'd never forgiven her for divorcing their father and assumed, as this boy did, that she and Charlotte were lovers.

"We don't break into houses." Charlotte declared. She was as fond of drawing lines as Veronica was of blurring them.

"And I don't throw rocks! Not at people, anyway. But I know who did!" He'd gotten to his feet now, and his voice gathered strength.

"Who?" Veronica asked, fearing Charlotte might dismiss his claim.

"Luke Branscomb, that's who. And his friends from that church group my mom made me go to back when we lived over here. That's who."

"And how do you know that?" Charlotte was still the prosecutor.

"I know everything that goes on in these woods. I see them sneaking around. And they hate dykes. Heard them talking about you—nasty."

Charlotte's hands dropped to her sides.

"God help us," Veronica breathed, her resistance to the church connection crumbling to dust.

"He won't. He don't give a damn for the likes of us." The boy bent to tie his shoes, then picked up his coat, blanket, and bundle and straightened. "You can call the sheriff on me, now," he said, hefting his pack. "'Cause I won't be here when they come."

They made no move to stop him. His thin form vanished into the woods, and they were left staring at each other. Charlotte pulled out her cell phone, looked at it, and put it back. "Later."

Veronica gazed at the scene, the image of her own son replacing the boy's, then lifted Constance and took a picture of the scramble of dust and rags on the floor where he'd been. Not to publish, but to hang above her desk, returning her to this moment.

They drove home in silence, absorbing the boy and their inclusion into his world of outcasts, plus the unasked for, unexpected connection with the church. Veronica repeated the name Luke Branscomb to herself, grateful that it reduced the angry mob to a single boy. A focus.

"I think he's right," Charlotte stated as they pulled into the gravel drive leading to their house.

"About what? Luke and his compatriots?"

"Mmhm. It fits." Charlotte pulled up to the garage and braked. "And you can bet the church group is Grace Bible. Plus it fits with our deputy's reaction and the whole mood of the country—mad as hell and looking for a target."

Veronica looked at the craggy face beside her with its disarray of graying hair. "Which I've now brought down on us." She climbed out of the car and followed Charlotte to the house, picking her way carefully around the broken glass on the porch.

Charlotte chuckled. "Your camera is always in close-up mode, my dear, insisting people see what's there."

"And now it's turned on me ..." She bumped into Charlotte who had stopped and was staring at the blinking answering machine. "Good grief, Lotti. You'll spook at the laundry basket next." She went around her friend and punched the playback.

The machine clicked without a message.

"No heavy breathing. No veiled threats. Someone trying to get hold of us, that's all. They'll call back." The sun broke through the gray, lighting up the shards of glass as though in celebration of the morning's attack. Veronica gritted her teeth and picked up Constance. "Do your work, kiddo." When she was done, she let out a hiss of relief. "Now let's get this cleaned up." She turned in time to see Charlotte's grim distaste. "All right then, I'll tend to the glass, and you feed Trix."

But the next hour, spent in sweeping and ordering, failed to restore the peace that had become their habitual companion. The cold invaded through the open space that had been a window. It smelled, as always, of evergreens and salt water, but the woods and sea no longer sheltered them.

To escape the exposure, Veronica returned to the sun porch to collect and reorder her photos. She stopped before returning the discard pile to the wastebasket. Instead she smoothed them out, her thoughts returning to the personal mysteries they contained and to the boy in the woods. Then her son's face, after the accident, replaced the boy's. Surrounded by monitors and tubes, and backed by the glaring white hospital walls, David's one eye burned into her from his bruised and bloodied face. *"Dad's dead! Dead, you hear? Dead! Because of you! Get out, get ..."* He broke into a sob.

"You're still thinking of David."

Charlotte's voice startled her, and she returned from the past. She nodded. "David, Laura, the whole mess ... But why now, Charlotte? After all this time? It's nonsense. Has nothing to do with this. Just raises memories that have no business here." She slapped her hand on the table to drive away the losses that had engulfed her. She'd learned to keep that door closed, and she wasn't going to open it now. "Let's get out of here for the day—off the island."

"We have to wait for the glass people; we can't leave the house gaping open that long." Charlotte settled on a stool next to the drawing table. "So just sit still. You're really worried it might have been David."

Veronica stared into those brown eyes, the same eyes she'd looked into the day of her first photo show. Charlotte had turned from studying a picture of a deserted high school parking lot strewn with McDonald's wrappers, gym shorts, paper Coke cups, and, off to one side against the fence, a syringe. "You have an eye for the truth."

The respect, even awe, in Charlotte's eyes was what drew Veronica to the lawyer's office when her husband, unemployed victim of corporate "lean and mean," began turning strange. *There's a crazy light in his eyes ... some desperate seeking.* Her words came back, clear as the day she'd uttered them. For the first time in her life, she'd been frightened, for Simon's desperation had turned to anger at her, and her children were breathing its poison. The tall angular woman seemed just the sort who would nail the problem to the floor. She counted on Charlotte's belief in her eye for the truth—in her sanity. Charlotte knew the rest of the family disintegration that ended in that deadly accident as well as she did.

Veronica gazed at a photo of a rubble-strewn beach and touched the image of the lone tennis shoe. "He's out there somewhere, Charlotte. And thanks to his father, he thinks I'm some sort of demon." She shoved away from the table. "Tell me it's kid stuff—the rock—and he's not a kid anymore. Tell me it's nonsense."

"What if it's not?" Charlotte's tone was gentle but insistent—as always. She brooked no denials.

Veronica turned, wondering afresh at Charlotte's ability to cut off all escape routes. "Because the boy said it's kids from that church—and you agreed."

"You're dodging. It never works."

Charlotte was studying her with quiet attention. "For all I know David's still full of the garbage his father fed him … about photography … that I was abandoning them …" She broke off as another memory hit. "That's when I named the camera, remember? 'Constance the spy.' Making light of it to stay sane."

Charlotte nodded. "And Simon called you a damned dyke when you started coming to me. I thought of that this morning. But you're right; David's no kid anymore. You don't think he's come to his senses about his father? I'd think the accident … I mean his father damned near killed him driving drunk through the mountains …"

Veronica shook her head. "David screamed at me to get out of his hospital room, Charlotte. Remember? He loved this new father. Simon never got mad at him. In fact, he acted as though he was saving David from me. From David's point of view, it was all just great. Simon took him rock climbing, taught him to ride a motorcycle. And he had his dad all to himself."

"That was then, Veronica. This is now."

"I know. And if Simon had survived that accident, things might have changed. But he didn't."

"And David never came home to discover that his misfit mother isn't a witch," Charlotte finished.

They fell silent. David had recovered then disappeared. She'd stared at that vacant hospital bed in disbelief. They'd spent days contacting friends, girl friends, shops, parks, until one morning, on a hunch Veronica had called her sister, Dorothy.

"You stay away from him!" Dorothy's shrill command had sat her down with a mixture of relief and horror. "Haven't you ruined his life enough? If you hadn't filed for divorce, he'd have a father …"

"He's with you." Veronica had cut her off, her voice choked with incredulity that Dorothy hadn't called her, told her, had let her spend days drowning in the horror of the search.

"He is, but I'm not even supposed to tell you that much. So just go back to your 'girlfriend' and stay out of it." The slam of the receiver came back as fresh as though it had been yesterday.

But a month later, Veronica had picked up the blaring phone to hear Dorothy yelling that she had stolen him. He'd disappeared again. Again the days and nights of searching. Nothing.

Charlotte's grim frown told her she'd been thinking through the same events. She sighed. "Well, I won't ask you to call Dorothy, but Laura might be in touch with him. Right?"

"I don't know."

The words sat in the silence between them, spelling out the burial of her family. Veronica gazed at the sadness on her friend's face and wondered if her story had made the death of Charlotte's only child and life with a chronically ill husband more bearable. It had been a long time before Veronica had learned of Charlotte's husband's fight with Parkinson's and longer still before her friend had told her of her little girl, Ellie, and their futile battle with cancer. In truth, they'd been a refuge for each other.

"Why don't you try calling her?" Charlotte looked at her watch.

Veronica let her breath out. "I swore I wouldn't." Her mind went back to Laura's last call—out of the blue.

"Is any of Dad's money left?"

That's all. No "hello, how are you?" Just the question uttered as an accusation. Veronica had been so surprised to hear from her she couldn't find words.

"Ted's lost his job so I need to know." Laura's words were clipped with the distaste of having to talk to her.

And at that, Veronica's temper rose. "No." She'd snapped the single word. "None." Which was the truth. Simon had spent the children's college fund on motorcycles, jet skis, a sailboat. That's when she'd filed for divorce. The last of their money had buried him.

She shook herself free of the memory. "Anyway, those ..." She pointed to the rocks that now sat on the bookcase, "have nothing to do with Laura."

"Yes, they do as long as you think it might be David. Call."

"She won't talk to me." She'd hoped, when they'd moved to the same island as Laura and Ted, that she could repair their relationship, but her response to Laura's demand for Simon's money had nixed that. She pulled another of her published books toward her and turned to the culprit, a photo of the "For Sale" sign in front of Laura's huge house, its yard filled with cars, boats, jet skis, and other paraphernalia necessary to their lifestyle.

"You did the right thing. Well, not the picture, maybe ..." Charlotte laughed as she pulled the book toward her, "... but not volunteering to dig her out. Twenty years from now she's going to look at that picture and say 'Thank God I got out of that world.'"

"So you think. It's the only world she knew."

"Who knows? Maybe she's wised up already. Call her."

"If I ask about David, I'll get another load of 'bad mother.'"

"You need to know, Roni." Charlotte's tone cut to the chase, as always.

Chapter 3

Veronica sighed and picked up the phone. She listened to the repeated rings then jumped as the instrument in her hand came to life.

"Ted and Laura Reilly can't come to the phone right now. Please leave your name and number, and we'll get back to you as soon as we can."

Veronica was relieved in spite of herself. "Laura, this is your mother. I need to talk to you. Call me, please." She paused, but could think of nothing that might break the ice and hung up. She could feel Charlotte's gaze on the back of her head but didn't turn to answer the question she knew would be in her eyes. How could anyone be unable to confront her own children? Because if she did, she would start screaming at them, making it worse. Her anger at Simon for the poison he fed them had worn to a heavy lump over the years, but at its core was a buried fury so likely to be rekindled that her mind clamped shut at the thought of any contact.

The blare of the phone cut through her thoughts. She put her hand on the receiver, gathering her thoughts as it rang again. And again. She picked it up. "Hello."

"Hello, Mother." Laura sounded as though she'd steeled herself for the encounter as well—or as though Ted had forced her to return the call. "What is it?"

Veronica opened her mouth, then stopped. Suggesting David might have flung a rock through her window would bring exactly the wrong response. "I called to ask you again whether you know where David is. I—"

"Mother," Laura's cut her off. "I've told you it's none of your—"

"Stop! Don't. I'm his mother. That makes it my business whether either of you like it or not." Her words were greeted with silence, and she turned to meet the approval in Charlotte's eyes. "I had a dream that David was in trouble." It wasn't a lie. She often had such dreams about both of her children.

"Well, he's fine," her daughter snapped.

Veronica closed her eyes, woozy with relief. Laura was indeed, as Charlotte had suspected, in contact with her brother. "How do you know that, Laura? Where is he?"

"He's found a home, Mother. Thanks to Pastor Bob he's turned his life around. So let him be." Laura's voice emphasized the period.

Veronica sat silent, letting the bits of information feed her greedy heart. Had she never pushed Laura this hard before or was Laura finally relenting? "Thank you," she managed finally. "I'm not going to bother him."

"Then why do you want to know? You can't do him any good." Laura's voice was rising with anger, and Veronica could hear Ted chiding her in the background.

Veronica clenched her teeth. "Then he can tell me so himself."

"He doesn't want you to know where he is! And I don't want to talk to you! Go—"

"Veronica?" Ted's voice broke in over his wife's. He'd taken the phone. "I'm sorry ... but you're upsetting her." His voice was half angry, half apologetic. "What's the trouble? Something to do with David?"

"I simply would like to know where he is, that's all. For my peace of mind."

"He doesn't want—"

"In the mountains." Ted's voice cut off Laura's yell and something slammed in the background. "Laura," Ted chided. "Take it easy. Up near Cougar Gap," he added to Veronica.

"Ted!" Laura cried.

"Thank you, Ted." She'd only met Ted once. At their wedding, where she'd shown up uninvited. Despite the corporate polish that reminded her all too sharply of Simon, she'd liked the man—sensed something more human underneath. "And is he all right, do you know?"

"Fine. He's doing—"

"That's enough." Laura grabbed the phone back. "Goodbye, Mother." The line snapped off.

Veronica put the phone down and sat in a daze, feeling long shriveled vessels fill with blood as he son took shape in the void. "She does know," she said, letting that confirmation settle.

"And?"

"Up in the mountains near Cougar Gap, Ted says. And he's fine." She gave a short laugh. "All this time, she knew. And let me …" she broke off as tears threatened. "Damn."

"Has she talked with him?"

Veronica shook her head. "I don't know. Thanks to one Pastor Bob he's turned his life around. That's what she said." She closed her eyes until the effect of the encounter drained away and she could think again.

"Sounds like he's found religion," Charlotte remarked.

"Which, I guess could be good if it helps him accept his father's death and get over the rest of the mess at long last."

"Mm." Charlotte's grunt expressed her skepticism. "Well, in any case it's something and a whole lot more than you've ever had before. I wonder what possessed her to give you that much."

"Ted. I had the feeling it's been a bone of contention—her refusal to tell me."

"Well, thank you, Ted." Charlotte stood up and put her arm around Veronica's shoulders. She sat herself next to Veronica on the couch. "It's the first time I've heard you stand up to her, too."

"Amen to both."

They sat silent absorbing the information. Through waves of relief, the name Pastor Bob kept grating against Veronica's elation, joining the billboard in front of Grace Bible Church and the outlaw boy's story of Luke and his Bible study class.

The doorbell interrupted them. A glass repair truck stood in the drive, returning them to the present.

"You wanted to get off the island," Charlotte remarked an hour later when a board shielded them from the world and cut off the light. Glass would have to wait until tomorrow. "Let's go for a drive in the mountains."

"To Cougar Gap, you mean." Veronica stopped, filled with both dread and excitement at the idea she might actually see her son again. "If David's all the way up there, he's got nothing to do with this mess."

"True. But he's on your mind, and you've just gotten your first lead in years. And if we find him, we can rule him out once and for all. We can't just sit here and stew."

"Right. Not our style." Veronica jumped to her feet. "I'll just shut Trix in." She opened the back door and called for her. The tiger cat didn't answer, which wasn't unusual; she was probably off tormenting some smaller beast.

Charlotte consulted her watch. "We can catch the two o'clock ferry."

Veronica paused only long enough to grab her coat and Constance.

Twenty minutes later, they stood on the open foredeck of the boat, letting the sea air wash through them. It was one of those crisp fall days Northwesterners live for when the air lightens the body and the mountains, already in their snow-caps, restore perspective and quiet the soul. By the time the boat drew in to the Anacortes dock, their mission felt like nothing more than a free-day's jaunt.

Once they left the freeway for the mountains, they leaned back and enjoyed the last of the autumn color, rushing streams, gleaming meadows with their crumbling, moss-covered barns. Then they arrived at Cougar Gap, and sat wondering what to do next.

"Pastor Bob." Veronica stared at a church across the street, its white steeple gleaming against the golden leaves and too-blue autumn sky. The image brought back quiet Sunday mornings listening to the choir, Sunday dinner with chicken and dumplings. Peace.

"We need a phone book," Charlotte decided, as though their mission was anything but preposterous.

They found one in the drug store, but the listings didn't give pastors' names.

"Well, that's that." Veronica took a step back, disappointed that their fool's errand had come to nothing but in some way relieved of tension. Her daughter's "Leave him alone!" had been riding her all the way.

"We'll just drive around." Charlotte stated. "The church signs will give the pastors' names."

Veronica smiled. This was Charlotte, taking charge when her energies failed, as they often had in the days when she was tangled in accusations.

The only fruits of the next hour were the many faces of religion captured by Constance. Promises of solace for the unemployed, the debt-ridden and those forced from their homes were interspersed with anger, demands to cast the moneylenders from the temple, sinners from the heart of the nation, murderers of infants from the hospitals. Some of the bulletin boards gave the pastor's name, some not, but no Roberts or Bobs emerged.

"We need to watch the time, Charlotte," Veronica said, half-relieved at their failure, "or we'll miss the last boat."

But Charlotte wasn't listening. She'd stopped the car to gaze at a pair of stone gate posts and, across a wide tree-shaded lawn, a Victorian house painted in soft greens and blues. "Serenity House," the sign beside the gate announced.

"A rehabilitation center of some sort," Veronica guessed.

Charlotte nodded and turned the car through the gates. The white stone of the drive crunched under their wheels. Veronica's heart sank at the notion that they might find him here, victim of who knows what addiction, but she couldn't argue with Charlotte's logic.

They joined other cars parked in a line across from the house and approached the veranda whose paint showed more wear than had been visible from the street. But the double doors were of polished oak with stained glass inserts, the gift of some generous donor, perhaps.

Once inside, they found themselves in a green-carpeted reception hall. At the desk beside a wide staircase, sat a woman of their own age but with a visage, Veronica decided, far sweeter than theirs. She smiled.

"Hello." Charlotte passed a pair of overstuffed couches with flowered upholstery and approached the desk with her usual firm stride. "We're looking for a friend."

The racks on the wall beside the desk, Veronica noted, were full of Alcoholic Anonymous pamphlets and brochures from various churches and camps.

"Many are," the woman said with an understanding smile.

"No, no, I mean—he's been missing. A David Lorimer. Would you happen to know whether he's a resident here?"

"We don't use last names here," the woman responded. "We've had many Davids, of course."

"Of course." Charlotte sighed. "He's been gone quite a while, you see, and we've just learned he's friends with a Pastor Bob. Do you know such a person?"

The woman's face changed. "Oh, yes. He's our minister."

The casual response caught them both off guard. The lack of a last name was evidently no impediment to identification in Pastor Bob's case.

Charlotte was the first to recover. "Could we speak to him?"

"Well, I don't know ..."

"Please," Veronica broke in. "David is my son. I need to find him."

"Oh." The woman's polite mask changed to alert caution. "I see. Please have a seat. I'll see if Pastor Bob is in his office."

A few minutes later a tall, balding man with a soft, round face and matching paunch entered the reception room and crossed to them. "Welcome," he said quietly. When they repeated their quest, he invited them into his office.

"You say David Lorimer is your son. Which of you?" He looked from one to the other.

"Mine." Veronica took a seat, her spirits soaring. He'd spoken David's name as though he knew it.

"I see." The pastor assessed her as if confirming some diagnosis. Veronica felt her flesh shrink.

"He's been missing almost ten years—since his father died," Charlotte began, reacting to his silence with characteristic impatience, "but David's sister said he'd found a home with a Pastor Bob."

He nodded. "You understand, I hope, that we protect our residents' anonymity."

"We do," Charlotte replied in her best cool lawyer voice. "But you can ask him—tell him we're here, couldn't you?"

"I could, indeed, if he was here ..." Pastor Bob spread his hands. "But, alas, we have no Davids at the moment."

"But ... he was here," Veronica guessed. The man's demeanor contradicted his vagueness.

He smiled. "That's confidential information, I'm afraid."

"I think you know the name," Charlotte asserted. "If so, could you tell us when the man you're thinking of left?"

Pastor Bob eyed her quietly, measuring her up. "If, as you say, the man I'm thinking of is Ms. Lorimer's son, I'm sure he would have contacted her if he wished to ..."

"He might have lost track of me. I've moved," Veronica interrupted. "Can you at least tell me whether he's well?"

"I appreciate your concern, Mrs. Lorimer, but we don't know whether the man I'm thinking of is your son, so I'm afraid I can't answer your question."

"And you have no idea why he left?" Charlotte tried once again to break through his guard.

The man spread his hands. "Again ... he was ready—that's all."

Veronica felt her spine tingle at the edge now in the man's voice. "Did he talk about his family?" she asked, in a flash of intuition.

The glint that came and went from the man's eyes and a straightening of his shoulders were the only confirmations that, behind the pastoral façade, he was fending them off. "I'm afraid I've told you all I can." He stood. "But do leave your names and a message at the desk, and we'll give them to any David we see. What he does with it is, of course, his own business."

Five minutes later, they returned to the car to salvage what they could from the encounter.

"He certainly kept us at a distance." Veronica slammed the door.

"He's bound to do that, Roni." Charlotte started the engine. "And at least we know Pastor Bob runs a rehab facility, not some religious cult. That's a lot."

"But he knew him, I'm sure of it."

Charlotte nodded. "Recognition was written all over the man." She pulled into the roadway.

Veronica sat back with a sigh. "That makes David an alcoholic."

"True. That's better than a religious freak, Roni. In AA, religion is of the 'take it or leave it' sort."

"I suppose, but the man was fencing with us." She drew her seatbelt across her chest, snapped it, then leaned back and closed her eyes. "Every time I come within a hope of finding him, I get this whiff of the stories Simon fed him about me—and I want to start screaming and throwing things."

"Which would reinforce Simon's tales about you." Charlotte smiled.

"I never did that, though. That's the ironic part. I think I probably should have—it might have cleared the air. At least the kids would have known why I was fed up. That it wasn't them. It was Simon's eternal cocktail parties and three-martini lunches. Photography was such a wonderful release. I could let the pictures say exactly what I felt and go home emptied out, ready to be a mother."

Charlotte laughed. "You probably would have gotten away with it, if it weren't for all that evidence you left lying around."

Veronica grunted, remembering those pictures—drunken colleagues with call girls on their arms, a toddler exploring the liquor cabinet—that had so eloquently expressed her rebellion.

"You were an enemy spy," Charlotte added.

"Look out! Mommy will get you, too!" Veronica's head echoed with Simon's voice. She shook herself free. "Enough of this. We repeat the same stories over and over, and they get us nowhere—worse, they take us back where neither of us wants to be. Are we going to make that boat?" She looked at her watch.

"Only with the help of Lady Luck." Charlotte swung out to pass a truck.

"Well, don't try her patience!" Veronica exclaimed.

By the time Charlotte had swung the car back into their lane, the truck safely behind them, Veronica's mind had returned to the scene just past. "So David's an alcoholic. I wonder how much of that Laura knows. When I said I dreamt he was in trouble, she said he was all right. She knew. And it sounds as though she's right. He found a home." She watched the fields fly by. "I'd like to think that. That he found some peace. Even if he never talks to me again."

"Well, we know considerably more than we did. Maybe our rock thrower did you a favor, making you mad enough to confront Laura."

"Mm. And if he's an alcoholic, where would he go?"

"If he was drinking, he probably had favorite haunts—friends who would take him in. If he's not—God knows, Roni."

"Ted sounded as though he's still up here, somewhere."

Charlotte nodded. "He may think he's still at Serenity House."

"Which he may be," Veronica added dryly.

They drove on without conversation other than Charlotte's comments on the traffic that impeded their progress. Once they were on the freeway headed north, she relaxed and glanced at Veronica. "What are you thinking?"

"That Laura knows more than she's told me."

Charlotte sighed. "It would certainly be helpful if you could mend fences with her. She's been angry at you long enough. Time to leave the past behind and move on."

"We were good friends when she was little. With David, too. They had cameras, and we'd go on photo shoots—the sloughs and tidelands were great places for kids to grow up."

"But then you made the mistake of becoming successful. Jealous bastard."

Veronica murmured her assent and fell silent. She hadn't seen Simon's jealousy. She'd only known things were coming unhinged. It wasn't until he'd thrown that first photo book across the room that she'd realized he resented her success. Too late.

Veronica stared at the road. The anguished rage at their accusations had subsided in the light of her new knowledge. "Simon had been unemployed for a year. My success was eating him alive," she mused.

"A lot of men have found themselves in that boat in recent years. They manage."

"He didn't. It's funny, you know. You never see those cracks deep inside people—weak spots that are going to make the whole structure give way if they get hit just so. Like a football player who gets smacked all of the time and then one day—boom—he's dead on the field."

Charlotte pulled to the right for the Anacortes exit and didn't answer.

"We all have those spots—we know we do. Know it could be us." Veronica spoke against the denial on her friend's face.

"Maybe we're coming apart—imagining we're being persecuted by angry mobs." Charlotte turned toward the ferry and gunned the motor. "It'll serve us right if we get left on the mainland tonight."

"All over a rock through the window." Veronica laughed, but as Charlotte raced the last twenty minutes for the evening boat, her mind returned to her son. The shock of David's disappearance from the hospital and the terror of the search had long since settled into a tension that was a part of every day. The mind-numbing despair when Laura had turned against her—screaming that it was all her fault—had faded into a lump she kicked aside every morning. Slowly, life had taken a new shape, simpler, satisfying, and she had little inclination to plunge back into the angers and resentments that had marked that other life. Simon was gone, and she was too brutally honest to pretend she hadn't, at some level, been relieved. But her children. They left deep holes that time never filled. Now the anguish burned fresh, as though the years had never been. Had she really thought David would throw a rock through her window? No, the boy in the woods had simply brought him back. No more.

Charlotte drove down the main street of Anacortes and turned the final corner toward the ferry terminal. "Seven minutes. We just might do it."

Veronica gladly forsook the grim thoughts that were weighing her down for the tension of the more immediate problem. She dug out the exact change for the fare so they could clear the toll booth in record time.

Six and a half minutes later, they rolled onto the tail of the ferry. The last car on.

Chapter 4

The last of the November day had faded by the time they reached the island, and once they left the terminal, the road was dark. Charlotte braked hard as a shape flashed in the headlights, and then gave an audible hiss as the deer fled unharmed into the woods.

"That's enough for today, okay?" she called after it.

Veronica laughed. "Almost home." Despite the morning's attack, the island still felt like a haven.

A few minutes later, their headlights flashed on the wooden heron that marked their mailbox, and they turned down the drive. The house sat at peace, its metal roof gleaming in the moonlight. The front porch hid the ugly patch of wood that had been a window.

Veronica raised her camera. "It would be a shame to ruin this with lights."

Charlotte waited for her to snap the shutter, then pulled into the garage.

"Maybe we *are* just a couple of hysterical old biddies," Veronica mused as they opened the door and stood listening to the ticking of the grandfather clock.

"Maybe. But I'm going to make a fire. We need one tonight. Shine a light for me, Roni. I'm going to get us some wood." Charlotte picked up the empty wicker basket from the porch and headed down the steps to the woodshed.

Veronica aimed the shaft from the electric torch on her path. "Get the apple wood," she called, to break up the silence of the night.

"Don't be picky," Charlotte answered.

By the time she was safely in the house, they were both smiling, happy to be home. Veronica wondered how long it would be before they really returned to their previous complacency.

She left Charlotte at the fireplace and went to the kitchen to fix them some soup. "Charlotte," she called, still standing at the door, her hand on the light switch.

"Hm? What?"

"Trix isn't back. It's past dinner time."

Charlotte came up beside her. "She probably found her own." Charlotte spoke without her usual conviction.

Veronica went to the back door. "Trixy!" she called into the night. "Come on, Trix! We're home!"

But no whining bundle raced out of the night to throw herself into their arms.

"Shut the door, Roni. She'll show up. She always does."

"Except that we shut her in after dark." Veronica closed the door. "Except when we forget," she muttered to herself, remembering Trix's outrage of the morning.

"I hope she didn't mix it up with a racoon."

But when they woke the next morning, the cat was still missing. They pulled on rubber boots and went in search. A half hour later they were staring in silence at the mound of orange fir only a few feet from the drive.

"I didn't hit her," Charlotte exclaimed. "I know I didn't."

"No. You didn't, but did someone else?"

They studied the silent form. There was no blood.

"Look." Veronica pointed to the foam around the cat's mouth.

"Poison!"

An hour later, the island vet confirmed their diagnosis. Trix had indeed been poisoned.

"Who would do that?" Veronica cried, holding the lifeless cat. "What sick pervert ..." She choked back tears.

"Can you tell what it was?" Charlotte asked the vet.

"Not without doing an autopsy, but I suspect it's rat poison."

"Bastard." Charlotte stood up, her eyes dark.

"Well, there is a rat problem on the island." The vet's tone urged reason. "And animals that roam free do get into it."

"But they don't throw rocks," Veronica countered.

"Rocks?" Dr. Graves looked confused.

"Someone pitched a rock through our window night before last," Charlotte explained.

"Mmm. This might or might not be related." He frowned at the cat. "In any case, I'd report this to animal control—they don't much care for poison being left around for whatever animal might happen across it. And the sheriff, too. Did you report the rock throwing?"

"Oh, yes," Charlotte responded. "But I intend to make them take it seriously now. Come on, Veronica."

It took them less than fifteen minutes, once they got home, to find the tin of tuna, half-eaten, at the edge of the wood near their drive.

"We don't get into civil matters," Sheriff Astor told them when they laid the tin on the counter. "You ladies have a quarrel with anyone lately?"

"A quarrel?" … "Certainly not!" They answered simultaneously.

"What are you suggesting—that this looks like a neighborly spat?" Charlotte demanded.

"Well, yes, ma'am, you'd be surprised how often these things happen."

"No I wouldn't," Charlotte assured him, "but we've had the same neighbors for five years. They are a hundred yards away, and I assure you they aren't into this sort of thing."

"Even if we'd had trouble with them, which we haven't," Veronica added. "Have you seen Deputy Hansen's report on the rock thrown through our window?"

He looked surprised, then shook his head. "I'll check that out, Mrs. Lorimer and have Steve keep a look out. We have your address."

"It's the mailbox with the heron," Veronica offered.

"Yes, ma'am." He made a note.

They drove off, painfully aware of Sheriff Astor's lack of interest.

"Well, at least one thing's for sure," Veronica said, gunning the motor. "It isn't David. I can't believe he'd do this. We always had dogs and cats, and he loved them."

Charlotte, beside her, said nothing. Her mind seemed elsewhere.

They spent the next three hours combing every inch of their property and found two more open tins of tuna, both near their property line. Whoever had done this had ventured far off the road. Except for the one by the drive, they were all out of sight of the house.

"Someone was serious about this," Charlotte mused as they went back inside.

Veronica returned to her pictures. Lightened by the knowledge that David was far away, her brain energized by anger at Trix's fate, she examined them with new eyes. She could see nothing that spelled cruelty, but she could revisit the scenes, and see if some memory would click. She climbed the stairs and found a heavy sweater, socks, and rubber boots.

"I'm going to drive around for a bit," she told Charlotte, who was bent over her computer at the desk in the living room.

Deeply engrossed in the screen, Charlotte nodded without looking up.

The tide was out, as it had been the day she took the pictures, and the beach was dotted with clam diggers.

"Getting anything?" she asked a young boy as she passed.

"Yeah—lots." He grinned and pushed back his cap with a damp sandy hand.

"Help yourself," an older man near him offered, pointing to their pail. "We've got more than we can eat."

"Thanks. Maybe I'll take you up on that." She returned to her car for the pail she kept in the trunk, then helped herself to a few.

"You want to dig?" the boy asked, offering her a spade.

"Well, for a few minutes. Why not?"

Her pail was half full when an old pickup full of crab pots drove up to the boat launch and a hefty man with a graying beard climbed out. He looked very much like the crabber whose picture she'd taken.

"Afternoon, Rafe," the boy's father called. "How're you doing?"

"Hanging in. It's a good season, anyway. You? Got work, yet?" He turned and began to haul pots from his truck.

"Nope. Not a thing." The father stood up and stretched, then stood watching the booted fisherman walk out onto the soft sand of the tide flats to set his pots.

"Can we go crabbing, Dad?"

"Nope. Out of season."

"But he is."

"Yep.'Cause he's part Indian." There was no mistaking the resentment in the man's voice.

"That's not fair."

The man gave a crooked smile. "Well some folks have a funny idea of fair, son." He looked at Veronica. "That right?"

Veronica smiled at the boy, rather than the man, and didn't answer. Abstract ideas of reparation seemed woefully inadequate when facing a ten-year-old boy, and in truth, she'd become weary, over the years, of bearing the burden of her race's past. She picked up her bucket and thanked them for their generosity.

She regained the road and drove on toward the ferry dock. The afternoon boat was just arriving, and she watched as early commuters disembarked and walked toward their cars. She could see no sign that any of them had any thoughts other than home, a warm fire, and dinner. She couldn't even see any that caught her eye the way the young lovers in her picture had.

A waste of time, and if she was going to fix clam chowder for supper, she needed milk. She revved the engine and drove off in exasperation. What did she hope to gain from this activity anyway? Busyness, she decided. Just busyness.

She collected her milk, added salad makings and headed for the cash registers.

Behind her, a pair of women her own age greeted each other.

"Coming to the meeting at church tonight?"

"You bet—if this nonsense doesn't stop, we're going under." The woman slammed her basket on the counter.

"Government's too busy taking care of all of those illegal immigrants and perverts to be worried about hard-working regular folk."

"Well, it's time to put a stop to it."

"High time."

Veronica turned and smiled. "Which church is that? Where the meeting is."

"Grace Bible, seven o'clock," one woman replied even as the other, who seemed to recognize Veronica, nudged her to be quiet.

"Thank you." She turned and paid for her groceries. Who was the second woman? She didn't know her, did she? In her mind, she scanned the faces of clerks, hairdressers, shopkeepers and receptionists—Doctor Barnoff's nurse. That's who.

But so what? She started the car. So the recession had turned people sour. Why not? They'd lost their jobs, were losing their homes. Anger wasn't hard to understand. She and Charlotte were angry, too. They'd lost half of their retirement funds in the Wall Street shenanigans. What did those people propose to do about it, besides vent? She pulled into the drive, frustrated by her own circling thoughts and knowing she was avoiding the woman's sudden silence of exclusion.

Charlotte was still bent over her computer and barely responded to Veronica's greeting.

"What on earth are you doing?" Veronica sat on the stool near the door and pulled off her boots.

"Trying to find someone. Several someones, in fact, but I've boiled it down to a couple, now."

"Who?" Veronica went up behind her and looked at the screen.

"Well, I've been on the phone with the court system. Finally managed to find out that Bruno Gutterman is on parole in Spokane, wearing a bracelet, no less. So he's probably out, and now ..." Charlotte clicked the mouse, "I'm focusing on one Marybelle Branscomb."

"Branscomb. That's the name the boy mentioned."

"Yep. It clicked at the time, but my mind was on Bruno, so it didn't come back until I started going through back cases. I'd been through a half dozen or more when I saw the name."

"What did you have to do with Marybelle Branscomb? And is it the same Branscomb?"

"Took her kids away from her. About six years ago. She was a drug addict." Charlotte's lips had closed into a thin line of distaste.

Veronica sighed. "Somehow I can't see a grown woman throwing rocks—it's wrong."

"No, no, you're right. Throwing rocks is greasy kid stuff—though I'm not so sure about killing cats. In any case, it's her kids I'm wondering about." Charlotte studied the screen then typed in a new command.

"Can you find out what happened to them? Either the adults or the kids?"

"I found my old case file—dated 2005. They lived in Monroe. Marybelle was sent to a rehab program. Her kids—come look."

"Joseph, fourteen, Luke, eleven," Veronica read. *"Remanded to juvenile authorities for placement ... then taken by Janine Manning, an aunt, who lives on Grafton Island."* She pulled up a chair. Her afternoon jaunt now felt like diddling away precious time. "Where was the father?"

"Don't know—not around." Charlotte scrolled through the text.

"There. James. Wanted for car theft, whereabouts unknown."

"Does the aunt still live on the island, do you suppose?"

"Think so. A Joseph Branscomb was killed in a teenage drunk driving accident on the island in 2007. I found the obit and an article in the local paper. Manning's a common name, but there are only two in the island phone book. And who knows? Marybelle may be around, too, and she may have taken them back."

"Charlotte, how would she, or they, for that matter, know you're on the island—particularly since you practiced under your maiden name?"

"They could have seen me." She spread her hands. "It's that simple."

Veronica fell silent, putting a story together in her head of a boy with no father, robbed of his mother. "Well, if that's what it is, I'll be relieved. He sounds like a kid with a grudge against the world—nasty, probably, but not dangerous."

Charlotte smiled. "Glad you're so sure." She leaned back and rubbed her eyes. "So what have you been up to?"

"I'm not sure. Digging clams for supper, for one thing."

"Really. What brought that on? The need to dig up something?"

Veronica winced. "Well, chowder sounds like a good way to take the sour taste out of this day."

As she chopped onions and potatoes and cleaned clams, Veronica recounted the rest of her wanderings and the overheard conversation at the grocery store.

"So you think we should plan to ruin our chowder supper by going to that meeting?" Charlotte asked when she'd finished.

"God, no. I'm not ready for that. I have a hard time believing that all of the years we've been living here as a couple of nondescript widows, we've been viewed as perverts—old dykes, as the boy put it—but I'm beginning to realize you've been right all of this time." She dumped the clams into the broth. "It makes my flesh shrink away."

"And if you had known, what would you have done differently?" Charlotte got up and went to the refrigerator to get salad makings.

Veronica blinked at the question. "Nothing. Nothing at all."

"You'd still run around taking pictures even if you knew they were seeing you as—an alien?"

Veronica burst out laughing. "An alien, Charlotte? Come on."

"Well, would you rather be a pervert? And what if you were?"

"You know what? You've just convinced me that oblivion has been a great blessing. I think I'll go right on being blind and deaf." She turned away and began to set the table.

Charlotte chuckled as she rinsed vegetables for salad. "Blind and deaf you aren't, but oblivious is fine with me. I rather like you that way." She dumped lettuce into the spinner. "But be careful."

They let the smell of simmering chowder replace conversation, and it wasn't until they finally sat back satisfied that they stole glances at the clock.

"I'd love to know who's at that meeting," Charlotte remarked, over coffee.

"Well, since they think we're spies, perhaps we should oblige."

Charlotte studied her. "'I thought you said you weren't up for that."

"I've recovered. I've gone from shrinking to not giving a damn. Let's go."

Chapter 5

Grace Bible Church stood on a knoll overlooking the Sound. The white frame building was steepled, but otherwise unadorned, though it was backed by a school building of impressive proportions. They were among the first to get to the church, so parked at the end of the lot, where they could watch the arriving populace. Through their open windows they heard people greet each other and exchange news of everything from the state of the clams to the health of ailing spouses.

Veronica leaned back and closed her eyes, sinking into the familiar comfort of the scene. She and Charlotte were greeted that way by islanders every time they went to the village. Surely they hadn't imagined the friendliness. Where, in this day, had they lost track of that? They weren't church goers, to be sure, but on any other day she wouldn't have hesitated to join the crowd.

When seven o'clock passed, and the parking lot was empty of all but vehicles, they went to the door and slipped in among the overflow standing in the back. The minister was giving an invocation, asking God to listen to the voices and guide the actions of the people gathered in His name.

For the next hour, they listened to speaker after speaker voice the grievances of people forgotten by a government run by Wall Street, bankers, and high-priced experts. They demanded respect for their work, their commitment to morality, and an end to government interference in their lives. They were tired of the mounting paperwork that earned them nothing in return but hours of waiting in government offices. Veronica heard nothing that made her uncomfortable.

Then someone at the side of the hall cried out an obscenity at the President. There was a murmur of assent, but he was otherwise ignored.

A local radio host took the stage to urge action—the staging of rallies, visits to the legislature, radio shows. The focus of the group shifted more and more to enemies—liberals, socialists, elites—leaders more interested in minorities, illegal aliens, and perverts than in the people whose taxes built the country.

Veronica stiffened. She'd been a civil rights leader once, in her college days, and she'd hated the arrogant smugness of her fellow corporate wives. But when she'd deserted and returned to liberal groups, she'd soon tired of their eternal guilt-mongering and culture bashing. She, too, was tired of being the bad guy.

In the crowd, she heard the escalation of her own sentiments. Served them right, she thought. Then she felt Charlotte jerk, beside her. Someone was waving a poster of President Obama with a Hitler mustache, another jumped up and charged that the country was being turned over to Muslims. There was some attempt to shush them, which succeeded temporarily, but the mood of the crowd changed. A different group of speakers took the stage, damning socialist commie lovers, illegal thieves, parasites bleeding the nation, perverts destroying morality, destroying families.

Charlotte took hold of her arm and they sidled through the crowd until they were free.

"What happened in there?" Veronica breathed when they'd regained their car.

"Anger and fear that has cooked far too long—give it a target and it explodes." Charlotte started the car and backed out.

"It was perfectly sane for most of the meeting," Veronica reflected, "then—it's as though they all breathed poison."

Charlotte nodded. "Scary."

"There were a lot of people trying to get it back to the economy, but when they started in on the President—it's like he's a trigger."

"Target. He's an outsider." Charlotte headed down the road for home, gunning the motor to put distance between them and the church. "You don't have to be a racist to feel that way if you've grown up in a place where everyone is the same color, the same faith."

"Mm. Like turbans and burkas. It adds another dose of fear." She watched the headlights light up the forest on either side of the road. Out over the bay, the moon rose, unperturbed. She opened the window and took a deep breath of sea-laden air spiced with evergreen, then leaned back.

"I'm glad we went," she decided, as Charlotte turned onto the lane leading to the house. "It's like learning how a perfectly good pot of soup can turn bad."

"Or like what happens when you suppress resentments and fear for forty years and let them cook away without air."

As Charlotte signaled and slowed for their driveway, a blast of a horn jerked them upright, and the dark shape of a vehicle barely missed their tail as they turned.

"Who the hell was that?" Charlotte breathed as the car roared off into the night.

"He didn't have his lights on." Veronica craned her neck but could see nothing through the dense screen of evergreens. There was little traffic on the island this time of night and even less in their lane.

"Who would drive these roads with his lights off?" Charlotte let out her breath, took her foot off the brake, and rolled toward the house.

"There was a car behind us, coming down the island. With lights. I didn't think a thing about it."

"You mean he switched his lights off when he turned into the lane?" Charlotte braked and cut the engine. "Someone who followed us from the meeting."

Veronica climbed out and slammed the door to shut off her rising fear. "Well, we know everyone on the lane. Tomorrow we conduct a survey." Even as they spoke they heard the car returning. Its lights reflected off the trees as he passed, and the sound of his engine faded as he turned onto the main road.

"Forget the survey. Tomorrow we get a dog." Charlotte mounted the steps ahead of her and put her key in the lock. She reached around the jamb and turned the overhead light on before she pushed the door wide.

Nothing had been disturbed.

"Time we calmed down, or we'll drive ourselves right off the island," Veronica shrugged out of her coat. "Let's put on the pot, for a start."

"If whoever that was had intended to do us harm, they could have driven in here after us." Charlotte hung her jacket on the hook by the door.

"So they only intended to scare a couple of grey-haired ladies." Veronica banged the teakettle into the sink and turned on the water.

"Right." Charlotte ran a hand through her disheveled hair.

"Which is a mistake." Veronica turned the heat on under the kettle. "I'll put Constance on watch." It was a long time since she'd used her camera as her protector. Once upon a time, she'd shrugged off people's objections to her pictures with a "Constance did it." Tonight, it was a comfort to have her around. "I should have taken her with me tonight. There were some terrific shots."

"Sure. What we needed was a flash or so to draw attention to ourselves."

Veronica shrugged. "Apparently we were spotted anyway."

"You know, Veronica, if you had a digital camera—just as an assistant to Constance, you understand—you could suppress the flash." She picked up Constance and hefted her substantial weight. "And you could shove it into your coat pocket—far more effective for a sleuth." Charlotte pulled her tiny digital out of her pocket and waved it.

"Don't tell me you got a picture." Veronica slapped her hand on the counter. "Did you?"

"I tried, but my view was blocked. Let's see …" Charlotte turned on the camera and shifted to display mode.

Veronica went to look over her shoulder. The pictures were far from perfect. Someone's coat sleeve blocked one side, and the first couple was blurred. A couple of shots illuminated the congregation from behind, showing a predominance of balding and grey heads. Only the minister, illuminated by the podium, was identifiable. Another shot caught the Obama-curser, fist raised in the shadow of the aisle. A big man, rendered featureless by the shadows. "Too bad we weren't standing around that side. But look—people are turned toward him in that shot—you can see a few faces."

Together they studied the profiles, a few grinned in agreement, but most only looked surprised.

Charlotte pointed to a man near the front. "Our neighbor."

"He's frowning. That's good. I wouldn't have put him down as rabble rouser."

"No. Middle-of-the-Road-Henry. That's what he calls himself."

The singing of the tea kettle brought them out of their thoughts, and they turned to their tea. The very ordinariness of the crowd calmed them, though the effect, Veronica decided, probably sprang from the backs of their heads. They turned their attention to their tea and the evening news.

A terrorist plot foiled in Jakarta and a tsunami in Haiti were followed by the face of their recently-elected senator blaming the gridlock in Washington on the other party.

"I'm going to bed," Charlotte announced, getting up.

"Amen." Veronica flipped off the set. "Schoolyard politics. It's a wonder more of us haven't gone off half-cocked."

They retired to their respective bedrooms. Veronica flipped through book after book, looking for a tale that would wash out the day's dramas. Her attempts failed and left her tossing and turning until the wee hours of the morning.

Charlotte, when she greeted her at the coffee pot at seven, looked as grumpy as Veronica felt. "We're going to put an end to this," she stated, "starting with lights and a dog."

They had to wait for the glass company to come and replace the board with a new pane, but arrived at the island animal shelter by ten. The only resident dogs were a terrier who leapt at the cage walls and a mixed-breed hound who cowered in the corner, but they left with a black and white cat who had rubbed against Veronica's ankles as they waited.

"All right," Veronica said, bending to pick up the cat. "You're not a solution, but you'll fill a hole." She studied the cat's swirling markings. "I think you're Yin-Yang."

Charlotte rolled her eyes but didn't object. With Yin-Yang in a carrier, they drove toward the ferry and the mainland shelters. It was midday before a brown and white spaniel leapt into Charlotte's lap and licked her face. "Good grief, she likes me!" she exclaimed, amazed.

Veronica turned from rubbing the ears of a mottled grey-brown and white hound of uncertain heritage and grinned. "Wonders never cease."

And so they arrived back at the house in the mid afternoon with two dogs, a cat, kitty litter, food, and assorted dishes, collars, and leashes.

"This is not what I intended," Charlotte declared. The brood sniffed around each other and Trix's empty bed, explored the house, then returned to sniff Charlotte's ankles. "And we never got lights."

"This crew will keep us safe without them." Veronica shook food into the dishes, amazed at how good it felt to have animals about.

"How do we know that?" Charlotte sank into a chair. "They might just greet everyone and wag their tails." The spaniel, who she'd now dubbed Molly after a client who'd once had a crush on her, jumped into her lap and put a wet nose to hers. "No, don't try to sweet talk me. You're going to have to be useful around here."

"So are you. Here," Veronica held out the spaniel's food dish. "Feed her," she commanded. "And then they have to go out—except for you, puss." She put the cat's dish in her kennel and closed the door to protect her from the dogs while she ate. "You're staying home until the dogs drive our nasty devil away." She turned and tripped over the flop-eared hound who looked at her quizzically. "And what do you want, Mortimer?" She didn't know where the name came from, but it fit. She picked up his dish. "Come on. You're eating on the porch."

At the threshold of the sun-porch the hound bolted for the back door, barking and jumping at the window. Veronica froze and scanned the yard.

"What is it?" Charlotte came up beside her.

Veronica shook her head. "I don't see anything." The dog was sniffing at the bottom of the door. "Has someone been here, boy?" She knelt, examined the floor, then stood up, checked the lock on the door and crossed the room to gaze at her work table.

"Anything disturbed?"

"Not that I can see." She turned back. "Come on, Morty, get your dinner, and we'll go out and look around." The dog came eagerly when she put the dish down.

As soon as they had hooked them up and opened the back door, the hound dashed for the garden shed, dragging Veronica behind him. Once there, he concentrated on the ground at one side, sniffing with great energy an area where the grasses and leaves had been trampled. Molly soon joined him, and they both huffed as they circled the spot.

"So we're being watched." Charlotte's voice was flat.

"Looks like it." Veronica shivered then took a deep breath. "Well, we need a fence anyway." She pulled the hound away. "Come on fella, let's take a tour."

They circled the perimeter of the property without further incident until they reached the south corner, where the dogs wanted to pull them further into the woods.

"This is Tower's land, isn't it?" Charlotte asked as they followed the dogs.

"I don't know who it belongs to, but it's vacant. It goes through to Cooper Road." Veronica came to a stop abruptly as the hound gave a bark and headed for a ring of charred wood—the remains of a campfire.

Charlotte let out her breath. "This we report to the sheriff."

Veronica nodded and looked around the small clearing. The light was fading now, the woods closing in around them. "And then we get a fence."

"Six feet topped with barbed wire. Let's get home, Roni."

"I'd like to see where this comes out. Look there's a path."

"Roni ..."

"We have time before dark. Come on." Veronica headed for the opening.

"We didn't bring a light." Charlotte grumbled, following her.

"It can't be more than a block or so to the road. Look, there are Frank Tower's lights." She pointed to the right.

They jumped as Mortimer and Molly yanked their leads, lunging for the underbrush, but all that followed was the skittering of some small creature.

"Tend to business," Charlotte growled, pulling Molly in.

They reached the road as dusk deepened, but they could still make out the sign marking their lane less than a hundred yards to the left. Heartened, they set off at a more confident pace.

As they approached their own drive, a car caught them in its lights. Startled, they pulled the dogs in and stopped.

"It's the deputy!" Veronica exclaimed and was even more surprised when he pulled up beside them.

"Good evening, ladies." Hansen stepped out of the car and tipped his hat. "I was just on my way to your place."

"Ah?"

"I have news. We think that boy, Norris Stoner, who was breaking into houses over on Drummond may be over here. Someone stole a boat over there, and we've had a call from a party who sighted him on the west side. That could explain the rock through your window." He bent down to scratch the hound that was sniffing around his boots.

"Ah." This time Charlotte's tone was disappointed.

"I thought that boy only broke into empty houses," Veronica said to cover the lack of interest in Charlotte's response.

"So far, but he's been getting bolder—and he may have thought your house was empty."

"Mm." Charlotte sounded doubtful. "Deputy Hansen, would you come to the house, for a minute. We have a few more events to report. And I'm afraid they don't sound like that boy."

"Sure. I'll follow you." He looked at them with interest for the first time. "It's pretty dark to be out here without a light."

"That's true," Veronica agreed. "And we'd appreciate your head-lights." She pulled Morty away from the sheriff's knees and headed down the drive.

When they reached the house and turned on the lights, Charlotte gave the deputy an account of the dead cat, the poisoned cans of tuna, the car that had followed them home, the trampled grass around the shed, and the abandoned campfire.

"Well …" Deputy Hansen scratched his head. "I'm not sure I'd put much stock in those things. You're probably just nervous after that broken window, yesterday."

Veronica, who'd found it far thinner on the retelling, wasn't surprised at his response. "The cat was poisoned," she protested.

"Not too unusual. And the campfire–well, kids make fires in the woods all of the time, I'm afraid. Not much we can do to stop them except give lectures on the dangers of forest fires—which we do. But it could be the Stoner boy. We'll have a look at that in the morning and see if we can spot anything."

"Why would he poison a cat?" Charlotte snapped.

He shook his head. "Can't say anything that boy does would surprise me."

Charlotte made a noise between a sigh and a raspberry. "All right. Well, thank you for stopping by, Deputy Hansen. We'll keep our eyes peeled."

He nodded. "Do that." He tipped his hat and was gone.

Charlotte let out an exasperated puff. "Stoner boy, my eye."

"I'm afraid we did nothing but support his belief that we're a pair of nervous broads." Veronica commented as she went to put the kettle on. "I wonder what he'd say if we'd told him we'd already talked to the Stoner boy."

"I was thinking about that." Charlotte sank down on the couch, and Molly jumped up beside her. "We never did report it."

"No, we never did." Veronica set out the cups.

"You don't sound very remorseful."

Veronica shrugged. "Well, no harm done. They know he's on the island, now—someone else did it for us."

Charlotte sighed. "Your civic conscience leaves something to be desired."

"Mine? Ours, you mean." Veronica smiled, watching Molly lick her friend's face. "Molly seems to think you're okay."

"I don't know what to make of this dog."

"No one told her dogs don't like you." Veronica got the teapot off the shelf. "Are we really going to fence this whole lot, or only a yard for the dogs? Maybe we *are* being a couple of nervous nellies."

They drank their tea and settled on the size of the dog yard, then Charlotte called Conrad, the handyman who'd rescued them when a tree fell on the porch.

"He'll try to find a helper and be here tomorrow," she reported.

"A helper." Veronica searched her mind for a name, snorted at the one that popped into her mind, then sat up. Maybe not so dumb. She tumbled Morty from her lap and took the phone from Charlotte. "Hello, Ted," she said when her son-in-law answered. "I want to thank you for your help, yesterday."

"That's okay. I understand that as a mother you want to know he's okay." He sounded relaxed, not afraid of being overheard.

"Right." She paused, wondering whether to tell him of their trip to Cougar Gap, then decided against revealing they'd actually gone in search of David. "Well, I thought if sitting around the house was driving you crazy, you might be interested in an odd job—for pay, of course."

"What sort of job—just a sec ..." He turned away from the phone. "It's your mother."

Laura grumbled something in the background.

"Help build a fence," she continued when he returned. "We've had some trouble here, so we're now the proud owner of a pair of dogs, and we need a fence."

"No kidding. What kind of dogs?" He sounded pleased. "We have a pair of Vizslas, you know." His enthusiasm broke through his usual bland facade.

"A spaniel and a hound of uncertain heritage—could have some Vizsla or Weimaraner, but I wouldn't swear to it. And we have a new cat, I might add." She was encouraged by his tone.

"Well, I guess I could do that—help, that is. But I don't know much about building fences, I'm afraid." He sounded uncertain now, in part, Veronica was sure, because of Laura, standing somewhere behind him.

"Help is fine. We have a handyman, Conrad, who will take charge. If you could just come ... around ten. Is that okay?"

"Right. Sure."

"Is Laura there?" Veronica asked on impulse. "I'd like to talk to her." About what, she wasn't sure, but she was changing courses now. No more being treated like the plague.

"Laura," she began when her daughter came on the phone. "Ted has agreed to help us build a fence tomorrow, and I'd like you to come with him."

"Why?"

"Why a fence or why come?"

"Both, I guess."

"The fence is for the two dogs we've just bought."

"Dogs? I thought Charlotte hated dogs." Her opinion of Charlotte came through whenever she mentioned her name.

"No, dogs hate Charlotte. But this one doesn't."

"Oh." There was a silence. "Well, I don't see what it has to do with me."

"No, but I have something to do with you. I'm your mother. And I need to settle a few things in my head."

"I don't see what—"

"Please." Her voice was a command, not a request. "Don't fight me. Just come."

"Well, I guess ... okay. For a bit." Laura's tone was doubtful and tentative.

Veronica thought it probable she'd think up some excuse before noon tomorrow, but tonight she would settle for the grudging consent. "Thanks. See you then." She hung up and sat back with a sigh, letting the tension of the conversation drain from her, then called Conrad to report that she'd found him help. "Now let's go to bed," she breathed, putting the phone on its cradle.

"What are we going to do with them?" Charlotte pointed to the trio asleep on the couch.

"Nothing. They look perfectly comfortable where they are."

Chapter 6

Sometime in the dark of the night, a thump on Veronica's bed sat her up in terror. She put a hand down and found Mortimer. She flopped back onto the pillow with an unladylike word or so, but let him curl up next to her, She warmed her hands on his warm, silken coat, breathing in listening to the whisper of mist, the ping of a twig falling, the far-off cry of a small animal—the night noises of the forest.

In the morning, Charlotte reported a similar experience. She, however, had scolded Molly and ordered her off the bed—without success. Only Yin-Yang the cat, curled on the back of the couch, remained aloof, immune to the smell of oatmeal and eggs. She did, however, deign to consume her own food, safely in her own crate away from the dogs.

Energized by a night's sleep and a hot breakfast, they booted up and trudged into the yard, measuring tapes in hand. They had a blueprint ready by the time Laura and Ted arrived.

"Morning." Ted sounded cheerful and energetic as he climbed down from the truck, then bent down to greet the dog at Veronica's side.

"This is Mortimer," Veronica offered, her eyes on the truck where Laura sat immobile in the front seat, staring straight ahead.

"Good morning, Mortimer. Glad to make your acquaintance." Ted scratched the dog's chest, then straightened and looked up at Laura. "Hey!"

Laura shifted her gaze to him, then grudgingly opened the door and got out, muttered a greeting and immediately turned her attention to the dog.

Veronica turned away and saw Charlotte on the porch watching. Molly, at her side, barked a greeting, attracting the newcomers.

"Morning," Ted repeated as he climbed the porch stairs. "And who's this?" He rubbed the second set of ears.

"Molly. She's a total stranger, but she thinks she has to be by my side—at all times, evidently."

"Hello, Molly. Tell her you just know your job." He straightened. "What possessed you two to get dogs, all of a sudden?" he asked.

"Someone threw rocks through our front window." Charlotte's tone was only conversational.

"What?" Laura stopped dead at the bottom of the steps. "When?"

"Day before yesterday," Veronica answered, following her. "Then someone poisoned Trix."

"And someone's built a campfire out back in the woods," Charlotte finished.

"Whoa," Ted burst. "Did you call the sheriff? It was probably that kid from Drummond."

"We called," Veronica answered, "but he's not too interested. Thinks a pair of single ladies shouldn't be living alone in the woods in the first place."

"Well, he's right," Laura shot. She cut herself off from further response.

"The dogs should take care of it, now." Ted broke the following silence, squatting to rub Mortimer's ears again. "You're a handsome fella for a mutt, aren't you?"

Conrad's truck rattled down the drive, cutting off the need of further conversation. After suitable introductions, they set to work. Laura watched from the porch as Ted joined Conrad pacing off the yard with Veronica and Charlotte in attendance, jotting measurements. Mist coated their jackets and smeared the blueprint as they laid out a fence that would both leave the dogs room to run and protect the house without interfering with their own comings and goings. Conrad calculated the materials needed, and he and Ted set off for the village and materials.

Veronica eyed her daughter in the rear view mirror as they drove behind Conrad's truck. "How's the job?" During one of her failed attempts to repair their relationship, Laura had informed her that she was a high school counselor—one of the few bits of knowledge that had pleased her.

"All right." Laura's tone did not invite further conversation.

Despite long effort and two miscarriages—which she'd only found out about because sister Dorothy had called to blame her for them—

Laura hadn't succeeded in having children. And Ted had yet to find employment. A job was undoubtedly only a poor third on Laura's list.

"At least I still have one—for another year," Laura added finally, as though to break the silence.

"That's a relief. It's been a rough year." Veronica pondered how to pursue the brief opening, but Laura didn't respond and silence seemed an almost welcome relief from the effort.

"Have you, by any chance, run into a Luke Branscomb?" Charlotte's question shot through the empty air.

Veronica caught her breath as she saw Laura's eyes widen.

"Why?" The word contained more surprise than challenge but contained both.

Charlotte pulled into the parking lot in front of the hardware-lumber yard-feed store that served the island. "The name popped up as a possible culprit—stone thrower." She pulled into a parking slot and cut the engine.

"Oh, no. That can't be. There's a Luke Branscomb in our church youth group, but it wouldn't be him, I'm sure."

Veronica gasped. "Youth group! You run a youth group?"

"What church is that?" Charlotte asked simultaneously, making no move to get out.

Laura chose to ignore her mother. "Grace Bible." She opened her car door.

Veronica clamped her mouth shut on her protest. But it fit, didn't it? Pastor Bob ... "he's found a home" ... They'd always gone to church, taken the children, but ... not that one. Please. "How long have you been doing that?" Her voice was a half-starved squeak.

"Since last spring." Laura got out then turned. "We started going to a couples group—a support group for people going through tough times—like us. And they talked about how the kids needed support, too. So Ted and I started one. We understand being abandoned." She shut the door and marched off.

"Ahh." Charlotte cast Veronica a look and laid a hand on hers. "Sorry."

Veronica could only nod. "Go on in. I'll be there in a moment."

When she'd gone, Veronica sank back into her seat, recovering from Laura's "abandoned." Why did Laura's hostility always catch her unaware? *And who, exactly, rejected whom?* she mouthed at her daughter's back. Laura had refused to talk to her for years—until her sudden need for her father's money. But she hadn't offered her own money, had she? No. Instead, she'd asked whether Ted had sold his boat, his jet ski, or his motorcycle. A mistake? Maybe. Spiteful? Probably. She sighed and got out of the car to join the others before the stacks of redwood.

But as her anger faded, it was replaced by a far deeper unease. The Bible Study group Stoner had told them about was Laura's. Luke Branscomb's group. The reality of the connection turned her feet to lead and made her head pound. She did little to help in the selection of materials.

It had subsided to a dull ache when, an hour later, the fence posts, wire, boards, nails, hinges, latches and bags of concrete had been piled into Conrad's truck, and they returned to the Honda.

Charlotte stopped, her key in her outstretched hand, and Veronica bumped into her.

A deep scratch ran the full length of the car.

They heard Laura's sharp intake of breath. "Good grief. What did that?"

"Who did that, you mean," Charlotte replied. "Someone who thinks we're a pair of dykes." She spat the words and clicked the remote to unlock the car.

Laura's shoulders jerked at the word, and she turned away.

Veronica and Charlotte exchanged a look, then climbed into the car and waited in silence for Laura to retake her seat in back.

"That's what these attacks are about, Laura," she said when Laura finally took her seat.

Her daughter looked pale and didn't answer. Charlotte started the engine, and they made the drive back a silence Veronica had no wish to break. Her mind fought the idea of a youth group fired up to do such things, much less one headed by her daughter. Something was missing. Something had to be missing. Luke. Her mind fished for details. Removed from his drug addicted mother. His older brother killed in a motorcycle accident. Not a happy story. Angry at Charlotte. Okay, but why against gays?

Her mind was still circling when they arrived at the house, and she was happy to turn her attention to unloading and marking for the next couple of hours. She took pleasure in the exertion, feeling her muscles respond as her head refused. She'd taken up a shovel and was digging holes when she noticed that Laura had joined in this time. Evidently she needed distraction, too. The sun burned the mist away, and she cast her jacket aside, expelling energy into the thrust of her digger until the sweat trickled down her forehead. She paused to get her breath and looked at her watch. Time for lunch.

She watched Laura, across the yard helping Ted stretch a line, and tried to retrieve the conversation she'd intended to have. Grace Bible Church and Laura's attack had blotted it out. But that was the point, wasn't it? She was done with those attacks. Tired of letting Laura have the upper hand out of guilt. Guilt for what? The break-up of the marriage, of course. She was the bad guy, the one who'd asked the divorce. *Enough of that. Now.* "Laura!" she called, heading across the yard. "Come help me with lunch."

Laura stopped and stared.

"Go on," Ted told her. "I'll get Charlotte to hold the line."

Laura opened her mouth to protest, but then, under Ted's steady gaze, shut it again and turned toward the house.

"It's time to talk," Veronica told her as she washed her hands. She turned and took lunch meat and cheese from the refrigerator in the quiet that followed.

"About what?" Laura was forced by silence to ask.

Veronica added lettuce and mayonnaise to the counter. "About your father's version of me in general, and in particular, Charlotte and me. That we're lesbians."

Laura, her back to her mother, had turned her attention to the cat. "Well, aren't you?" It was a challenge, not a question.

"You know what, Laura? That isn't the question. The question is whether I abandoned you for Charlotte—which is nonsense. It's your father's story. Your father was desperate to keep you away from me. You know that, right?"

"Only for our own good." Laura rose and turned toward the kitchen. She picked up a knife and started spreading mayonnaise without looking at Veronica.

"How's that?" Veronica kept her voice casual—merely interested— and continued slicing cheese without a pause.

Laura slapped her knife down on the counter. "Because he didn't want us around … perverts, for heaven's sake. Do I have to spell it out?"

"Ah." Good God. Had she really found a church that reinforced Simon's twisted version of the world? "And if we are lesbians does that make it okay to persecute us? Is that what your church says?"

"I didn't say that," Laura snapped. She ducked her head and slapped meat and cheese on the bread.

"No. You just treat us like lepers—particularly Charlotte." Veronica blotted the lettuce too vigorously and made herself slow down and take a breath. "I've had enough of it. It's time you saw your father's opinions for what they were—the venting of a bitter man."

"He was having a tough time. I understand that now—because of what Ted is going through."

"He was. No argument. And like your father, Ted has to cope with the fact that you are supporting the family." The word that implied the existence of children was out before she could stop it, and she bit her tongue in regret. "Ted seems to be dealing with it more gracefully than your father did," she continued to cover her mistake. "But I agree, it's tough."

Laura put cheese and meat on the bread without answering.

"I'd like to give you the support I know you need, Laura. But I'll be damned if I will until you decide to look at us through your own eyes instead of your father's." She reached over Laura's head for paper plates.

"You just left us to Dad as though you were glad to be rid of us."

"That's your father's version." Veronica carried paper plates and napkins to the dining area. She returned to find her daughter staring at the knife in her hand, as though fishing for a response. "I tried to tell you your father was … suffering from the strain … from not having a job, but you'd always been a daddy's girl. You wouldn't hear of it. I don't believe in tearing children apart in a divorce, Laura. I wasn't going to rip you apart by grabbing at you."

"You did tear us apart." Laura's voice carried the memory of that hurt.

Veronica didn't answer because there was no answer.

"Then there was no one."

Veronica stared out of the window. Her eyes saw Ted and Conrad pouring concrete around a fence post in the sunshine. Her mind saw the two gurneys in the hospital emergency ward, the face of her son blood crusted, the other lifeless—Simon. She'd leaned against the wall, shaking. Someone had led her to a seat, pushed her head down between her knees. In the fog, she'd realized that Laura wasn't there. Wasn't with them. Where was she?

The next moment returned with a shock untouched by time. Laura running through the emergency entrance toward the gurneys, crying out for her father. Dorothy running behind her, grabbing her away. The pair turning, seeing her ...

"You did it! You killed them!" Laura pounding on her, screaming, until someone pulled her off.

Dorothy taking her daughter away—never looking her way.

She shook off the memory. "Not true, Laura. There was me. I was there. You don't remember, do you?" Veronica said softly into air between them. Tears she couldn't shed then rolled down her cheeks.

"Remember what?"

"At the hospital ... seeing me there."

Laura shook her head. "Not really. I remember them—Dad and David—I saw their faces in my dreams for years."

Outside, the men had finished the post and taken the shovel from Charlotte, who'd been digging the next one. The scene seemed unconnected to anything she knew. Again she looked at her daughter's back. "Well, I guess I have to be grateful to my sister for being there for you." She started to reach for her, then dropped her arms and turned away. "Even though I hated her for it." Her voice was far rougher than she intended. She swallowed and shook her head to bring herself back to the present.

She reached a bag of chips down from the top of the refrigerator and dumped them into a basket, then went to the sink to wash fruit.

"I didn't want you anywhere near me."

"I know that." Veronica polished an apple far more than it needed. At least Laura had used past tense. That was something.

"Dad wouldn't have been driving drunk if you hadn't divorced him."

Veronica nodded. "You thought that then. And I understand—you were twelve, and the family was coming apart. Do you still think it now?"

Laura frowned at the plate of sandwiches. "It's a terrible thing you did to him—leaving him for a woman ..."

"And if I told you you were wrong?" Veronica burst in spite of her vow that she wouldn't take that coward's out.

"I wouldn't believe you." Laura tossed her head and headed for the dining room.

Veronica stared after her. So much for that. But she was relieved she hadn't been invited to go further. For those who believed, denial was futile anyway. She'd intended to ask about David, but the conversation had veered off on its own, and it was too late to call it back. She watched her daughter's back as she distributed silverware and plates. Her heart told her she'd accomplished something, but she couldn't name what it was. She gave it up and went to call the yard crew in for lunch.

She sat during the meal mulling over what her daughter had said. So Laura had driven Veronica away in anger and then there'd been no one. Who but a twelve-year-old girl would get so tangled up? And trust sister Dorothy to take advantage of it. With a puff, she drove the image of her sister away and looked across the table at Laura, who was smiling at something Ted had said. Well, she had Ted now, and Veronica was beginning to like the man. Maybe there was hope—except for the untouchable subject her church had labeled perversion. Her flesh shrank from such a religion as it, evidently, shrank from her. And Laura's connection to it— her mind shut off the thought. Yes, it was high time to have it out. And she had. She'd said her piece. Let her words sink in for a while.

The conversation around the table carried none of her struggle. It was the light talk of people who had released tension through hard physical work.

Charlotte was studying Laura, looking, Veronica guessed, for a chink in her armor. "I don't know how you do it." Her friend shook her head. "I always found work with the youth authorities exhausting, and here you're running a youth group, too … on your own time."

"Ted's found he's really good at it." Laura's tone was barbed.

"Caught me by surprise, I can tell you," Ted said. "Never had time for religion before—always go-go-go in the financial business." He laughed. "Well, I guess this is go-go-go, too, but in a different way. Kids suit me." He reached for another cookie. "And the church—well, that feels good, too." He put an arm around his wife's shoulder. "It's brought us a lot closer, too, knowing what Laura deals with every day."

Laura nodded. "It's our family."

Veronica's sandwich stopped halfway to her mouth. So much for peace.

Charlotte shot Laura a look of outrage. "Well," she said, pushing back from the table. "We'd better get back to work if you have to be gone by four." Her tone was icy.

"Gone where?" Veronica asked, as the others left the house for the yard.

"Church youth group," Charlotte snapped, shrugging into her jacket.

Veronica sat on, dashed hope rooting her to the chair. When she finally got up and joined the others, the afternoon's work felt long and tedious. She tried to persuade herself she was imagining Laura's rejection as the time for their departure neared. Five posts later, she threw down her shovel and stretched. *Now stop it,* she scolded herself. *You stood up to her. Let that be enough.* The problem was, she knew, that she'd let herself become vulnerable, hopeful of achieving new understanding with Laura, and now it was hard to settle back into acceptance, a state she'd never had much success with, anyway.

She decided she needed to take some pictures—family pictures of fence building. That's what. By the time she'd retrieved Constance from the house and returned to the porch, they'd set the last post and Ted and Laura were carrying tools to their car. Conrad and Charlotte stood several yards down the fence, deep in consultation. Veronica took a picture she knew she wasn't going to like.

"Wait a minute," she called. She hooked leashes on the two dogs who'd spent the day in the window watching humans play in their yard. "Molly and Mort want to say good-bye." How transparent can you be? She grimaced as the pair pulled her across the yard. Pathetic, in fact.

"Conrad says he can finish it up, all right, with your help," Ted assured her as the dogs received their necessary rubs. "If he doesn't, I can come back Monday."

Veronica nodded. So Sunday wasn't a work day. She didn't mind; she'd always secretly approved of the day of rest. "I'm sure we can get it done now. Thank you both for today."

"'Bye." Laura gave a wave and ducked into the car,

"That crack about family was colossally rude," Charlotte commented as they watched the car depart. "What did you two talk about in there?"

"About whether I was trying to get rid of them."

Charlotte made a noise of disdain.

"So I could have my lesbian affair."

"Which was always total bunk, Roni, and you know it."

"All too believable, if you knew Simon." She broke off. "Hi, Conrad." She greeted the handyman as he came up. "Done for today?"

"Yep. The posts need to set overnight. I'll be back after church tomorrow to hang the rails and run the wire. I'll bring my boy with me to help."

"Okay." Veronica smiled. "If you want to wait until Monday, my son-in-law said he could come."

"Naw, I have another job on Monday. We'll do it tomorrow."

Apparently for Conrad, religious commands were balanced against the need for work. "Good enough," Charlotte agreed. "Let's get the rails and wire out of your truck."

"No, no, they're too heavy for you ladies. Tell you what, I'll call my boy to come pick me up, and we'll just leave the truck where it is, if it isn't in your way. I don't want anyone snitching rails on me."

"It's fine," Veronica answered. The truck was well off to the far side of the garage door. "But there's no need to call your son. We'll give you a lift home."

"Oh, I don't like to—"

"Nonsense," Veronica exclaimed. "We need to stop in the village for bread, anyway." Veronica put the dogs into the back of her car, and Charlotte climbed in beside them to supervise.

Chapter 7

After more demurring, Conrad accepted the ride and directed them to a hamlet of manufactured houses and cottages hugging the beach on the west side of the island. Neat lawns and flower pots faced the road interspersed with canvas shelters for boats and RVs.

"Do you happen to know the Mannings?" Charlotte asked from the back seat.

"Sure do. They're neighbors ... that's my place ..." He pointed. "The yellow one, there, with the Chevy in front."

Two boys emerged from the house and stopped, staring at them as they pulled into the drive.

"That's Mannings' nephew, Luke, with my son," Conrad commented, climbing out of the car.

Veronica jolted and heard Charlotte rustle to attention behind her. They studied the stocky boy with a buzz cut and the tall skinny blond boy in T-shirt and jeans jacket who could have been mistaken for any other tall blond boy on the island.

"Well, thank you ladies, see you in the morning." Conrad opened his door with a wave.

The boys relaxed and waved when they saw him, then headed for the Chevy.

"You on your way to church?" Conrad called as Veronica backed out of the drive.

"Yeah." The boys waved as they climbed into the blue Chevy truck.

"What's Conrad's last name?" Charlotte asked as Veronica drove off.

"Stevenson. But I don't believe Conrad's mixed up in this, Charlotte. Nothing in his behavior to us—we know him, for heaven's sake! We can't be that wrong ..."

"Amen. No I don't believe it either—not Conrad—but adults don't have a clue what their adolescents are up to."

"Except they send them to church groups, so they can tell themselves they do know."

Charlotte grunted. "Would you please stop, so I can get into the front seat? These animals are soaking me with slobber. They think they're going to get a walk."

"Well, we do need to give them that." Veronica pulled into a farm road and stopped.

Charlotte settled beside her with a sigh of relief. "Okay, drive around by the church. Grace Bible. There's a park next door. We can walk them there."

Veronica let out her breath, slowly. "I don't think I like the sound of this."

Five minutes later, she pulled the car into the park entrance.

"Park over there, out of sight of the church," Charlotte directed.

Veronica shot her a look.

"They know our cars, Roni. There's a lovely scratch down the length of mine to remind them."

Veronica felt her stomach churning. Her renewed ache for her daughter wasn't ready for this. She sighed and pulled the leashes from under the seat, snapping them to the dogs' collars without further protest.

"I don't think it's Laura, Roni, really I don't." Charlotte took Molly's lead from her. "But we have to put a stop to this. It's just, as you said, kid stuff—not criminal—but ..." Molly bolted for the path before she could finish.

"It's driving us nuts," Veronica finished for her, following with Mortimer. "The trouble is it isn't just kid stuff now. It's mean—scary." Not Laura, she wanted to insist, but her daughter's "It's our family" had been uttered in a tone too cruel to be ignored.

Charlotte nodded.

They walked on in silence. The day's flat light was dimming by the time they reached the bay. The lights of the mainland emerging from the gray did little to cheer them, and they turned and went back through the darkening woods. The path emerged against the fence separating the park from the church parking lot, which was full now. Lights on the lower level of the school building marked where the youth meeting was being held.

"Come on." Charlotte stooped to climb between the rails, then stopped and pulled back as the blue Chevy pick-up sped into the parking lot and braked. As they watched, Colin and Luke emerged and hurried into the building. Veronica let out her breath in relief. They hadn't been spotted.

"Okay, let's go." Charlotte climbed between the rails and snaked Molly's lead behind her.

Veronica forced herself to follow. She prayed the dogs would remain silent as they pressed against the dark building, making their way toward the lighted room.

Charlotte stopped. Beyond her, Veronica could see Ted and Laura, hands joined in a ring of about fifteen girls and boys, heads bowed. Veronica searched for the boys they'd seen emerge from the truck. There were several buzz cuts; two of those were stocky, one wore an orange shirt, she remembered. At least three were as tall and blond as Luke. Her attention became fixed on one of them, drawn by the straight shock of hair that hung over his brow. Before she could decide it was Luke, Molly gave a low growl and dove at the crawl space. They were forced to pull back before they were discovered.

"Would you recognize them again?" Charlotte asked when they'd regained the car.

"Conrad's boy was the one in the orange shirt. I think I spotted Luke, but I'm not sure about that. How about you?"

"I agree about Colin. Luke was the one in boots. I remember those. We'll make sure about Colin tomorrow when Conrad brings him to finish the fence." Charlotte turned the wipers on to clear the mist that was fogging their windshield. "And we'll go find Mrs. Manning."

Veronica started. She'd forgotten Mrs. Manning and Charlotte's past involvement with the family. "What are you going to ask her? 'Hey, remember me?'"

"Something like that. Unlike Marybelle, she has no particular reason to hate me." Charlotte peered into the murk ahead.

"Except you gave her a pair of kids to raise."

"She volunteered, which makes her a decent sort."

"Makes her a hero, if she knew what she was getting herself into." Veronica, aware of Charlotte's sharp look, stared into the night until the heron that marked their mailbox emerged. Charlotte turned into their drive then braked to an abrupt stop.

"FUCK DYKES" was painted in black across the white of their garage door.

It was a long time before either of them spoke. They simply sat stunned by the raw hatred that blanketed them. Veronica felt the heat of rage rising in the woman next to her. Her own stomach had turned into a hard lump.

"At least it can't have been anyone from the youth group." Veronica grasped at the only straw she could find.

"Why not? Those boys were late. We saw them leave for the church over an hour ago. Where were they while we were walking in the park?"

Veronica opened her mouth to protest, but the words wouldn't come. The idea of those clean-cut boys stopping on their way to church to paint hate signs was too macabre to contemplate. But their house was only a brief detour between Conrad's and the church, and they'd been walking in the park for at least a half hour.

"It wouldn't take but five minutes, and we had the dogs with us." Charlotte got out of the car, walked to the door and fingered the paint. "Still wet," she reported.

Veronica swallowed her nausea and punched the garage-door opener. When the words disappeared overhead, Charlotte moved out of the way, and Veronica pulled in beside the car with the blazing scratch. Never before had she wished for a place to hide.

Charlotte came into the garage behind her and fingered the ugly gash. "Don't close the door yet, Roni. I want Morty and Molly to have a good sniff of the ground out there."

They leashed the dogs who went immediately to the drive and snorted eagerly at the spot where a painter or painters would have stood.

"Good," Charlotte told them. "Now, we're going to see how they behave when Conrad's boy comes tomorrow."

"I want to hear Conrad's reaction when he sees that." Veronica pushed the button to close the garage as they turned the dogs to the porch. A moment later her foot hit something in the dark, almost sending her down. "What the ...?"

"It's the paint can," Charlotte exclaimed, shining her key light on the spot.

Veronica bent down to pick it up.

"No, leave it. Right where it is."

The top was only loosely closed, the can almost empty. "It's the brand Larry sells," Veronica said, naming the island's only hardware store. "There's probably a can like that in every garage on the island."

"All the same, leave it. It's evidence."

The next morning, Veronica rolled from her bed after a night when sleep came only in fits and starts. Bleary eyed, she pulled on jeans, heavy socks, and a wool shirt and headed for the stairs, knocking on Charlotte's door as she passed. A wariness she feared would become habit now beset her as she descended, but no cold draft attacked her ankles, and Yin-Yang sat gazing through an intact window. She sighed in relief and filled the coffee pot, then remembered the scrawled words on the garage door.

She picked up Constance, grabbed a coat, and went out. As she stood adjusting the camera, the sun cleared the trees and turned the door into a blazing sign. Perfect. Rage rose afresh as the snapped her pictures and returned to the warmth of the house. This was a morning that called for oatmeal.

Mortimer was nudging her legs by the time she put the pot on. "All right," she told him, "You're next." She pulled her cell phone from her pocket and rang Charlotte's number, saving herself from yelling up the stairs. "We need Molly," she told the grumble that answered. "And stay up when you let her out. We're having oatmeal in five minutes."

"What's the rush? It's the middle of the night."

"Hardly. It's almost nine, and Conrad will be here by ten."

There was another grumble Veronica took as assent, and she closed the phone. A door opened and closed above, and Molly rushed down stairs. For a half hour, Veronica occupied herself feeding and chatting with the animals, absurdly pleased with the way they filled the empty spaces of the house.

They were finishing breakfast when they heard a car on the gravel of the drive and stood watching as Conrad got slowly out of the car, staring at the door.

"Morning, Conrad." Veronica stepped out onto the porch.

"Where did that come from?" His voice croaked.

"That's what we'd like to know." Charlotte spoke from behind her.

Conrad was shaking his head. "That's not cool." He shoved his hands in his pockets and turned toward his car. His son, sitting in the driver's seat, had made no move to get out. "You see that?" he called.

The stocky boy with the buzz cut opened his door and got out. "Yeah."

"My son, Colin," Conrad said. "Colin, Misses Lorimer and McAllister."

From the porch they nodded and studied the boy's too-blank gaze.

"You know anyone would do something like that?" Conrad asked his son. He sounded both angry and worried. "Looks like kids."

The boy shrugged. "No. Sure don't." He slammed the car door but didn't come closer.

Conrad turned, and his gaze fell on the paint can. He stiffened. "What's that? The can?"

"It is." Charlotte descended the steps.

"'Spect they could've taken that from anyone's garage," Conrad muttered.

"Probably."

"Yeah. That kind of thing shouldn't happen. That's what I say. I'll have Colin here paint that out for you as soon as we've finished with the fence."

Veronica saw the boy jerk and read defiance on his face, but he said nothing.

"We'll just walk the dogs then we'll be ready to help," Charlotte told them. She, too, was eyeing Colin.

When they'd hooked up the animals and returned to the yard, Colin and Conrad were unloading rolls of wire. Mortimer put his nose in the air, lowered his head, and pulled Veronica toward the boy. The dog emitted a low growl. Molly, restrained by Charlotte on the porch, barked up a storm.

"Whoa, there!" Colin cried, jumping back.

Veronica pulled the dog to a stop.

"He don't like you." Conrad come forward and reached a hand out for the dog to sniff. Mortimer obliged by wagging his tail.

Charlotte, who'd been watching from the porch, approached with the still barking Molly, who promptly bared her teeth at both men.

"So sorry," Charlotte said in a voice that said she was nothing of the sort. She stood watching the boy, waiting for his response.

His gaze challenged her to make something of it.

"Okay, Molly, let's go." She pulled the dog away and glanced around for Veronica.

"Well, that was pretty clear," she muttered when they'd reached the end of the drive and headed down the road.

"Damn." Veronica could manage nothing more in the way of agreement. She wished she could even say it was a surprise. "Conrad suspects it, too, I think. He's at least worried—and the dogs' reaction wasn't reassuring."

"Amen."

By the time they returned to the house fifteen minutes later, the sound of hammers greeted them at the drive.

Chapter 8

By the end of the day, they had a redwood rail fence lined with wire grid. A gate opened into the drive and another in the back at the end of a path they used frequently to go through the woods.

"That's going to take another coat," Conrad commented as he watched the boy finish painting out the letters on the garage door. "You can come back tomorrow after school to do that."

"Got football practice."

"Okay, Tuesday, then." Conrad's tone settled the matter.

"That's going to mean painting this whole door," Colin complained.

"Bring Luke with you. You can count it as your week's community service." Conrad's tone suggested this was more than helping out widow ladies.

When they'd driven off, Charlotte let Molly and Mortimer out and walked the perimeter while the dogs raced about sniffing, reclaiming their turf.

"I never went to see Mrs. Manning," Charlotte commented as they reentered the house. "Tomorrow I do that."

"We—you're not going alone." Veronica closed the door with a snap, satisfied with ending the last two days.

"I hardly think she's dangerous, Roni." Charlotte released her wild hair from her cap and ran her hands through it.

"Everyone's dangerous," Veronica snapped. "It's my new mantra. Besides, if Luke and Colin happen to be there, they'll think you're being downright nosey." She hung her jacket on the peg next to the door and headed for the kitchen.

"We'll go during school."

Veronica smiled at the indirect concession as she gazed into the refrigerator and tried to focus on dinner.

***

The woman who answered the door the next day was not the motherly creature Veronica had expected. She was as tall as Charlotte and slim, though her face showed the years and her blond bob was faded and dull. "Yes?"

"Mrs. Manning? I'm Charlotte McAllister. I don't know if you remember me."

"I know who you are." The woman's tone was a shade short of hostile.

Charlotte smiled. "I stopped by to see how you are doing with the Branscomb children."

"We're just fine." Mrs. Manning's gaze flicked from Charlotte to Veronica and back again, her eyes and tone walling them out.

"This is my friend, Veronica Lorimer," Charlotte explained.

"Know who she is, too." Janine Manning crossed her arms over her chest.

"We live here on the island, now," Charlotte persisted in a neighborly tone. "And I noticed you in Albertson's," she lied with a smile. "I just wondered whether you still have the children with you."

"One of 'em. The oldest, Joseph, is dead." Her tone was that of a woman being questioned by the authorities.

"Yes, I read that in the paper. I'm so sorry. But Luke is still with you? Does he see his mother? She's your sister, as I remember."

Veronica blinked. She'd seen Charlotte in the courtroom, but the skill of this unwaveringly friendly interrogator was new.

"He's with me, mostly. Marybelle takes him sometimes." Mrs. Manning was still defensive.

A husky blond man appeared at Janine's shoulder. "What do you want with him?"

"With Luke? Nothing, Mr. Manning. I just stopped to see if he's still with you. And to see how he's doing."

"Well, I tell you. He don't much understand what a dyke is doing breaking up other people's families—taking kids from their mother. Otherwise he's doing fine." He reached an arm in front of his wife and took hold of the door to shut it.

Charlotte put her foot out, stopping it. "In that case, Mr. Manning, would you know whether he had anything to do with painting "FUCK DYKES on my garage door?" The interrogator was gone. This was Charlotte.

"No, ma'am, I wouldn't. Nor would I care."

"I see." Charlotte nodded and withdrew her foot. "So there you are," she declared to the closed door.

"Indeed. So you're the target, now. They hate you for saving the children from an addict. That makes a lot of sense."

Charlotte gave a huff of disgust. "Well, don't knock it. At least it lets David out." She turned away from the door.

"But not Laura." Veronica plunged her hands into her jacket pocket and followed Charlotte toward the car.

"Not Laura." Charlotte got in, slammed the door shut, and sat staring at the house they'd just left. "Or Grace Bible Church. I think it's time to pay a visit to the pastor."

They selected the small frame house next to the church as the parsonage and rang the bell. A pleasant-faced, dark-haired woman comfortably settled into middle age answered their ring. She looked startled, as though she, too, recognized them, but her "good morning" was far friendlier than Mrs. Manning's.

"Is Reverend Starkweather in?" Charlotte asked, taking the name from the sign out front. "I'm Charlotte McAllister and this is my friend Veronica Lorimer. We live here on the island."

"Do step in." She opened the door further. "I'm Thelma Starkweather." She held out her hand. "I'll see if he's busy." She waved to the parlor. "Have a seat."

The man who appeared a few minutes later was tall, lean, and bald. His clean-shaven face bore creases alongside his mouth, spectacles on a small nose magnified blue eyes that tried for friendliness but were mostly curious.

"Good morning, ladies." He held out his hand.

"Charlotte McAllister," her friend replied, rising and extending her hand.

"Veronica Lorimer," she said, wondering why she felt pinioned by his gaze.

"Welcome to Grace Bible," he said, when they'd taken seats. "And what can I do for you?"

"We've come for help," Charlotte began.

"Ahhh." The word was a sigh of either relief or pleasure. "That's what we're here for."

"No, no," Veronica intervened. "You don't understand. We're being harassed by someone—or several someones—who seem to think we are lesbians."

"We believe they may be young people from your church," Charlotte finished.

"Oh, come now." He stiffened. "We're good Christians here. That's …" He sputtered, waving his hands as he searched for words.

"We're not suggesting you approve of such behavior," Charlotte reassured him. "Which is why we thought you might assist us in putting a stop to it."

He raised his brows. "A stop? I don't see what it has to do with us. And what have these young people supposedly done?"

"Someone pitched a rock through our front window, poisoned our cat, and painted 'FUCK DYKES' on our garage door, for starters." Charlotte recited the list in her best prosecuting attorney voice, and Veronica watched the last of the politeness fade from the pastor's face.

"Well." He pulled his spectacles from his nose, wiped them, then put them on again. "That is, indeed … we certainly don't approve such behavior."

"I thought not," Charlotte replied, her voice now softened into friendly-witness voice tones.

"Not at all. But before we go further, may I ask … are you …?"

"Lesbians?" Veronica asked, cutting off Charlotte's reply, which she was sure would be a denial. "What does it matter? Are you suggesting it's all right to do those things if we are?"

"No, no, of course not." He floundered, then put his hands firmly on the wooden arms of his chair. "But the Bible forbids such unions, you understand, and it might be a case of a member—or youth, as you suggest—not of our church I would hope—becoming overly zealous." He sat back, satisfied with his answer.

"It might, indeed," Charlotte agreed. "And if that were the case, what would you do about it?"

"I would certainly speak to our youth leaders."

"Good. Do that." Charlotte answered, rising. "We would appreciate it."

The pastor blinked at this sudden concluding of their visit.

"And if they are being encouraged by adults?" Veronica asked, feeling the need to persist a bit.

"Let me be more specific," Charlotte stopped her progress from the door and turned. "The Mannings are members of your church, I know. Do you also know Marybelle Branscomb?"

The pastor stiffened. "Marybelle Branscomb?" he stressed the first name. "No, and I don't see what the Mannings have to do with this." His words were clipped now.

"Well, it might mean you are familiar with my professional name—Charlotte Browning." Charlotte smiled.

Reverend Starkweather gazed at her a long time before answering. Then he nodded. "I have heard it, yes. But I don't see what it has to do with—your current problems. Mrs. Branscomb has found God's way and wants to undo the harm done to her family." He gave a tight smile.

"Ah." Charlotte nodded, wordless.

"Then I suggest you talk to them about the evils of vengeance, Pastor." Veronica stood up. "And to their nephew, Luke Branscomb."

"You're suggesting the boy is responsible for the attacks on you? Preposterous." The reverend's mouth tightened into a straight line.

"Along with other members of your youth bible study group where you teach that gays are sinners." Charlotte slammed the period on her sentence.

"That is not the same thing at all." He rose in protest.

"Unless someone was over-zealous , perhaps?" Veronica insisted.

"Well!" He let out his breath. "Sinners do bring it on themselves, don't you think?"

Veronica saw Charlotte's jaw drop. "Are you saying hate crimes are justified, Reverend?"

"Not at all, Mrs. McAllister. But I think God is more merciful toward those who are over-zealous in preserving His laws."

"That would include men like Hitler," Veronica stated, taking Charlotte's arm and turning her toward the door. "Thank you, Reverend Starkweather, for your time."

"May Our Lord show you the way," the Reverend snapped as they closed the door.

"Whew!" Charlotte exploded as she got into the car.

Veronica started the engine and pulled out of the parking lot. "That man is scary."

"Why were you so determined not to tell him we aren't lesbians? We need that man on our side if we expect any help."

"On our side? When you're a destroyer of God's families? Small chance." Veronica stepped on the gas, putting distance between them and the church. "Telling him we're not feels like cowardice. Like we're on his side—saying it's okay to treat lesbians that way, but not us. We're not guilty."

Charlotte fell silent.

Veronica drove up the hill and along the ridge that separated one side of the island from the other and gazed at the still-emerald fields dotted with farm houses and ringed by forest. Beyond them lay the blue of the Sound. Then the road dipped into the village with its ever more frequent empty store fronts and "For-Sale" signs. She pulled into the Albertson's parking lot, stopped, and turned off the engine. "We need bread and coffee," she said to the windshield. "And I don't want to go in."

"Right." Charlotte sighed and opened the door. "But that's the way it's going to be if you refuse to set them straight."

Veronica watched her friend cross the lot. "Damned if I will," she said to no one but herself. Laura's "Well, are you?" came back with new discomfort. Her daughter was all too clearly in the Reverend's camp. And would she accept her daughter if she shared the Reverend's attitude that lesbians were perverts who brought hatred on themselves? Her being rebelled at the prospect.

By the time Charlotte came back, she was pushing away the belief that Simon had so poisoned her children that there was no pathway back. Oddly, some part of her had begun to accept that over the years. The gulf between them had become her normal—a fact of life to be lived with the way Charlotte lived with the absence of children. Now that wouldn't do. She and Charlotte had become targets. She had to know whether Laura and Ted were a part of this cruelty.

"I'm going to have it out with Laura." The decision somehow freed her from the tangle of emotions the morning had left. She started the engine.

Charlotte gave her a sharp look. "She's at work, isn't she?"

"Probably, but I'm going to be waiting at her door when she gets home." She stopped for traffic at the road, looking for some diversion, some return to normalcy. "And while we're here, I'm going to pick up a digital camera."

"Really?" Charlotte's eyes widened. "Good idea!"

"Of course. It's yours," Veronica retorted, crossing the road to the strip of stores on the other side that served as the island's shopping center. Short of a ferry ride, Walgreen's would have to do.

They gazed at the meager offerings, and Veronica shook her head. "I should at least look them up on the Internet."

"That Olympus gets good reviews," Charlotte offered.

"What are you doing looking at camera reviews?"

"I was going to take my life in my hands and get you one for Christmas," Charlotte confessed.

"Were you, now? Well, all right, let's take it. I'm not, after all, trying to replace Constance."

When they arrived home, she hooked Mortimer to his lead, and set off through the new back gate with her digital camera to pass the hours until Laura got off work. She stopped at the deserted campfire and noted that a couple of soda cans and a McDonald's sack had been added to the scene. Their watchers had returned. Newly chilled, she let Mortimer sniff, then pulled him away and took a picture, then another. It didn't matter how many she took, she realized, so kept shooting until the camera had caught the sinister aura of the blackened charcoal, and abandoned containers, in an already gray light dimmed further by the surrounding trees.

She took a side trail toward a derelict RV she knew lay deep in the woods and shot a picture of that. Ever since childhood, she'd been drawn to abandoned buildings and the stories they told. But this one was not so abandoned. The damp earth bore fresh tire marks. The camera clicked again as Veronica backed out of the clearing. At the edge of the trees, she studied the decrepit motor home for signs of life before turning and followed the tracks down the old fire road.

When she headed back toward the house, Frank Towers waved from his yard. "Morning, Veronica. Out shooting again, I see."

"Morning, Frank." She headed through the trees toward his fence, welcoming his friendly hail. "Got myself a new camera—a digital. I'm trying to come into the electronic age." She showed it to him.

"How about that? Nothing to it, is there?" His weathered face wrinkled with his bewildered smile.

"That's how it feels, all right. By the way, have you seen anyone in these woods? Or heard anything?"

"Can't say I have, but I don't hear much. Daughter says I should get hearing-aids—electronic ones," he said, pointing to her camera with a chuckle, "but I'm still holding out."

"Well, keep a look-out, will you? Someone's been watching our place. There's a campfire over there near the back of our property." She pointed through the trees.

"Hm. Come to think of it, I did smell wood smoke the other night. Thought someone had fired up their stove for the winter—you smell those fireplaces about this time every year."

"That's true. We've smelled it, too and thought nothing of it." She rubbed her forehead. "But you might be able to see it from here. You have our number, don't you?"

"Yep. And I'll sure keep watch. We don't want anyone messing in those woods, especially at night." Frank picked up his rake again.

"It's probably just kids, but we've had some trouble. Someone poisoned our cat and painted rude words on our garage."

"No kidding. What sort of words?"

"Fuck dykes."

His eyes widened. "Well, if that ain't the bees' knees." He shook his head. "Who'd do something like that? As nice a pair of neighbors as anyone could wish for. Some folks just don't understand ladies being able to take care of themselves, do they?"

"Is that what it's about?" The idea surprised her. "You could be right."

"Well, I'll keep an eye out, you can be sure. I sure don't appreciate that kind of trouble around here."

"Thanks, Frank. Well, I'll get on with my electronic adventure."

He nodded. "You take care, both of you."

Veronica walked away warmed by the utter normalcy of the neighborly encounter. How had they become so transformed in a matter of days? She headed to the crest of Cooper Road, gazed down at the Sound and distant San Juans and breathed in the green-laden northwest sea air. Racing clouds shifted light and dark in an ever-changing pattern—a daily light show that kept hundreds of painters and photographers on a life-long quest to capture the awe the sight inspired.

By the time she returned home, her universe redeemed, she'd almost persuaded herself her morning's upset was the vapors of an old woman. But she would go see Laura, just the same. She needed to know her reaction to the latest events.

"Well?" Charlotte asked. "How did you do?"

Veronica took the camera from her pocket and handed it to Charlotte. "I don't know. I admit it's kind of a kick to be able to just shoot with such abandon. It's probably going to disintegrate whatever discipline I've managed to maintain."

Charlotte turned the camera to display mode. "That's our campfire."

"Mm. Someone's been there since we saw it last. See the soda cans and hamburger wrappers?"

"Let's look at them on the computer." Charlotte opened the camera and removed the card.

A few minutes later, Veronica was viewing her afternoon's work in some surprise. "They're not bad, are they?"

"Luddite. See what you've been depriving yourself of?" Charlotte flipped on through. "Where is that?"

"Back in the woods between here and Cooper Road," Veronica responded, looking at the old RV. "It's been there for years."

"But there are fresh tire tracks."

"You're so right. I stopped and asked Frank Towers whether he'd seen anyone. He hadn't, but he's not happy that we've been targeted. I think he'll really keep an eye out, now."

Charlotte frowned, but went on through the pictures, stopping at those of distant views. "You are a marvel with the camera, Roni. I've seen shots of that scene a hundred times, but you catch the motion as well as the light. I don't know how you do it."

"The camera does a better job than I expected," Veronica conceded.

"Maybe I'll get you a fancier one for Christmas."

"Now, now, don't be trying to replace Constance. She's more demanding, which is a good thing, in the long run." She glanced at her watch. "Four thirty. Laura is probably home by now."

Charlotte sat back in her chair. "Is your mission fence-mending or confrontation, Roni?"

Veronica stopped with one arm in her coat. "The truth. Cutting the crap. Finding out where she stands."

"If you pick a fight, she's not going to tell you any more about David," Charlotte warned.

Veronica put her other arm into her coat more slowly. "All right. I'll keep that in mind."

Chapter 9

Laura's white SUV was in the drive of the stone and redwood house overlooking the Straits. Much too much house for a couple of kids just starting out, it stood now as the shell of Ted's ambitions in the world of finance. The realtor's sign at the end of the drive bore a "Price Reduced" tag in red. A rectangle of matted grass marked where their boat had been.

Veronica went to the door, and rang the bell, then studied the open garage as she waited. The jet ski and motorcycle were also gone.

"Mother!"

The jolt of the word spun Veronica back to the door. Her daughter's hostility always stabbed her afresh. "Hello, Laura. I hope you don't mind my dropping in unannounced, but I need to talk to you."

Laura blinked—wary. "Okay. I guess." She stood immovable for a long moment then backed away from the door.

Veronica went in and looked around the nearly empty living room. She'd been here just once before—at Laura and Ted's catered wedding reception. She'd been astounded—well, appalled, really—at the opulence of the leather couches, granite coffee tables, and hand woven rugs. They'd surrounded the great stone fireplace in excellent taste, but from a universe Veronica hadn't inhabited since her days as a corporate wife. She'd known, in those days, how much these objects cost because Simon had been drawn to them every time they'd shopped. She'd insisted they couldn't afford them, didn't want them, couldn't feel at home surrounded by them. He'd smiled and told her she'd grow into it, and she'd clenched her teeth and muttered, "God help me if I do."

Now the great room looked as though someone was in the process of moving out. The leather couches were gone. In their place was an old sofa Veronica recognized. It had been hers. The armchair on the other side of the fireplace looked familiar, too. She'd thought the offer of hand-me-downs would be welcome to newlyweds setting up house-keeping—an olive branch. She'd been disabused of that notion when she'd found them in the rec room of this great barn of a house.

"Looks different, doesn't it?"

Veronica turned at Laura's question, examined her daughter's face for resentment, and found instead a hint of challenge.

"We're going to be glad when it's all gone—this monstrosity of a house most of all." Laura waved her hand. "Ted sees it for what it is, now." Stocking-footed, she padded across the room to the arm chair.

Astonished, Veronica sank to the couch, fishing for words. "Tell me," she said, finally. "What is 'it'?"

"Trying to fill a hole with stuff—more and more stuff. Every time you get something, it's a high, then it fades away and you're empty."

"And now?"

Laura folded her arms across her chest before answering. "You'll laugh at me, but it's Jesus—the church people. Loving each other."

"When did I ever laugh at love?" Veronica fought an overwhelming sense of failure she only half understood, but there was no doubt that "loving each other" was directed at her.

Laura stared at her, unmoving. "You always laughed at church people."

"That was your father, not me. But he loved you. As did I."

"When we were little." Laura jumped up, her hand dropping to her sides, then went to the window and stared out at the empty November yard. "It's like getting that back."

"I'm glad you've found something to believe in, you and Ted." She spoke to Laura's back, willing it to soften. "Something other than stuff, as you call it."

"I have." Laura's voice was both defensive and certain. Buried in the tone was a command to leave her alone.

"And what about people outside your church, Laura?"

"What about them?" Laura folded her arms across her breast again, but didn't turn.

"When I was young—just out of high school, as a matter of fact—I almost became a Catholic," Veronica began, changing direction to get around the road block.

"You!" Laura swung around in surprise.

"Mmm. Me. I loved the music, the feeling of holiness—that kind of place. The dedication to preserving that kind of space."

For the first time, Laura seemed to be listening.

"I went to mass, learned the liturgy … but then, one day, I listened to the priest tell the faithful not to associate with non-Catholics. People like me. That people like me were a threat to their faith—to that holy place." Veronica stopped and filled her chest with air, dispelling the constriction she'd felt at that moment. "The whole thing turned sour. I never went back."

"But if you'd converted, you'd be changed, Mother. You wouldn't be one of those outside the church. And we'd have been religious, too!" For the first time, Laura's voice carried passion.

Veronica had broken through the barricades and ached to cry. "True, and raised you to believe outsiders were a danger to your holiness. I couldn't do that, Laura."

Her daughter shrugged and didn't answer.

"So I began to look elsewhere for my bits of truth. My camera finds them for me."

"Truth!" Laura stiffened. "Your truth!" She swung back to the window. "Not anyone else's."

Her venom took Veronica's breath. "Ah? So you've seen my last book?"

"No! But I've heard enough people talking about it to know I never want to see it."

Veronica stared at the rigid back. "I see. And what were they saying?"

Laura swung around. "That they desecrate the church. That's what. I was ashamed! Glad no one knows you're my mother!" Tears sprang to her eyes, and she clamped her mouth tight to stop them.

"But you didn't look at them yourself. You don't know what picture they're talking about." Veronica persisted out of some drive she didn't fully understand. Just a need to keep this conversation going.

"I don't want to see your pictures! Ever again. They just shut us out!" Laura's voice cracked. Her eyes showed the pain her anger sought to conceal.

"Us. You and David?" Veronica asked softly, surprised by the change of tack.

"All of us." Laura turned her back again.

"Is that what your father said about them?" Veronica trod gently. She felt as though they'd shifted back in time to a conversation she'd longed to have ten years ago.

"You always want to blame it all on him. You were the one who was gone. Anyway it's over, and I don't want to talk about it anymore." Laura turned and walked toward the back of the house.

Veronica sagged in disappointment, the moment gone. She got up and followed her daughter to the kitchen. "It would do us good to get the pain out, Laura."

"No, it's over. I've found something better, something that grows with other people. Swells in your heart."

Veronica knew she should let it go, simply depart before Laura kicked her out, but she wasn't ready to do that. "That's fine, Laura, as long as it doesn't turn ugly."

"It's not ugly! Why would you say that?"

"Because someone threw a rock through our window, killed our cat, and scrawled FUCK DYKES on our garage door, Laura. And it looks very much as though it was members of your youth group. One Luke Branscomb, in particular."

"Luke?" Laura stared at her for a long moment. "He wouldn't do that."

"Are you sure? We went to talk with your minister, Laura. He seemed to think it might be someone's overzealous hatred of sin."

"What does that have to do with Luke? Because he's religious? Just because your friend Charlotte messed up his life, you think he's some sort of delinquent?" Laura gripped the back of a bar stool, her knuckles white. "You need to go. Right now. David and I have found something beautiful. Healing. And I won't have you ruining it. I don't want any-thing to do with you!"

Veronica stood frozen in the doorway. "David? What has he to do with this? Is he a member of your church?"

"He has his own place. On the mainland, and I'm not going to tell you where. He doesn't want you in his life!"

Veronica continued to stare at her daughter, fitting this news with Laura's earlier comment that David had found a home. Their visit to the Cougar Gap rehab center was the explanation of that—he was an alcoholic. But that didn't connect David to Grace Bible church. Laura was that link. Laura wasn't telling her more, but she knew of Luke's connection to Charlotte. That could only have come from Luke himself.

She remembered Charlotte's warning about starting a fight. Had she squandered that one moment of connection by bringing up the attacks? Yes. But the whole point of her visit was to find out where Laura stood. The answer to that was clear in Laura's clenched hands and white face. "Ted already told me he was around Cougar Gap."

"That was a mistake. I should have known you'd go snooping."

"Who told you? Pastor Bob?"

"None of your business."

"David is my son. He's as much my business as yours." With that, Veronica turned and left. Once she'd regained the car, she sat and rubbed her eyes, then pinched her nose, cutting off tears of outrage enough to absorb the sudden re-emergence of David's name into the middle of this mess. This morning, she'd convinced herself he had nothing to do with it. She pressed her hands to the sides of her head to unscramble her thoughts. Finally, she started the engine and drove home.

Once she'd recounted the visit to Charlotte, she lay back in her chair, exhausted. "I don't know why she suddenly brought your name and David's into it. I don't think she meant to, really. But she's opened a door I don't want to walk through," she confessed. "Neither does Laura," she realized, seeing again the white-knuckled hands.

Charlotte didn't answer. She'd turned to her computer and was surfing the Internet. From her seat on the couch, Veronica could see the image of Grace Bible Church on the screen. Charlotte started punching links.

"I'm taking the dogs for a walk." Veronica rose and turned away. "Be back when I settle down enough to think." She shrugged back into her jacket. "Morty! Molly! Come!"

"Roni, it's dark," Charlotte objected, not removing her eyes from the screen.

"I have a light." She grabbed a flashlight from the shelf.

"Don't go out on the main road. There's not enough shoulder. You'll get picked off in a flash."

"Okay, so I'll patrol the fence. I just have to get out." And away from that screen, she concluded to herself.

She was less than half way around the perimeter, when the absurdity of what she was doing overcame her. What did she expect to find? Evidence of what? A coon? A mole? A deer? That was enough to interest the dogs, but no sinister footprint appeared in her light. No, she was succumbing to the feeling of being watched. She reached the back of the property and peered into the black wall of trees, searching for a flicker of camp fire, sniffed for the smell of smoke. Nothing. Reluctantly she turned back to the house.

Charlotte was still at the computer. On the screen was a log lodge set against the mountains. *"Eagles' Rest, a Place of Rebirth,"* the banner read.

"It's a camp or retreat of some sort," Charlotte said as Veronica came up.

"How did you find it?"

"It's linked to both Grace Bible Church and Serenity House."

"Those two are connected?" She searched the site for names and found none.

"Not necessarily. The church is just linked to other Christian organizations. But Serenity House is linked to AA also." Charlotte clicked on the "Contact us" button, which gave only the email address for the camp, a post office box in Cougar Gap, and a phone number.

"No names. And is this place linked to AA?"

"Yep. Through Al Anon."

"You think Eagles' Rest is connected to David, somehow?"

"I haven't a clue, really. At first I thought it sounded like a place for families to reunite, but now ..." She clicked another button, "... look at this."

Discover the strength the Lord gave you.
Reconnect with the glory of God's world.
Breathe in pure air that washes away all sin.
Year round explorations into God's work.

"And this." Charlotte clicked the "About Us" button.

Dedicated to helping youth find the true path by discovering God's creations.

"A camp for troubled youth," Veronica mused. "Well, that would connect to the Branscomb children. But to David, you think?" The possibility was calming. It brought back the small boy who'd loved the woods. The words spoke of a gentle, healing God, not the vengeful rock thrower, the poisoner of cats.

"I don't know, Roni. I'm just digging. Laura's comment about his having his own place suggests he's found a group. I'm just looking for groups that would fit."

Veronica nodded. "Makes sense. It truly seemed a David sort of place. Where is it?"

"There's no map. That looks like Glacier Peak in the distance, but that's as close as I can get. Which is odd, don't you think?"

"Um. Like they don't want people checking out the place."

"Reverend Starkweather could tell us," Charlotte mused.

"But won't." Veronica searched the link buttons for some clue. "Conrad. We can ask Conrad."

"True, but why would we want to know? What's our ruse?"

Veronica sat back in her chair and considered. "Would your brother Jonathan help? He had a hell of a time with your nephew, didn't he?"

"With Philip? True. The boy's been sober for a long time, as far as I know—though Jonathan still treats him like a fragile soul because Philip is—or was—in AA."

"So that's our ruse. Tell Conrad you're looking for a place for your nephew."

"It's November, Roni. Why would I be looking for a summer camp in November?"

"It says year-round activities," Veronica insisted.

Charlotte sighed. "You know, we're making this far more complicated than it needs to be." She clicked her way back to the contact screen and dialed the phone number.

Together they listened to the repeated rings until voicemail came on. *"You've reached Eagle's Rest Camp, a home away from home for youth. Please leave your name and number and we'll get back to you as soon as we can."*

"This is Emma Becker," Charlotte replied. "I'm interested in your camp for my nephew and would appreciate a call." She gave the number and hung up. "If David's at the other end of that phone, he'd recognize my name," she explained in answer to Veronica's raised eyebrows. She sat thinking for a moment, then picked up the phone again and dialed another number.

"Hi, Phil, how are you?"

Veronica could hear the surprise in her nephew's reply, though she couldn't make out the words. Charlotte and her corporate executive brother, Jonathan, had little in common and saw no reason to pretend they did. She sent Christmas presents to Philip out of habit, but had little other contact with the Bellevue family.

"Oh, we're good, as always. Listen, a colleague called. She's looking for summer camps for a couple of foster kids. Connected to AA or Al Anon if she can. I've been browsing the Internet and came across a place called 'Eagle's Rest.' Do you know anything about it?" She punched the speaker button.

"Yeah, sure. I know a couple of kids who went there. Sounded too religious for me, but they said it was a great place. They did lots of cool stuff like rock climbing, building huts out of logs—that kinds of thing."

"Sounds like the kind of place they might go for. Where is it, anyway?" Charlotte's voice was merely interested.

"Somewhere up around Cougar Gap. If you want to go see it, I could ask them."

"I'd appreciate that, Phil." She gave him the phone number and hung up. "Okay, that's a start. We'll see what pops."

Veronica turned and gazed at Constance, sitting neglected on the sideboard. Instead of her faithful friend, the capped lens was a hooded threat, exposer of secrets, truths best left buried. That wouldn't do. She couldn't let that happen. "I'm having island fever." She crossed the room and picked up the camera. "What do you say we get away from that screen and get off this island tomorrow? Constance needs a nice innocent photo-shoot."

"Probably a good idea. Where should we go?" Charlotte rose and stretched.

"To the ferry. We'll decide in the morning when we hit the mainland. Right now, I want dinner and a good movie on TV.

Chapter 10

The next morning, Mortimer and Molly milled around their feet as Veronica and Charlotte gathered their things, sensing a different sort of activity. "Let's take the dogs," Veronica said on impulse. "They need a change of scene as much as we do."

"We got them to guard the place, Roni." Molly turned at Charlotte's voice and jumped up against her leg, whining.

"All right, all right," Veronica conceded. "You're right. You have a job to do," she told Molly.

A half hour later, they were waiting at the ferry dock. Veronica sat behind the wheel, scanning the distant mainland, looking for some beckoning sign while Charlotte, beside her, rested her computer-burned eyes.

They disembarked on the mainland forty minutes later without a plan. Veronica was content to let the car find the way across the wetlands, then down the interminable interstate to Everett. Beside her, Charlotte dozed. Finally, they headed away from the suburban sprawl along the Sound toward open country and the foothills.

"Where are we?" Charlotte murmured a half hour later.

"On Highway 2, heading for the mountains, looking for a place to put Constance to work."

"Did you bring the Olympus, too?"

"I did. I'm going to compare the results."

Charlotte nodded. "You're headed toward Cougar Gap." She gave Veronica a knowing look. "But you know that."

"I'm just heading into the mountains."

Charlotte sighed. "How about a map?"

"What for?"

"Other roads in the area. There can't be that many, up here. You've always liked the back roads."

Charlotte was still rummaging in the side pocket when Veronica spied a road leading toward the Glacier Peak highlands and turned off. A few minutes later she stopped to photograph an abandoned barn framed by foothills high enough that their crevasses were already marked with snow. A pasture gate swung in the wind. The sun burst through, lighting the scene in racing shadows, a fast forward of passing time.

Using a fencepost as a tripod, Veronica lost herself in the imagery, shifting from camera to camera.

"Here, let me." Charlotte appeared beside her and held out her hand for the digital. "It doesn't take an expert to point and shoot."

"Okay, you're on." Veronica handed over the Olympus. "Hurry!" she exclaimed. "Look."

A deer appeared in the open doorway of the barn, as though taking it back as its own.

The animal was gone seconds later, and Veronica shifted her focus to the brown milkweed dancing around the fencepost at her feet. A spot of bright yellow flashed for a moment, and she climbed through the rotting rails to get a closer look. It was a biker's glove, mud-spattered but not old. Blown off the road when some cyclist stopped to fix a flat? She looked around and spotted a path—not really a path, but the sort of matting of weeds made by animals.

"Roni!" Charlotte called after her as she headed off.

"Come on!" A dozen paces later, Veronica paused. Another path intersected hers. Electing to go straight, she found herself heading toward the barn, passing two more lateral paths as she went. She stopped and waited for Charlotte to come up panting beside her. "The place is laced with them." She pointed to yet another path crossing theirs.

"Not animals," Charlotte decided, wrapping her arms around herself as the wind cut into her.

Veronica set off more rapidly now, across the clearing to the barn.

"This is not a friendly place, Roni," Charlotte said to her back.

Veronica didn't answer. She was standing in the open doorway of the abandoned building looking at the rotting stalls and rusting machinery, all of it dripping in blood.

Beside her, Charlotte uttered an unprintable sound.

Veronica moved forward and looked more closely. "Paintballs."

Charlotte closed her eyes and uttered a gasp of relief. "Nasty, but better than the alternative. What are you doing?" She watched Veronica adjust the setting on Constance. "Surely you don't want a picture of this."

"Surely I do. It's a mate to the picture of the deer." She looked around for something to set the camera on. Finding nothing, she headed for the car to get her tripod. "Do you have the digital?"

"Yes. Do we really have to do this—smash up that lovely picture of the deer, I mean?"

"Yes. Because I want to make people angry." She opened the car door and took out the tripod.

Ten minutes later, Veronica finished time exposures with both Constance and the as yet unnamed new camera, and they turned back toward the car. Veronica took a final look at the woods. "I really should go back there for a few shots of paint-spattered trees."

"Roni, no. We're not going into those woods." Charlotte took her arm and turned her away.

"I suppose you're right." Veronica allowed herself to be led to the car.

"Where do we go from here?" Charlotte fastened her seatbelt.

"We follow this road, I think. I'm curious now." She started the engine and accelerated, giving a sigh of relief as the barn disappeared in the rear view mirror.

The road took them through mossy, lichen-coated stretches of wood; then the rush of glacial water down a rock-strewn stream broke the silence. They followed it, passing a pair of anglers along the way, and came out into the sunshine of open meadows and a working farm. The peaks of the North Cascades rose in the distance. They took deep breaths, watched an eagle play on the thermals, and let the enormity of this land shrivel the barnyard scene. Constance and the new camera seemed happy to be put to work. Finally, they returned to the car and drove on.

Veronica braked in the middle of a right turn, as the sign she'd just read registered on her consciousness. The letters were carved in relief on a slab of wood and painted green. "Well, well. Look what we just found." She backed up around the turn.

"Eagle's Rest," Charlotte read. "Now if we had any idea where we were …?"

"We're on Jason Creek Road," Veronica answered, reading a half-tipped road sign. "Remember that." She drove another half-mile and they arrived at a clearing ringed by a cedar post and rail fence bearing the same sign. A pair of carved eagles sat on either side of the open gate. The log lodge of the website was set at the edge of the clearing, and next to it, a barn and a pair of smaller out-buildings. A pick-up truck was parked in front of the barn and there were a couple of off-road vehicles scattered about the yard, but no other signs of life.

"Are you ready for this, Roni?"

"No. Not really. But here I am." She turned the car into the drive and stopped. Her hands were icy. She clamped her mind shut on all thought.

Charlotte got out and came around, opening the driver's door. "Come on, then, let's get it over with."

They climbed to the front porch of the lodge, and Charlotte gave the leather bell pull a jerk. The cascade of bells from inside sounded friendly enough, but no one came to the door.

Veronica let out her breath in relief, more than ready to beat a retreat, but Charlotte eyed the pickup and headed for the barn. A horse whinnied from within, and Charlotte yanked at the heavy double door. A warm blast of hay and horse washed over them as they blinked to readjust to the dim interior.

"Can I help you?"

The voice turned them around.

A slim shape stood in the doorway of the neighboring shed. It wasn't David. Veronica moved from shock to a mixture of relief and disappointment.

Charlotte approached him. "We're looking for David."

"Ah? David who?" He was of medium height, with a balding pate and pleasant face, but his voice was cautious.

"I don't know," Charlotte confessed, shutting off Veronica's reply. "I was looking for a place for my nephew, and Serenity House told me about Eagle's Rest—told me one David ran it."

"That so? Usually they just refer folks to the web-site."

"Oh, they did. And I left a message there. We were just out on a photo-shoot and came across your sign by accident." Charlotte gave him a bright smile.

He nodded, reassured. "I see. Well, I can give you a brochure of the place, if you like. David won't be here till the weekend."

They followed the man across the yard to the lodge. Inside, the stone fireplace was surrounded by comfortable, if worn, couches, scarred coffee tables and threadbare rugs. The walls sported the expected deer-head and painted Northwest Indian masks.

"If you want to leave a number, I'll have him call you." The caretaker handed them brochures.

"I left it on the website. Emma Becker."

"He'll call you," the man assured her.

"Thank you for letting us drop in like this." Veronica closed the brochure and took Charlotte's arm. "We'll wait to hear from him."

"That's okay. Hope the camp suits your need." He held the door for them.

They were descending the porch steps when a green van with the camp's logo drove into the yard.

A moment later, Veronica confronted a man so familiar it brought unbidden tears. His now more mature face looked like more like his father but with her dark eyes and tousled curls. There was gray at the temples, now and a crease on either side of his mouth. The relaxed expression on his face, however, had frozen. "Hello, David."

Beside her, Veronica heard the startled exclamation of the caretaker.

"Hello, Mother." He barely moved his lips, and his glance flicked to Charlotte and back again. "How did you find this place?"

"By accident—mostly." She was amazed at how easily the words came, despite the hostility on his face. Was she getting used to this confrontation mode? "I need to talk to you."

"I've nothing to say to you." He turned and opened the rear doors of the van. "Mark, give a hand with this stuff, will you?" David lifted a case of toilet paper and tossed it to him. "When the hell did they get here?"

"Five-ten minutes ago." Mark's voice was apologetic. "The other lady gave her name—"

"That's okay," David interrupted. "Not your fault."

Veronica cut him off as he came around the truck. "It's not anyone's fault, David. And I didn't come to do you harm. Relax."

"What do you want?" He pulled a bag of potatoes from the van, slung it over his shoulders and marched toward the house.

She followed and felt Charlotte at her shoulder. "To talk."

He pulled open the lodge doors, crossed the living room to the kitchen, through the kitchen to the pantry behind it, then swung the bag from his shoulder and straightened."Why?" He shot the word without turning.

His bearing—that stubborn set to his shoulders, the defense of the backside, the arms folding across his chest—were so familiar she felt tears come to her eyes again. This was the same small boy she remembered defending his attack on a boy who'd bullied him. "At the very least, to understand." And she was the same mother, accepting the defense.

But he didn't turn around. "What's to understand, Mother? I've made a life out of the tatters you left. A place for abandoned boys where they're loved." He swung around, his eyes hard. "So why are you here? If you came up here crawling on your knees for forgiveness, why did you bring her?" He flung an arm out toward Charlotte without looking her way. "Just leave me in peace." He pushed past them and left the pantry.

"Then you tell your minions to leave *us* in peace!" Charlotte could hold her peace no longer.

"What's the dyke talking about?" He stopped in the kitchen door and turned to face Veronica.

The grossness of the insult made a stranger of her son. "If you want to know, you turn and ask her." Veronica didn't recognize the voice, emptied of all but teeth-clenching anger, as her own. She fought the urge to turn and walk out.

"Rocks through our window, a poisoned cat, obscenities painted on our garage door." Charlotte moved in front of Veronica, where he couldn't avoid facing her.

"What has that got to do with me?" He looked over her head at the opposite wall.

"That's what we came to find out." Veronica took a step to the side so she stood next to Charlotte. "Is Luke Branscomb a camper here?" The change in his eyes told Veronica the answer. "And friends of his—from Laura's and Ted's youth group?"

"I have no idea what you're talking about. Now get out."

They stood staring at him for a long moment before turning to leave.

"But if they did, God bless them!" David Lorimer cried as they reached the door.

Veronica stopped. Charlotte gave her a push.

They were down the steps to the car before either of them spoke. Charlotte led her to the passenger seat and took the wheel.

"I'm sorry." Veronica put a hand on her friend's, fighting for breath enough to speak. "I don't know that man …" She closed her eyes. "I would not for the world have let that happen. You know that."

"You aren't responsible for what he says—or does." Charlotte started the engine with a roar, then calmed herself, turned the car and headed out between the eagles.

"Yes, I am. Mothers are always responsible." The words came from memory. Charlotte had uttered them as her daughter lay dying of cancer.

In the silence that followed, Charlotte gave her hand an answering squeeze. "Sometimes I wonder what pain I was spared," she confessed. "But you still have hope—so you hang on. Death of a child kills that. Something deep inside breaks loose … has to turn … find another path to survive."

Veronica opened her eyes and watched the passing trees, listened to the cascading water beside them. She tried, and not for the first time, to imagine what it had been like for Charlotte—to have motherhood torn away, but she couldn't reach around the anger shaking her. "That's what Laura and David say—that they've found a path to survive." She gave a small laugh. "In fact, I used to tell them that—to respect—even be fascinated by the multitude of paths people find to keep going." She rubbed a hand down her face. "I'd show them pictures I took—a fortuneteller in her turban, reading her cards, a young man leaning over the handlebars of his bike, a hawker at a carnival, a beekeeper …" She closed her eyes as memories flooded—a small boy with a camera following her around a muddy swamp, proudly showing a blurry picture of a heron, a small David pasting pictures into his own book.

"Religion has saved a lot of people, Roni. After Ellie died and I was floundering, unable to get my breath, I used to recite the Twenty-third Psalm. It was like throwing an anchor. I wasn't alone. Others had walked that path."

"I suspect you yelled at Him, too, which is what I feel like doing right now." She rubbed her eyes. "I want Him to explain how this could have happened to my little boy."

Charlotte made a turn, and they continued through a lichen-coated swampland. "Well, at least David's not drunk under some bridge or dead of liver disease in some hospital."

"True." They drove out of the woods and across farmlands in silence. Veronica closed her eyes again, seeking calm in the hum of the tires. She felt the car slow and turn, bringing her out of her half-numb daze. They were back at the abandoned barn where they'd begun this adventure.

"We need a map, but if I'm not mistaken, we're behind the camp." Charlotte turned the engine off.

"Really? I wasn't paying attention." Veronica looked at the woods beyond the barn, then at her watch. Only two o'clock. "Want to take a walk?"

"Not very badly."

"Come on. We need to know the worst of this mess." She opened the car door and stamped her feet to shake off the lethargy that anger had left behind. Then she reached into the back seat to retrieve Constance.

"All right, all right," Charlotte called as Veronica set off down the road toward the barn. "Wait up."

They passed the barn and headed for the woods. As Veronica had guessed, the trees were spattered with imitation blood. Like the meadow, the area was laced with paths, some bearing the tracks of off-road vehicles. Veronica vented her anger by putting Constance to work. "Tell me, Charlotte, what is the point of this?" She waved a hand at the surrounding imitation carnage.

"Channeling anger."

"I suppose." She snapped a picture of a pine sapling flattened by a tire, and they went on.

Ten minutes later, they came to a fence and a gate marked with a "No Trespassing" sign.

"So." Charlotte considered situation. "Is it the camp or not?"

"There's only one way to find out." Veronica lifted the wire loop that held the gate shut.

Charlotte sighed. "How did I ever get hooked up with a vandal, anyway?"

"It's the hidden side of you. You love it." Anger at her son's abuse of Charlotte drove her feet, stamping the hurt of it underfoot. She was going to find out the worst of it—now.

The woods around them were unmolested and smelled of red cedar and damp earth. The light was tinged green by the moss. The ground beneath their feet crackled with the fresh coating of fallen leaves. "This is better." Charlotte took a deep breath and let it out. "And it fits with their website promises—finding His way."

Charlotte made a noise that might have been assent. "Except that those ..." She pointed at the trail, "are off-road tire tracks." She put her arm out, stopping Veronica. "Hush."

Distant voices floated through the trees. They moved forward with greater caution until they could see the light of a clearing ahead. A few more steps and they glimpsed the log lodge through the trees. As they watched, David Lorimer appeared in the clearing, talking to the man behind him as he headed for his truck.

Charlotte grabbed Veronica's arm and pulled her away. "Quick!" She headed back down the path at a near run.

Veronica followed. "What's wrong?" she muttered. "They didn't see us."

"He'll see the car."

Veronica blanched at the idea, and they raced for the gate—a broad enough gate to accommodate an off-road vehicle, she noted—and took off through the blood-spattered battlefield. Veronica expected to reach the clearing at every turn, but every turn produced another stretch of trees. Gasping, they were forced to slow down. Finally, at the edge of a clearing, they spied their car, a glaring advertisement of their presence. And beyond the car, the green van sat in the road. They froze, watching David climb out, circle the van and then gaze toward the woods.

After a moment that stretched interminably, he turned and went back to his van, which jerked and sped away with an angry burst of gas.

Veronica let out her breath. "He didn't see us, at least, or come after us."

Charlotte headed for the car without answering.

"And why does it matter if he knows we were here ...?" Veronica tripped over a snag and regained her balance.

"Snooping," Charlotte finished for her.

"So he's angry. So am I. So what?" They reached the car, and Veronica sank into her seat. "He's my son, for God's sake, Lotti. And if his camp has anything to do with this ..." She waved a hand at the barn and woods, unable to go on.

"You know it does, and so do I." Charlotte started the engine and backed onto the road, then sped off. "Let's get the hell out of this Janus-faced paradise."

Veronica's mind brought up the Christ/Lucifer image familiar from history. "I had an uncle—a great uncle really—who was a preacher. I only saw him once or twice. He died when I was little, but I remember him holding me on his lap. Then I saw him in the pulpit—just once—but his face changed. He was yelling at the congregation about hell and his face was red and sweaty, contorted with rage. I was terrified."

"Like that picture in your last book."

Veronica stared at the memory of David's face and final words. "And if they did, God bless them!" She leaned back and closed her eyes again. "I want to go home, please."

Chapter 11

The sky turned slate gray as they drove toward the ferry. They said little. Charlotte frowned at the road, her lips compressed.

The scene at the lodge dropped its full weight on Veronica. She pressed her fingers to her eyes to stop the tears, which only intensified the pain. When her children were adolescents, she'd borne their anger as normal and returned it with anger of her own. But the adult she'd confronted at the lodge was a stranger. The son she remembered was gentle. Did that David return when he counseled lost boys? Had he found a place for that compassion? If so, she was to have no part in it. She'd been a trusted ally—the one he'd come to when tougher boys called him a wuss. He'd turned morose, nursing his hurt for long silent days in his room. She'd bring him out of it by suggesting a day out in the open, looking for eagles—a bait he could never resist. Where was that boy? That trust?

The word triggered a memory. David was thirteen. A gaggle of toughs had gathered around him behind the school, where he'd gone to retrieve his bike. They'd knocked him off, kicked him, and left him bleeding, screaming in pain from a broken arm. A teacher had found him there, but when they'd called Veronica, she didn't answer. She was out with her camera, and some accidental jab of a button had turned her cell phone off. So it was Simon who retrieved him, a recently laid off Simon, betrayed by the world, who told him his mother was off doing her own thing, now. Liberated from all of them. David, he said, had to fight his own battles, now.

She'd come home to find Simon teaching his white-faced son to punch. David, his arm in a cast, wore a boxing glove on his good hand. His face was swollen on one side where he'd hit the pavement, his dark eyes flat with shock, and he was returning punches with a viciousness she had never seen. David saw her at the door and turned his back, throwing another punch with his good arm. Simon flicked a glance at her, then he, too, turned back to the lesson. She stood there, shut out.

Veronica closed her eyes against the memory, but the feeling persisted. Had she ever regained his trust? No. And that beating changed David. It was as though it had jolted him into adolescence. His friends changed. David had always had good friends, but singly; he'd never hung out with a group. Now he had three or four who came to the house together and barely acknowledged her as they went up the stairs to his room. They had a harder edge—boys who had learned far too soon that the world didn't give a damn.

When she tried to get through the barrier by inviting him to a day out with the camera, it felt like wheedling, and she wasn't surprised that he snorted.

Other mothers assured her that this was normal adolescence, but it wasn't. The difference hit her in the face every time she walked into her house. The rooms looked abandoned, as though the bonds that had given it life had disintegrated. Memories that marked each chair, the scratches on the coffee table, the pottery hand prints of small children, brought only the pain of loss. No one spent more time here than they had to, anymore. Laura lived at her friends' houses, Simon at the sports bar. David occupied his room, nothing more. More often than not, Veronica ate alone.

The darkroom in the basement became her refuge when she wasn't out with her camera.

Then, one night, Simon came in only half-drunk, bearing pizza and calling for his children. She went upstairs and found them gathering at the kitchen table, and for a moment her heart sang with hope.

"You here?" he said in surprise when he saw her. "Only brought enough for *us*." The stress on the last word made it clear that "us" did not include her.

She stayed only long enough to see the satisfaction in David's eyes and the averted head of her daughter. Embarrassed? Ashamed? The next day she went to see a lawyer. Charlotte McAllister.

Veronica opened her eyes and looked at her friend. Charlotte had never accused her of abandoning her family, and in the years after she knew Charlotte's story, she'd often wondered why. For her friend, death and illness had cemented the bonds of marriage. If Simon had become ill rather than being cut adrift, would their lives have been different? No. Simon was created by his confidence in himself, his certainty that life would always go his way. It anchored his character. Illness would have been no different—being thrown out of that world, without recourse. Deprived of his goals, he would have been consumed with the same bewildered anger that could only flail around, seeking a target. And she wasn't there. She had found a goal beyond the walls of her marriage. It had never, in her mind, replaced family, only substituted for the increasing independence of growing children. Or helped her survive their rage.

But for Simon? Abandonment. Her being acknowledged her crime. If he had been ill, would she have stayed? Yes, if his pride ever let him acknowledge his need for her. Which it wouldn't. She would have become a target. Charlotte had told her stories of care-giving clients who were victims of their ill spouse's helpless rage and humiliation. Later—years later—she'd learned that Charlotte had been one of those. But she hadn't left him. For Veronica, that explained the stoic, unbendable exterior that made Charlotte the toughest lawyer in the docket.

Veronica had been unable to watch her husband come apart like a house whose foundation had given way. Would she have been able to take the ravages of illness? She'd asked herself that over and over without coming to a conclusion. Maybe, if illness hadn't revealed his lack of inner resources the way unemployment had ... That was what she had run from. Leaving her children. How could she have done that?

"You haven't left them, Veronica," Charlotte had told her over and over. "They made the choice, not you."

"But his drinking. I can't just leave them with him and tell myself ..." Memory of the exchange faded. She couldn't remember what she'd told herself—many things, over the years, but nothing had ever convinced her she'd done right. Now she watched as the car reached the freeway and was swallowed in Seattle suburban traffic. The day was darkening and a fine mist blew against the windshield. Laura's words came back. "David and I have found something beautiful." *We're all right*, the words said. Make that enough.

For a brief moment, she released herself from the past, but the image of the lodge was blotted out by the paint-splattered trees, the defaced barn. The placid face of Pastor Bob at Serenity House became the patronizing gaze of Reverend Starkweather as he excused the overzealous. The two preachers merged with her uncle's face from the pulpit, calling his anger the Voice of God.

"Perfect." Charlotte's voice brought her back to reality, and she realized they had left the freeway and crossed the valley to the ferry terminal. The boat was loading as they paid the fare. Charlotte had stared straight ahead, saying nothing the whole way.

She examined her friend's face, searching the cause, but saw only an attentive driver, following the signalman's directions onto the boat.

Veronica settled into a seat in the lounge. Charlotte went first to the restroom, then to the front outdoor deck, then, driven back by the weather, she resorted to pacing.

Veronica watched with mounting concern. Pacing wasn't Charlotte's style. Charlotte made decisions and acted. "For heaven's sake, Lotti, sit."

Charlotte heaved a sigh and complied, but turned her head to the sea. Strain stiffened the lines of her face.

"You're acting like a trapped tiger—which isn't like you."

"No." Her friend turned to her. "But I *am* trapped."

"Go on."

"Because you have to let go of this, and I don't know whether you can. Which makes me helpless." She slapped her hands on the table.

"Which is definitely not your thing," Veronica quipped, trying to lighten the mood.

"It's not funny, Roni. It's dangerous. For Godsake, tell them we're not lesbians."

"Laura and David?" She remembered Laura's reaction to her offered denial. "What makes you think they would believe me?" Even as she said it, she realized she'd tangled Charlotte in a story not her own.

Charlotte reached across the table and took her hands. "But if they did, you'd get them back, wouldn't you? And maybe that damned church would become less important. It's worth a try."

"They'd stop harassing us, you mean. And go after someone else?"

"We don't know that. We don't even know David's behind it all. All we know is Luke and his friends are members of the church and the camp—which is not what anyone would call evidence, Roni."

Veronica turned her eyes to the sea this time. "Just our guts."

"Just our guts," Charlotte agreed. "Because it all ties in so neatly with your personal past. But what do we have, really, Roni? A couple leading a Bible study group for troubled youth. A man running a camp for the same purpose. Angry boys taking it out on the trees behind the camp. A psychologist would probably tell you that's a healthy thing. Far better than ..." She broke off.

"Killing cats? Painting obscenities on garage doors?"

Charlotte gave another sigh and ran her hands through her hair. "If they're the culprits—which we don't know. All I do know is you have to let go—walk away from the mess and let them ... be."

"Before we rile them up any further? I know ... or part of me knows. The other part is just plain scared of what Laura and David are into. And I don't see how telling them we're not lesbians would change that."

Charlotte fell silent, and they both gazed past the wind-splattered window into the gray waters of the Sound.

"It would change you, Roni. Release you." She spoke to the water. "For a year—more than that—I wore Ellie's old blue flannel shirt around the house. Every evening I'd pull it on. I never asked myself what I was doing, what it meant. I just had to do it." She turned and faced Veronica. "Then, one day, I packed it away. It was over."

Veronica looked at their still-clasped hands. *And you want me to have that day.* "Is there a way to do that when they're still alive?" The words came without thought, leaving her appalled. She gave Charlotte's hand a squeeze of apology. "Come on, we're docking."

They drove home chatting about domestic details, relieved to have at least unburdened themselves and restored communication. Charlotte turned into the grocery store parking lot. "Let's have ourselves a spit-roasted chicken. No cooking tonight."

"I'll second that. " Veronica examined the baked goods by the door. "And cinnamon rolls for breakfast," she decided.

Armored against the fading November day, they headed down the island toward home. Charlotte sniffed. "Smells as though everyone's fired up their wood stoves tonight."

Veronica frowned. The cloud ahead wasn't mist. "More like burning brush."

Charlotte turned into their drive—"Oh dear God, what ...?"

The car jolted to a stop.

"It's us! Oh no—no, please no ..."

Ahead was a fire truck, and the stench of charred wood hit them in the face.

They were out of the car in a flash. A fireman approached as they stood staring at the house. It stood. No smoke blackened the windows or yard. Where were the dogs? Yin Yang?

"Hello, ladies, you the owners?" He held out a hand. "Captain Wilson. Your shed out back caught fire."

"The shed," Veronica repeated, relief flooding her voice.

"What on earth ...where are the dogs?" Charlotte looked around, trying to get her bearings.

"And the cat?" Veronica added.

"We had to get animal control out here. They weren't going to let us in." The fireman smiled. "You can go get them anytime. Fire's out. We're just doing clean-up now."

"When did it happen?" Veronica started for the back of the house.

"Long about four, I'd say. A neighbor called it in. Saw the smoke and heard the dogs howling."

They reached the back yard. Eyes stinging in the smoke, noses covered against the smell, they stared at the blackened mess that had been their shed.

Veronica felt everything inside her—grief, self-incrimination, compassion—incinerate. "This is one too many. This is it." She clenched her fists in mounting rage, then turned and walked away, taking deep breaths to calm herself.

"How did it start, do you know?" She heard Charlotte ask, behind her.

"Not yet. Do you keep paint or gasoline out here?"

"Probably both," Charlotte conceded, "but there's plenty of ventilation ..." She broke off and Veronica turned. The fireman was handing the chief the remains of a quart jar.

The fireman sniffed, then frowned and walked over to the ruins. A few minutes later, he was back. "Does this look familiar to you?"

Charlotte shook her head and Veronica joined her and sniffed, her nose confirming her suspicions. "Gas."

The fireman nodded. "I'd say it was a Molotov cocktail."

Charlotte's hands dropped to her sides. Veronica closed her eyes, words she'd never uttered pressing against her lips.

"Do you know of anyone who'd set your shed on fire?"

They stared. "How? The dogs would keep them out." Charlotte's voice was harsh with disbelief.

"They could pitch this from outside the fence. Easily." The fireman pointed. "And the dogs were raising Cain. We know that." He turned to the second fireman. "Go look for footprints, Tom—outside the fence behind the shed." He turned back to them. "If this is arson," he began again, "we need to investigate."

"Thank you. Absolutely, yes." Veronica spoke through clenched teeth.

Charlotte nodded. "I suggest you start with whoever poisoned our cat, painted 'Fuck Dykes' on our garage door, and threw arocks through our front window."

Wilson's brows went up. "Have you reported those things to Sheriff Astor?"

"We have." Charlotte folded her arms.

"Except for the 'Fuck Dykes,'" Veronica added. "We didn't see much point—he thought the other things were just kids."

"This time 'just kids' isn't good enough." Veronica crossed her arms over her chest. "We're lucky the woods didn't catch. Probably would have if it hadn't been raining all afternoon. Or if there'd been a wind."

"Do you have any idea who those kids were?" Wilson asked.

Veronica and Charlotte looked at each other for a long moment.

"Yes. You bet." Veronica restrained the anger that was pushing at her vocal chords.

"We have ideas," Charlotte moderated, "but no evidence."

"So tell me."

A breeze sprang up, blowing the stench into their nostrils as the shed faded into the dark.

"All right, we will." Charlotte's voice was determined. "Come in and have a cup of coffee."

Frightened of the pressure that had built up in her chest, Veronica let Charlotte tell the story in more reasoned tones than she could have managed. She only wanted to grab Luke around the neck and scream at him, push his nose into the ashes. And she was terrified that her children had some hand in it. Outraged that she'd spent an hour justifying David's ugliness.

Charlotte was interrupted only once, when Tom came in to report that there was a trampled spot outside the fence and a couple of possible prints leading into the woods. At that point they lost them in the bed of pine needles that carpeted the forest floor.

A half hour later, Captain Wilson put his pen and pad away. "So you think David Lorimer called the Branscomb boy to tell him you were nosing around up there?"

"I don't know that," Charlotte replied. "But I think this was meant to scare us away."

Veronica said nothing. She should be horrified at implicating David in this. She wasn't. Her outrage had left her numb.

The fireman nodded. "Okay, I'll let you know what we find." He looked around. "And you'd better get those dogs. They were doing a very good job of keeping us out of your yard." He smiled and tipped his hat.

A minute later, they listened to the roar of the fire truck backing out of their drive.

They drove out soon after and headed for the animal shelter. Molly and Mortimer barked, howled and whined all the way home, recounting the insults of their afternoon. Yin Yang just glared. When they turned thedogs loose into the yard, they raced for the back, where they sniffed and howled at the charred remains of their shed.

The roast chicken was cold. Wet ashes had so permeated their senses that everything they put in their mouths tasted. The stench had soaked into their clothes, gagging them.

"I'm about ready to evacuate for a motel," Veronica exclaimed, sniffing a clean dish towel.

"We don't dare leave." Charlotte washed the last pan and set it in the drain.

"It's going to stink for days." Veronica dried the pan and shoved it into the cupboard, slamming the door after it. "Making me madder by the minute."

"That's not the effect they intended."

"Too bad."

Charlotte drained the dishwater and dried her hands. "Roni ..."

"What?" She sank into a chair, exhausted, and pulled Yin Yang into her lap.

"I think ... you wouldn't have given the fire captain David's name— or mentioned the camp. So how much do you mind that I did?"

"I should mind … but I don't." She slapped her hands on the counter. "All the minding I had in me burned in that fire. I'm so angry it scares me."

"I know. It's been coming off you in waves. But when you cool down … what then?"

"You had to do it. I know that." Her last words slapped the air. "Lotti, I never protected my kids from the consequences of what they did, and parents who did made me furious. Believe me, I was angry enough to tell him myself." Veronica turned away, choking at the idea of doing that. "Dear God, I hope …"

"Hope what?"

"David's not behind this—and maybe he isn't. Maybe Luke acted for him without his knowledge. Maybe he doesn't know his boys are going through the back gate to the paintball range. Maybe Luke's target is you, not me, for taking him away from his mother. Maybe … maybe, maybe, maybe. But their religion justifies that—" She pointed. "And I'm going to—" she broke off and closed her eyes. "Just give me a straw to grab that will keep me from going off after them all, including the Reverend, and pushing their nose into those ashes until …" She gave a huff and sank back. "Until someone stops me."

"We need answers." Molly jumped into Charlotte's lap, distracting her. She rubbed the dog's ears. "Maybe the sheriff will listen to Chief Wilson."

"Another maybe." Veronica was suddenly very tired, drained. She leaned back and closed her eyes. Her mouth tasted of the sodden ash. She heard Charlotte get up and opened them again. She was standing at the window, looking out at the blackness. "What are you thinking?"

"I'm wondering what kind of an arm it would take to pitch a jar through this window without coming into the yard."

Veronica rose and joined her at the window. A heavy calm had replaced her anger. The fence looked far too close. "Well, they won't do it when we're here. The dogs would alert us. In fact, I think Frank will be listening for them now and come investigate." She turned away, determined to close the door on the combination of anger and fear that was, like the smell of ashes, beginning to sour the house.

She crossed the room and turned on the television. "Come on, let's bury ourselves in a lousy movie."

When their noses had finally cleared of the stink left by the day, they retired to their chill beds. Veronica dreamt of swimming in a gray swamp that grew thicker and thicker, her limbs heavier and heavier. She fought free and swung. Then there was a boy on the ground—headless. She woke with a jolt as the foul mixture of terror and ash filled her mouth and invaded her nostrils. She leapt from the bed, shaking her head free, and sat, unable to stop trembling. Finally, she headed for the shower to drive the dream away.

She emerged ten minutes later, reveling in the few moments of freshness she would have before the stench soaked into her flesh. She dressed quickly and took Constance to the back yard. Action, any kind of action, was vital to control the anger simmering at the fringe of consciousness. Focusing on the hatred emanating from the charred wood, the blackened remains of a rake handle, the twisted form of a half-melted fertilizer bottle gave physical certainty to the assaults and legitimacy to her rage. She let the camera roam until Constance found her target: the remains of the tool-caddy David had made for her in shop class when he was ten. David's name in his childish hand was still visible on its blistered red paint. It was full of black water. Anger broke and she sobbed.

Chapter 12

Shivering, she returned to the house. "Sometimes, you're not a friend," she told the camera as she set it on its shelf.

"You've been out already?" Charlotte asked, coming down the stairs.

"Only to the shed." She took a breath to get past the image that wouldn't fade. "I was going to go out and take a look at that RV, but ..."

"Alone? Don't be stupid, Roni."

"Okay, then get your clothes on. We do need to see if it's occupied."

"After breakfast," Charlotte pronounced. "Coffee first. Did you put the pot on?"

"No. but I will; go get dressed." Veronica had fed the dogs and warmed the cinnamon rolls by the time Charlotte returned, dressed for the woods.

"Let's take Morty and Molly," Charlotte suggested as they cleaned up.

"No, I don't want them barking—broadcasting our presence." Veronica hung up the dishtowel and went to get her coat, boots and cameras.

They started by examining the footprints the fireman had found yesterday outside their fence then tried to follow them into the woods. They might or might not go toward the campfire. As Wilson had said, pine needles obliterated the arsonist's footfalls. The fire-ring, when they reached it, showed no sign of recent use, nor were there any footprints in the clear space around it.

"Which means nothing, of course," Charlotte remarked, "Since our fire-bug was here in broad daylight. No reason for a fire."

The morning brightened as they continued through the woods, and the RV, sitting in the sunshine of a clearing, looked equally innocent. The derelict was silent, its rusted siding and boarded windows telling nothing. They circled the clearing, keeping well behind a screen of trees. The tire tracks leading into the woods on the far side looked fresh.

Charlotte put a hand out, stopping Veronica. "Look. The door's ajar."

The metal door was indeed open a crack, as though stuck.

"Was it that way before?" Charlotte asked.

Veronica shook her head. "I don't think so."

They waited, motionless, as though something was bound to happen. Nothing did.

Charlotte started forward just as Veronica's ears picked up a faint shuffling, and she grabbed her friend's arm. "Wait ..."

But Charlotte's foot cracked a stick as Veronica breathed the word, and a moment later a boy appeared in the doorway, his head swinging from right to left.

"Well, well." Charlotte's words were soft as the rustling leaves of the forest. "Look who we have here." She stepped from the woods. "Hello, Norris."

But Norris Stoner, object of island-wide manhunt, wasn't staying around to talk this time. He was down the steps and into the woods to their right before they were half way across the clearing. They could only stand watching. There was no point in chasing after him.

Instead they mounted the rusty stairs and went inside. The walls of the musty interior were covered with graffiti. A bare mattress that had obviously provided a home for vermin lay along one wall. On the other, a pair of chairs sat on either side of a small table, spilling their batting through splits in the green vinyl of their cushions. At the other end of the room were a filthy sink and a rusty stove. On the counter between them was a bright red gasoline can.

Without a word, Charlotte pulled out her cell-phone and punched in the number of the fire station. "Captain Wilson, please."

Veronica looked around the room for the blankets and pack the boy had had at their first encounter. "He didn't have anything with him."

Charlotte, waiting on the line, looked around. "True. It doesn't look as though he was staying here ... Hello? Captain Wilson? Charlotte McAllister, here. I think we've found our arsonist's headquarters." She went on to describe their find, then stopped. "Roni, do you have any idea where the hell we are? This damn cell-phone's too old to give a GPS signal."

Veronica blinked. "Somewhere along Cooper Road. We'll have to find out more exactly and call him back."

Charlotte nodded, transmitted the message, and flipped the phone closed. "He'll have Sheriff Astor send a deputy as soon as we call back with the location. Whew! Let's get out of here."

Veronica put both cameras to work before following her friend outside.

"It doesn't make sense—that it was Norris." Charlotte was looking in the direction the boy had taken.

"I agree, but—there he was." An irrational relief flooded Veronica as she said the words. "And we know the police are looking for him." She walked toward the rutted drive that led to the road.

"Careful. Don't mess up those tire tracks." Charlotte followed. "And how do you explain those? Norris Stoner was on foot—he always is."

"Except when he steals a car." Veronica reminded her.

"That was on Drummond. No one here has reported a car stolen. We would have heard it on the evening news."

"Is that you, Lotti, proposing we conceal evidence—again?" They reached the road, and Veronica looked one way, then the other, trying to spot familiar signposts.

"If we tell them the whole thing—everything that's happened will be due to Norris Stoner. You know that. It's so much easier that way."

Veronica spotted a mailbox and headed toward it and away from Charlotte's words. "But it lets David and Laura off the hook," she muttered, giving voice to her elation. And Charlotte, bless her heart, was calling that for what it was. Shame replaced relief as she trudged to the top of the rise.

She reached the box and could see a street sign in the distance. "This way!" she called.

They reached the intersection with what was clearly a more major road.

"Our road?" Charlotte asked doubtfully.

Veronica shook her head. "Wrong way. It's Roger's Crest, I think." She started off to her right. "I'll know if we come to the Grange." She tramped in silence for a while, searching her mind for some middle ground. "We can say we saw a boy—not that we know it was Norris Stoner."

"Who's going to buy that? His picture has been blazing from the front page for a month."

Veronica sighed. "So, who says we read the paper?" She paced on ahead, avoiding the argument she no longer had the heart for. "Well, there's the Grange," she said a few minutes later. "So we know where we are, anyway."

"You do. Here …" She handed Veronica the phone. "You tell them."

Veronica conveyed the information, and they retraced their steps. They passed the rutted entrance to the clearing twice before they spotted it. Once they'd made sure it led to the RV, they posted themselves at the end of the driveway to wait.

"If they catch him, he's going to tell them he talked to us before, and we'll have to explain that. They'll going to argue that if we'd reported finding him in that abandoned house, none of this would have happened to us."

"Which neither of us believes." Veronica concluded.

"What we believe doesn't matter."

"It'll matter, if they don't look further." Because it wouldn't stop, Veronica knew. It wouldn't stop, and no one would listen.

They heard a car in the distance, and the cruiser appeared over the rise a moment later.

"Hello, ladies." The pleasant-faced deputy who'd answered Veronica's call when the rock came through the window stepped out of the car.

"Deputy Hansen, isn't it?" She held out her hand.

"That's right." He looked pleased she remembered. "I hear you've had more trouble."

They led him down the drive to the RV. He gave a short laugh at the sight of the gas can. "Well, well. That's pretty obviously our culprit, isn't it?" He looked around the room for other signs of occupancy. "I'll have that fingerprinted, and you'll get your answer. All we need to do is keep an eye on the place. He'll be back, I'd guess." He made notes on his pad, then drew on gloves and picked up the can. "Haven't seen anyone around, have you?" he asked as he turned to leave.

"We saw a boy when we first got here." Charlotte's voice tried to give the sighting little importance. "He saw us and headed for the woods. We think it was Norris Stoner—or could have been."

"Aha!" He pulled out his pad again. "And what time was this? Which direction did he go?"

"That way." Veronica pointed, sure the boy was long gone.

Deputy Hansen pulled his radio from his belt and reported a spotting of Norris Stoner off Roger's Crest Road. His voice was excited and pleased. "Well, I think that's your answer, ladies, and I'm grateful to you for the information."

"He's never done anything like setting fires. He just breaks in, takes a shower and steals food." Charlotte's voice conveyed the logical certainty of a judge.

"We've been waiting for him to do other stuff—just a matter of time. Looks like he's started. We'll get him now." He stuffed his notebook into his pocket.

"How about those tire tracks?" Veronica pointed. "The boy we saw was on foot."

Deputy Hansen looked at them and shrugged. "Could've been made by someone just looking around."

"No one would ever find that drive unless they knew where it was. We missed it ourselves when we walked back." Charlotte's exasperation rang loud and clear.

"We'll take a cast of them, but this ..." He held up the gas can. "His prints on this'll do the trick."

They watched him head for the road and his cruiser.

"Shit." Charlotte's voice was barely audible.

"Double that." Veronica sighed. "Well, there's nothing we can do about it. Let's go home."

They tramped back through the woods in silence.

"Is it possible we've been off searching in the wrong direction?" Charlotte muttered as they opened the gate to the yard. "Maybe it was Norris. He's a delinquent kid, after all, so ..." She broke off as Molly raced across the yard to greet her.

"Who considers us fellow outcasts, as you remember," Veronica added. Mortimer raced up and put his paws on her shoulders. "And he knows which house is ours. He wouldn't choose it by mistake."

Charlotte made a sound, muffled by Molly's fur. "A bit of information we aren't going to share with the police."

"Who might be interested in where we got it." Veronica rubbed Mortimer's neck. "We've been neglecting you, haven't we?" she told him.

They spent the next hour throwing Frisbees for the dogs in a vain attempt to revive their spirits. Then, winded, they went inside to fix lunch.

"Whose prints *are* going to be on the gas can, do you suppose?" Charlotte mused as she set out soup bowls. "Why would Norris Stoner touch it?"

"I don't know. But if his prints are on it, he's done for." Veronica stirred the soup. How could anyone knowingly let the wrong person stand trial? Go to jail? The thought sickened her. The impact of such an act—to say nothing of living with it—made her initial relief more and more appalling.

Silence fell again as they ate. Outside, the clouds had vanished. Sky was blue; sun break had turned to sunshine, as though God had released them from their cares. Veronica closed her eyes against the onset of a headache. "I'm going to the darkroom," she announced as they cleared the table.

"Would you like me to retrieve the pictures from the digitals?" Charlotte asked.

"Please. That would be great.

"I'll print them out then I'm going to dig up what I can on Norris Stoner." Charlotte put their plates into the dishwasher and dried her hands.

Veronica retrieved the film from Constance's belly and spent the afternoon in the little room behind the kitchen. She'd always loved watching the images emerge from darkness into the red glow of the safe light, a process the digital camera would deprive her of. But, as she hung the grim pictures one by one on the drying rack, the process became a forced march.

Earlier views of island pastures backed by Mount Baker gave way to the glitter of broken glass on the floor before the shattered front window. A woodland path was followed by a disheveled pile of blankets and rags shoved into a corner of an abandoned house. She had no picture of Trix, lying beside the road. Her shock had blotted out all thought of the camera, but the glare of black words on the garage door made the point vividly enough. Scattered among the churches of Cougar Gap, their varied steeples framed in evergreens were their sign boards promising solace to the unemployed and targeting the sources of their grief. Views of the Sound framed against the white-tipped Cascades appeared and disappeared throughout. The deer emerging from the moss-laden barn gave way to the blood-spattered interior. The next picture was of the charred remains of the shed, followed by the home made toolbox, David's blistered name on its side.

By the time the morning's photos of the old RV interior with its bright red gas can joined the others on the line, her hands were icy and her head throbbed. She bottled her chemicals, pulled off her gloves and rejoined Charlotte in the living room. "Let's see what the digitals produced."

Together they viewed the pictures of the church crowd, the shadowed man in the aisle, arm raised in rage, the abandoned campfire, the blood spattered barn, the eagle-crested gateposts fronting the log lodge.

Veronica caught her breath. "When did you take that?"

"When I followed you in. That's with my camera."

Veronica sat back letting out a long breath. "Go take a look at Constance's."

When Charlotte returned, she was shaking her head. "They tell a story, don't they?"

Veronica nodded. "As do these. Put them together and …" She let out her breath with a huff. "But it's not the story the sheriff will see. He'll draw a straight line from the pile of clothes, through the attacks, to the gas can, to Norris Stoner." But for her they would eat at the part of her that still wanted to grab at the alternative offered by the elusive boy. The television news had built the boy into an outlaw hero. "Terrorizing the island!" they'd proclaimed. The appeal was inescapable.

"Probably." Charlotte agreed. "Speaking of which, you need to look at this." Charlotte returned to her computer. "I still have the passwords to get me into the Juvenile Court records."

The fatherless boy had taken himself off into the woods and trouble when he was twelve. He'd become an untraceable woodsman, breaking into unoccupied summer homes for shelter and food, then vanishing. He'd been captured only once, only to escape the group home where they'd placed him and return to his island. As the heat increased, he stole a boat, fleeing to other islands in the Sound. His stature grew in proportion to the law's inability to apprehend him. He began to live up to the folk hero the media had created, thumbing his nose at his pursuers, daring them to capture him.

But nowhere in his considerable history had he vandalized any of the homes or attacked anyone. Quite the opposite, his talent was for escaping notice. He'd never even broken into a house where the occupants were home.

"It all fits the boy we found that day," Veronica muttered. "Not our harasser."

"Unless he turned and started getting back at the world, but he's never left any evidence of that." Charlotte flipped through screens. "He's the sort of boy your son would take in. Do you suppose they've connected somewhere along the line? He's the son of an alcoholic … another lost boy …"

"What are we doing, Charlotte, turning David into a modern Peter Pan?"

Charlotte laughed. "With a very ugly twist. But I suppose it's possible."

"But why us?"

"Indeed. Why us?" Charlotte cut the connection to the Internet and sat back, rubbing her eyes.

Outside the shadows of the evergreens had crossed the yard, encroaching on the house.

"Roni, let's go out to dinner."

"And leave this place for someone to throw a bomb?"

"Yes. Exactly that. We can't just sit here waiting for the phone to ring to tell us they caught him—or for the dogs to warn us someone's afoot. We'll become as crazy as they all think we are already."

Chapter 13

The North-End Grill was quiet. A member of the local photography group of which Veronica was a sometimes-member raised a hand and smiled a greeting, but otherwise the few diners paid them little attention. As usual, Charlotte and Veronica chose a table by the window overlooking the sound and settled to look at the lights just coming on across the bay.

Veronica leaned back and breathed deeply, filling her nostrils with baking bread and her ears with soft muzak blended with the muted babble of the television hung in one corner. "This was a wonderful idea."

"Mm," Charlotte answered, engrossed in her menu. "And I think I'll indulge in crab, just to celebrate."

"An excellent idea. I think I'll do …" She ran her eyes down the familiar menu, as though in search of some new discovery. "Mussels … the steam bucket."

The waitress came and went, and a few minutes later they were sitting over their wine, watching the arrival of the ferry below. The deli, they knew, would soon fill up with commuters too tired to face cooking their evening meal.

"The rhythm of the island," Veronica murmured.

"Soporific." Charlotte yawned, then looked around the restaurant, stretching to stay awake. "Here come our salads."

The noise level of the grill rose as diners, fresh from the city, flowed in, filling the space with voices raised in the greeting of friends, then subsiding into a murmur filled with release from the day. Veronica, like Charlotte, ate slowly, letting the human warmth of the sound soak in.

Their dinners arrived, smelling of garlic, butter, and the sea. They dug in without conversation.

114

Halfway through the meal, someone turned the television up, and the blend of voices was replaced by the evening news. "... new leads in the notorious case of Drummond Island's outlaw, Norris Stoner. We turn to Grafton Island Sheriff, Dan Astor for the details."

They put their forks down, as did most of the diners, and turned to watch the familiar face of their sheriff, standing in front of the rusty RV. "Local residents spotted Stoner fleeing the mobile home behind me, here, and heading into the woods. We believe he's also responsible for a fire set yesterday at a nearby home."

Veronica's mouth went dry. She scanned the faces of the café crowd, but none were turned in their direction.

"What are your chances of catching him, do you think?" the reporter asked.

"Close to ninety percent, I'd say. Local residents are on the alert now."

The camera shifted to the reporter. "We were unable to locate the residents who spotted Stoner, but the sheriff assures me we'll soon be bringing you news of the capture of the elusive outlaw."

The television was turned down again. Eager voices broke out across the restaurant, devouring the news and the celebrity status, however momentary, of their island. The tone was rich with excitement at the island's moment of fame, laced with the sense of justice his capture would bring.

Veronica looked at Charlotte. "Did you know this would happen—that they'd come looking for us—when you suggested we go out to dinner?"

Charlotte shook her head. "Serendipity. I swear it."

Veronica chanced another survey of the diners. No one was looking in their direction. She breathed in relief then looked down at the litter of empty mussel shells. Evidence of celebration. For feeding Norris Stoner to the crowd. Her fists clenched at the incongruity—the notoriety attached to the pallid defiant boy they'd found in that abandoned house. She felt Charlotte watching her and looked up. "Well, you were right—and it's so damned wrong!"

Charlotte nodded and looked around the now-buzzing space. "Witness the public appetite."

"Oh, stop it." She picked up her fork and made a stab at a piece of broccoli. "And when they catch him, that's it? There's no way they're going to listen to us?"

"The question, is, Roni, do you want them to?" Charlotte's voice was gentle.

The broccoli formed a pasty lump in her throat. She swallowed it down. "How hard will I try, you mean?" She wiped her mouth and put the napkin on the table. "I don't know." She looked at Charlotte's empty plate. "Are you ready to get out of here?"

Charlotte nodded and signaled for the bill. They said nothing more until they were back in the car, headed for home. "If I know you, Roni, you're not going to be happy until you know the truth."

"I know I'm not. And now—I have to know David and Laura aren't responsible. I can't let that place—that retreat—settle in the base of my stomach and molder." Veronica rolled down the window to the chill of the night breeze. "But that doesn't mean I want it all on national TV!"

"So I guess we just keep looking ourselves." Charlotte's voice conveyed a decision made, and they fell silent.

As they approached the house, they heard the dogs barking. Charlotte slowed, listening, then speeded up. They were within a hundred feet of the drive when a white van shot out into the lane, oblivious to traffic. Their headlights lit up the Channel 5 TV on its side.

"Bye bye," Charlotte intoned softly then drove past the driveway entrance as the dogs clamor subsided.

"Where are you going?"

"I don't want to chance their seeing us turn in." Charlotte watched the lights of the van turn in at the first available driveway and stop. She passed them then watched in the rear view mirror as the vehicle backed out and headed for town.

"Sheriff Astor gave them our name and address." Veronica turned and watched the red tail lights disappear.

"Looks like it. Damn him." Charlotte jerked the wheel, and they rounded the corner with a squeal of tires.

"Will they be back, do you think?"

"Probably not. Unless there's news of Stoner's capture, and I have a feeling there won't be. That kid is good at what he does." Charlotte turned in at a drive and backed around, heading for home once again.

"I daresay you're right. I hope so."

"News has a short shelf-life." Charlotte turned in at their drive, and this time the dogs' barks were welcoming.

"Well done, guys," Veronica cheered as she opened the gate. "Even Auntie Charlotte will agree you earned your keep tonight."

Behind her, Charlotte gave a laugh and didn't grumble when Molly licked her face. "Didn't even let them in the gate, did you?"

"It's going to be cold tonight," Veronica remarked, gazing up at the panoply of stars. "Let's build us a fire." She headed for the woodpile, Mortimer at her heels. When she'd filled one of the wood baskets, she stood and breathed in crisp air laden with evergreen, letting its pure clarity reach her bones. She heard a faint rustle beyond the fence and Mortimer charged as she turned and met the glowing eyes of a deer. *Ah ... we've fenced you out, haven't we?* she asked silently. *The price we've paid.* The deer vanished, leaving her nothing to do but lug the basket across the yard to the house.

Charlotte had the tea kettle on and was filling the dogs' dishes. "Where's Yin-Yang? I called her, but she didn't come."

"Oh, no, not again." Veronica dropped the basket by the fireplace. "But she was inside when we left. I know that." In her best commanding voice, she called the cat and heard a faint meow in return. "Ha." She crossed the room and opened the closet door. The cat streaked out, scolding them at the top of her lungs, and Veronica enjoyed her first laugh in days. "We shut her in the closet. You didn't hear her crying?"

"Nope. Not a thing. I yelled and yelled."

"One of these days, you're going to have to break down and get new hearing aids, my friend."

Charlotte looked down at the cat now demanding her supper. "It'll take more than a cat to get me to pay their price," she retorted, setting Yang's food dish on the floor. "Get that fire started," she called, shifting her attention to Veronica. "The kettle's hot."

"I think I'll do hot chocolate instead of tea, tonight." Veronica pulled the kindling basket over and got to work.

"You are feeling wintry, aren't you?"

"Decidedly. The idea of the media banging at our door makes me feel naked. I want my island home back."

Charlotte chuckled and dug in the back of the cupboard for the cocoa. "It does sound like a good idea."

Ten minutes later they were settled before the fire with steaming cups and gave themselves over to watching the pop and crackle of the flames.

"They're so friendly, enclosed in stone," Veronica remarked. "Even the smell is different."

Charlotte put her head back and breathed deeply. "Essential, in fact. Basic."

They fell silent again. The dogs curled up on the hearth and went to sleep. Yin-Yang, now fed, had forgiven them and curled up in Veronica's lap.

The chill of the house wakened them an hour later, and they climbed the stairs to bed.

The next morning, Veronica was jolted back to consciousness by the blare of the news on her clock radio. They'd found an empty house broken into on the southern tip of the island, but no trace of the boy. Good, she thought. In another day, Norris Stoner would drop out of the news. Meanwhile ... Her anger rose with the memory of yesterday. She rolled onto her back and stared at the ceiling, restraining herself with Charlotte's insistence that they discover the truth.

How? The police were happy with Norris. Laura, David, Reverend Starkweather, Pastor Bob? All of those doors had shut in their faces. Nor was Janine Manning likely to be helpful. Astonishing how worlds closed around themselves to protect their version of the truth. Impervious cloisters. She and Charlotte were intruders.

Frustrated, she threw back the covers and headed for the shower. No sound came from Charlotte's room. She'd stopped setting her clock to the news when she retired. Smart woman. The warm water mellowed her mood and let her think, but by the time the coffee was made, and she heard Charlotte on the stairs, she was no further on devising a plan of attack.

"Good morning." Charlotte looked out of the window. "Looks like a bright day."

"Well, I'm glad something's bright. I'm certainly not." Veronica set a cup of coffee down in front of her friend. "I feel absolutely stalled."

"When in doubt, go to the Internet." Charlotte took her coffee to her favorite chair and set her laptop on her knees. "Let's start with the paintball crowd."

Veronica gave a laugh of appreciation. She was right. On the Internet, everything became public. She pulled her laptop from the corner of the cabinet where it had sat neglected for days. A half hour later, Charlotte had become "Chuck" and was chatting on Facebook about good battle sites, and Veronica, "Nicky," had found a gay-lesbian blog comparing harassment experiences. The current topic was the high school scene.

She was deep into a world where scrawled obscenities were routine, too commonplace to be worth more than passing mention, while trashed lockers, stolen gear, and bloody noses were almost as common. The voices were young, high school students from Florida to Washington, emerging from total isolation to find companions on the blog. Some were timid, just discovering their difference and hoping to be saved from membership in this group, while others, emboldened by parental support, wore stigma as a badge of distinction. The blogs were full of references to support and political action groups, but short on suggestions for stopping the hatred. Veronica, suffocating from the pain that emanated from her screen, finally composed her own response, asking how members identified the high school harassers and what they did about it.

Then she switched off, escaping back into her own space. Charlotte was busy at her keyboard. "Let's take the dogs out. I need air."

"What did you find out?" Charlotte punched the send button and leaned back.

"That high schools are hell holes—which I knew—but for gay kids, they're torture chambers. The blog is long on companionship in misery, but short on action. I finally wrote asking what the hell they did about it. And you?"

"That childhood turns some kids into animals—which I knew—but that paintballing is a high art extension of video games. Just good fun." She sat back. "Some of the authors are full of strategy, others are full of hate."

"You were writing."

"I was. Asking for local groups and battle locations around Seattle. Said I just moved here." Charlotte pushed her laptop away and sat back to stretch. "Okay, doggies, you're on." She rose and looked out the window at the Washington drizzle. "Yuk. Are you sure you wouldn't rather be a couch potato?"

"Very sure. I've spent the last hour being gay. I'm shriveled and need to re-inflate."

"I imagine. I'm full of the joys of combat. Anyone that looks weak is fair game."

"A perfect pair." Veronica went to the door and pulled her coat off the hook. Mortimer and Molly leapt to their feet.

Molly was the first to spot the nose of a white van waiting at the end of their drive. "Shit." Charlotte yanked her lead.

"Guess we go out the back way," Veronica muttered, pulling the straining Mortimer back into the house.

The trail through the woods was soggy and the green canopy soaked them. When they came to the campfire clearing, they found it barricaded with yellow tape.

"So we're surrounded," Charlotte muttered. "Swell."

"Feels like a noose." Veronica hunched her shoulders against the seeping cold. "Well, tough. I'm going out to Cooper Road. If I don't walk, I'm going to freeze." She turned and headed away.

They reached Cooper Road and found a police van parked on the shoulder. It was unoccupied, but excited the dogs. "They're searching the woods," Charlotte said, pulling Molly away.

"Mm. With dogs. Well, let them. We'll take the road." Veronica started off to the right. "Not that way," she called to Charlotte who had headed away from her. "Or you'll run into the RV. That's sure to be guarded."

Cooper Road took them a long way from home, and by the time they circled back to their own road, Veronica felt restored.

"The van is gone," Charlotte remarked as they approached their drive.

Veronica breathed a sigh of relief. "Thank goodness. I don't know another way to get home, and I'm hungry."

"How long do you suppose we're going to have to live like this?"

"I don't know, but it sure makes anonymity idyllic." Veronica pushed open the gate and released Mortimer. She was grateful to Charlotte for not pointing out that it was her photo book that had triggered all of this attention. What would she give to call it back?

By the time they'd eaten and returned to their computers, they had a flood of replies to their entries. Veronica scrolled through.

"You've got to be kidding."

"Nothing, unless you want a lecture on sin."

"I found a neat counselor, once, who tried, but it's like most people see harassing weirdoes as normal, you know?"

"Tell your folks. My Dad went in, and it got better, for a while."

"Tell my Dad? No way. I wouldn't live to go to school."

120

"I knew who was doing it, but the authorities wouldn't touch them."
"Principals and teachers are blind, and kids don't rat on each other."
Veronica turned off her computer and sat back. "Whew!"

"What did you get?" Charlotte was still scrolling.

"Total helplessness. No one will do anything—well, with the possible exception of one counselor. I guess you said it—behaving like animals is 'normal.'" She rose and went to the kitchen. "I guess I can go up to the high school and talk with a counselor—see if he or she at least knows who the harassers are. Not hopeful," she acknowledged, filling the tea kettle.

"Well, our battle site is on my bloggers' list." Charlotte pushed back her chair. "And one of them mentioned that if you go on weekends, there's a group from the camp that's always game to take on visitors."

"Really. Well, that confirms our guesses."

"Sure does. The guy says to ask for Luke. He'll set things up."

"Well, well. Let's have a cup of tea on that. We're not bad sleuths for a couple of old broads."

Chapter 14

The next morning, Veronica left Charlotte searching for more blogs and set off for the high school. Clouds of moisture, too light to be called rain, periodically baptized her windshield as she drove north. It was going to be the sort of day Washingtonians called normal, when clouds, shredded by the Olympics, waft over the state in streaks, puffing moisture, interspersed with sun.

A sunbreak greeted her as she arrived at the squat stucco building on the north tip of the island. She paused to take a digital picture of the Sound rimmed by the snow-clad spires and ridges of the North Cascades. How could the ugliness she'd buried herself in yesterday take place against a backdrop like this? Laura was a counselor here. It looked like a lovely place to work. What did Laura know of the off-campus activities of her charges? She wished for the umpteenth time that she could simply ask—talk with her—that Laura wouldn't see her questions as nosing into her life. And what would she do if she ran into Laura today?

Veronica blew the possibility away with a raspberry, gritted her teeth and mounted the steps to the double doors.

The clamor was deafening. The walls hollowed out the voices raised above the clang of locker doors into a ringing affirmation of young energy. She stood inside the door as students flooded past her to and from the row of portable classrooms along the edge of the parking lot. This is a small high school, she kept telling herself. Only island kids come here. The cavernous city high school her children had attended had been twice this size. Was there a time in her life she'd found this din normal?

She stood watching as students emerged from classrooms, scattered, then formed clots, leaving only a few alone, eyes fixed on their destination. Yes. Familiar. She identified the popular, the geeks, the rowdies, with no trouble, struck only by the dominance of blond and fair—mark of the Scandinavian heritage of this region.

She drew the camera from her purse again. She might make friends with this gadget yet. But when she raised it to catch a pair of girls sharing a juicy bit of news, she felt a tap on her shoulder and turned to face a uniformed officer. She started.

"No cameras allowed, ma'am."

"What?" This was different.

The buzz of the class bell drowned out his response, but there was no doubt he was directing her to the office. Rattled by the encounter, she crossed the emptying foyer, aware that his eyes were following her. She took a breath and let it out. A sign of the times, she told herself. Just a sign of the times.

"My name is Veronica Lorimer," she said to a woman with a great cloud of black hair who sat beyond the counter. "I'd like to speak to a counselor." What would she do if they gave her Laura's name? Go home?

"The student's name?" The secretary punched keys on her computer with scarcely a glance at Veronica. "Is this a requested visit?"

"No, no, I'm not a parent. It's about harassment—I don't know the students' names."

"Ah." The woman's hands fell to her lap. "you need a student's name to talk with a counselor."

"Oh." She muttered a rude word and turned away, then stopped. On the reception area wall in front of her, the black letters of a poster proclaimed "TOLERANCE!" along with the date of an upcoming assembly. She turned back. "I'd like to speak with the principal then, please."

"I'll see if he's available." She punched another button, this time on the intercom of her phone.

Forty minutes later, Veronica was sitting before John Holloway, a man of imposing size. Football in his past, she guessed. "My friend and housemate, Charlotte McAllister, and I have been harassed by someone—or someones—who believe we're lesbians. We have reason to believe the culprits are high school students, and I'd like your help in putting a stop to it."

"By harassed, you mean …?"

"A rock through our window, nasty words painted on our garage door, our cat poisoned, our shed burned." She was pleased to see the bland politeness fade from the man's face.

"Have you reported this to the sheriff?"

"He believes it's the work of Norris Stoner." She grimaced. "Who hasn't harassed anyone, so far as I know."

"So you think it's our students? Why?"

Veronica opened her mouth to answer then realized the path of their suspicions was far too tangled to make sense. "Some boys were seen in the woods near our house—down at the south end—and at least one of them was a boy who may bear a grudge against my housemate. She's a lawyer, and before she retired she was instrumental in removing him from his drug-addicted, alcoholic mother."

"The name?"

"Luke Branscomb."

Holloway gave a jerk and frown of surprise—incredulity even. "Luke? I think someone's mistaken." He stopped to give a short laugh. "Luke is a group leader—of a Christian group that meets after school. In fact, they're applying for permission to meet at school like official school groups. I can't imagine ..." He paused, reading something in her face. "But I'll pass your information on to his counselor, if you like."

"Please do." She was about to continue when the man rose and held out his hand. "And do feel free to come in if there are further incidents. We aren't responsible for behavior off school grounds, of course."

"Of course." She stood and shook the proffered hand. "But I noticed you're having an assembly on tolerance, so I gather such behavior isn't unknown to you."

"Too true. The foulness of the Internet—the places kids go—spills over everywhere."

"That sounds ugly." Veronica opened the office door.

"Not like anything I ran into when I was in school, that's for sure," Holloway agreed. "Simple civility is a challenge."

She left on that note of sympathy. The man had enough on his hands keeping order in his halls to worry about what students were up to in the woods. And Luke Branscomb wasn't on his list of troublemakers. That was clear. So how was she going to get access to a counselor?

The bell blasted her, signaling another change of class, and within seconds, she was inundated. A group of boys in football jerseys collided with her and uttered obscenities before realizing she wasn't one of their own. They went off punching each other in embarrassment, and, deliberately she thought, collided with a group of Hispanic students who shoved back. Veronica wished her camera could catch the language. The tension around her turned sour with a hostility that hadn't been visible from afar.

At the door, she passed the security officer who faced the crowd, stony faced. When she reached the car, she leaned back and closed her eyes, sorting through the mix of energy and emotion she'd been a part of, and decided it had been a long time since she'd experience the un-impeded hormones of adolescence, but there was a hostility between groups that was different. When she opened her eyes again, she realized she was looking at the portables marked "Counseling."

She waited until the campus was quiet again, then got out of the car and approached a lone man standing outside his door, enjoying a cup of coffee. He was a sandy-haired and paunchy, dressed in chinos and a faded plaid shirt. His whole being suggested "approachable."

"My name is Veronica Lorimer. I'm a photographer. Are you a counselor?"

"I am. Ed Stein." He shook her hand. "What can I do for you?"

"I'm doing a photo essay on harassment, and I suspect, as a counselor, you've had some experience with that sort of thing." The ruse, wherever it had sprouted from, felt so right she almost gave a chortle of appreciation. *Brilliant, Veronica.*

Ed Stein gave a lop-sided grin of assent. "That's me."

"Tell me about it. Has it flared up lately?"

"Flared up? A good word." He nodded. "And what can you expect when students watch political rallies and listen to talk radio where every group screams that anyone different—black, Asian, Muslim, Indian, gay—is a threat to their way of life. Do people think kids don't bring that stuff to school?"

"The principal blamed the Internet."

"That, too, for sure. Not that adolescence wasn't always a trial by fire. Kids have always had it tough and some a lot tougher than others. But now, instead of talking to some adult who can help—Aunt Sarah, their camp counselor, me—they find allies in anger on the Net, which only raises the temperature."

"Talking to their parents doesn't help?"

"Their parents are at those damned rallies. Or they're holding down three jobs—they just plain aren't there. No, kids have developed their own sealed off world."

"Churches?"

"Some churches. I've held meetings with pastors and group leaders of various denominations and some of them really try to broaden the kids' view of the world. Other churches—well, they have very different goals. They're part of the problem."

"I've been up to Grace Bible, talking with the pastor there. He seems to think harassment is simply the overzealous pursuit of the Good."

"Ha." Ed took a last swallow of coffee. "You didn't hear me say that, okay? Not professional."

Veronica smiled. "I didn't hear a thing. But you've had a run-in with him?"

"Not a run in, no. More like a brush off. And there's an after school church club here—actually started by one of our counselors—made up mostly of kids who go there. They want to meet at the school—which some have a problem with."

Veronica's blood chilled in recognition. She didn't need to ask that counselor's name. But Stein didn't appear to notice. "And you're one of the 'some'?"

"One of the few, I should have said. "They've set themselves up as …" he paused and scratched his head "… how shall I put this …? Let's say 'activists for Christ.'" He threw his cup into a nearby trash bin. "And since we encourage groups of every other type, why not them? You'll see them around, talking to this kid or that. Holloway thinks they're a great influence, and he may be right—for some. But I've had kids complain that if you turn them away, you find your locker trashed or your bike tires flattened. And a couple of my gay kids … well, they're plain scared. One of them is close to dropping out."

"You've reported that?"

"Sure. But I'm not getting much support. And I don't blame them, in a way. The faculty, that is. That kind of thing doesn't fit the group's MO—or the school's, for that matter. John's a good guy, and he really tries to keep the place civilized. But he's also a good church member."

Veronica was about to ask about Luke, but realized privacy laws would prevent him from answering. She'd have to be content with generalities. "Ah. Of Grace Bible?"

He nodded. "It's one of the biggest churches on the island. And the kids who go there are fine, by and large, but ..." He stopped and shook his head. "It's strange, you know. I've talked with them—the group. In their minds, they're the good kids. They go to church, volunteer for community work, do their homework. Why aren't I talking to the thugs—the drop-outs, druggies, the bullies? Isn't that my job? To keep kids like them safe in school? Then they talk about ridding the school of gays and Muslims—of which we actually have a couple—and they just don't see anything wrong with it. In their minds they're promoting God's way."

"I had much the same experience talking with Pastor Starkweather."

"I bet you did. Well, here comes my next appointment. Good luck on your work."

"I'd like to talk with them—those gay kids."

He shook his head. "Can't give you names, I'm afraid, but I'll mention your project to them if you like. They can contact you."

"Wonderful. I'd appreciate that." Veronica handed him her card just as Ed greeted the student, a gangling youth with pimples and an engaging grin.

Back in the car, Veronica sat without turning on the engine. She'd just set herself up as a spy, subverting her daughter's mission. Her mouth felt like tin. Could Laura not know about those trashed lockers and flattened bike tires? Ed Stein said he'd talked with the group. She had to know. And if she did?

Then it was war. Veronica turned on the engine and drove away from the school. Anger flared then was replaced by elation as she realized she'd found an ally. She remembered the 'aha' moment her own story about a project had given her. A photo essay. Elation doubled and spread from her core to her fingertips—an indescribable surge that came only when a book came into being. The grimness of her subject matter would return, she knew, but with purpose now. She'd taken it by the horns.

She started the engine and pulled out of the parking lot, her head alive with the passions that drive the hunter, select the hunted. The pictures in her head centered on the high school. Because they were freshest? In part. But more because human passions were so naked in those hallways, newly minted and not yet under adult restraint. Raw. The image of thirteen-year-old Veronica rose before her, a too-tall blond whose only distinguishing feature, other than her height, was a sharp nose. Hanging around her neck was her escape from the impossible social demands of high school. Her camera.

That camera had taken her onto the yearbook board and into the company of student leaders she would not have dared approach in her own behalf. In college, she'd piggybacked into adulthood on their gregarious whirlwind confidence, denying the introverted loner residing in her core. And one of those leaders had been Simon.

And David? As a little boy, David had been more like her, studying the beetles that crossed the porch, satisfied with his own company ... but no, maybe not. Maybe longing for the easy ways of others. He'd forsaken that lone child, latched onto groups—science groups, music groups—they swept him through the treacherous waters of high school. His very busyness made his father beam. They became pals. David gave off a light that was more gratitude for being noticed than confidence.

Then his horse collapsed under him. She'd divorced his father—sent David off into that fatal crash—stranding him. The eyes she'd stared into at Eagle's Rest still accused her. Are our choices so shaped by the whipping winds of adolescence, a time when passion and need aren't yet under control?

Veronica braked, narrowly missing a car pulling out from the shopping center. She shook her head, returning her attention to the road. Why was she so focused on adolescence, anyway? Her subject was harassment. Because the two seemed locked together. The terror of stepping beyond the fortress of family and being spotted as a misfit. The desolation of loneliness. Worse. Of becoming isolated and thereby targeted for destruction.

The chill of the last week returned. But she and Charlotte weren't isolates—were they? She shook her head as she turned into the drive. No. They weren't social butterflies or dowagers given to church suppers and quilting groups—simply a pair of widows who had found companionship and support in the course of a bumpy ride through adulthood. There was none of that fear of being a misfit that plagued all adolescents. And if she and Charlotte were lesbians, would they feel differently? She tried to step into those shoes and could come up with no more than a "So what? Whose business is it?" In fact, she couldn't imagine who would be interested enough to care.

What she had, she decided as she braked and turned off the engine, was enough of the experience suffered by the isolate to get a dose of that reality. She slammed the car door, welcomed the charging beasts, and climbed onto the porch.

"Guess what, Charlotte," she said bursting into the room. "I've got myself another book!"

Charlotte turned from the counter where she was making a sandwich. "A book?" She blinked. "From where? What are you talking about?"

"From the high school. Make me one of those, and I'll tell you." She picked up Yin Yang and sank into a chair.

When she'd finished her story, Charlotte sighed. "It sounds great. I wish I had your talent for turning shit into gold. I really do." She headed for the living room with the plates. "So you found out the Bible kids have a club, and the gay kids are scared of them. Anything about Luke and company?"

"They won't discuss individual students—privacy laws. But he's going to give the gay kids my card. They might name their attackers." She reached around the purring cat for her sandwich.

Charlotte nodded. "Progress."She crossed the room to her own chair. "What did you find out this morning?"

"That there's something called 'doing a job' on selected people—non-Christian, non-heterosexuals or immigrants—who are all a threat to the American way of life." The jangle of the phone put a period on her description. "Oh. That's probably your sister. She's pissed at you—as usual."

"She called?"

"She did. So you can answer this time. She doesn't care for me."

Chapter 15

She reached for the jangling phone. "Hello, this is Veronica."

"Veronica. This has to stop!" Her sister's voice sounded just like their mother's, a characteristic, Veronica had decided long ago, of eldest daughters.

"What, exactly, is 'this'?"

"You know full well. Snooping on David." Her voice forced Veronica to hold the phone away from her ear.

She bit down on her retort. For once, she'd try not to respond to the air of triumphant ownership Dorothy's voice carried when talking about Laura and David. Dorothy had been widowed young, without children, and her eager mothering of her niece and nephew was more unfulfilled need than hostility. Or so Veronica told herself until she realized her sister was reinforcing David's and Laura's sense of abandonment. "I beg your pardon, Dorothy. I went to visit him. He's my son."

"You went to make trouble for him. You were nosing around the property after he told you to get out, and if that doesn't stop, he's going to get a restraining order against you." The words came in a torrent.

"A ..." Veronica sat down. "Did he tell you that?" She was aware that her voice had become a squeak and took a deep breath to cure it.

"I advised it, and he agreed."

"Did you, now?" Charlotte looked up as the venom in Veronica's voice spelled the end of civility. "It's not your business to give advice to my son, Dorothy. I went up there to patch things up."

"Some things can't be fixed." Her sister snipped the words.

"Like what?" Veronica snipped back.

"Death."

Veronica stared opened-mouthed at Charlotte, as though her friend could provide words where Veronica could not. Finally, she shook her head clear. "I assume you mean Simon, who drove drunk off a cliff."

"Because of you! You had everything and ruined it!" The telephone slammed down.

Veronica stared from the dead receiver to Charlotte. "Did you hear that?"

Charlotte nodded. "Same old Dorothy."

"No." Veronica frowned. "There's something more ... or I just heard it ... at the end. Tears. She was bursting into tears!" She sat back, remembering Dorothy's lighthearted quips that she'd take Simon if Veronica changed her mind. Or she'd thought they were lighthearted. "She was in love with him."

"With Simon?"

Veronica nodded. "There were other comments ... they come back now ... that she didn't see what he saw in me." Dorothy's barbs pierced once again. Some part of her had always understood her super-responsible, super-serious, older sister's resentment of her younger, more carefree self. But she'd never understood why Dorothy hadn't grown past it. Now she did. "I met him in college. I'd worked up the courage to go to a frat party with a friend from the photography club. Dorothy wouldn't go. Said she had to study—as always. The next day, he came to the boarding house where we were living to ask me out." Dorothy's face, animated and lit up, came across the years. "She flirted with him! Dorothy never flirted. She was the good girl, the responsible one, never allowing herself to—come alive."

She remembered other days when Dorothy was always the first down the stairs, racing for the doorbell. "I remember feeling as though I was stealing her guy."

"Oh, come, Roni. I expect Simon was capable of making his own choice."

"Mm. But Dorothy always thought he'd made the wrong one. 'You had everything—and ruined it.' Her words just now." Veronica rose and crossed the room and grabbed her digital camera. "I need a walk. Want to come?"

"I guess so. Do me good. Come on, Molly. Morty ..."

"I never met Simon," Charlotte said as they started off into the woods behind the house, "but if he's anything like you describe, I can't imagine his choosing Dorothy."

"Well, thank you. I guess. Can you imagine his picking me? I never understood it. Whoa, Morty! Hold up!" But the dog paid no heed. He barreled down the path and ended on his hind legs against the tree where the squirrel chattered at him from above.

"You were beautiful, my dear," Charlotte answered, catching up. "I've seen pictures."

Veronica snorted. "Come on, Morty, don't you hear that fella gloating?"

"Well, you were." Charlotte continued as they started off again. "Maybe striking is the better word. And you had an air about you."

"An air." Veronica let Morty lead them onto a side path.

"Of ... defiance ... no, that's not right ... devil-may-care ... I don't know, but I imagine it would appeal to a guy. Where are we going?" Charlotte brushed an encroaching bush from her path.

"Wherever Morty takes us, I guess, but we don't have any other destination." Veronica remembered the pictures Charlotte was referring to. "I was defying my own shyness, but I don't suppose anyone knew that but me." Morty made another turn, taking them to Cooper Road.

"And me." Charlotte restrained Molly and looked both ways for traffic.

They fell silent, as they entered the woods on the other side of the road. Ferns rather than brush carpeted the ground on either side, and the encroaching cedars were laden with moss. Black spires of lichen-coated dead trees dotted the interior, and the ground beneath her feet was spongy. The air smelled of wet leaves and mold. This had once been swamp. A quarter mile on, the ground became drier and a spot of sun glowed from a clearing ahead. Now she recognized the path.

"We're headed toward the old RV."

"Really? Do you suppose we'll find our friend Norris?" Charlotte pulled a blackberry vine from her coat.

"I doubt it. I think that boy is long gone from these woods."

As they reached the clearing, Molly began to growl, then let loose with a short bark, followed by another. "Hush!" Charlotte yanked the leash, pulling her back into the trees, and put her fingers around her muzzle. "Quiet."

Mortimer's ears flicked in this direction and that. He gave a barely audible rumble. They both knelt, restraining their dogs between their legs, hands around their muzzles.

A moment later, a boy appeared in the doorway of the RV. Bare-chested, he was buttoning his jeans and looking from left to right.

Veronica didn't recognize him. His buzz-cut was red and he was smaller—younger, she guessed—than Luke and Colin. She released Mortimer's muzzle, pulled the digital from her pocket and snapped his picture, though even with the zoom he was probably too far away to be identifiable.

As they watched, the boy said something over his shoulder then ducked back into the van. A moment later, he emerged wearing a jacket, and fled into the woods to their right.

Veronica put a restraining hand on Charlotte's arm.

Sure enough, another half-naked boy, lanky and blond, appeared in the doorway, his gaze darting about. Veronica jerked, her brain denying her eyes. Luke Branscomb.

"So that's it." Charlotte breathed, her voice barely audible.

"What?"

"Luke is gay."

Veronica closed her eyes. Impossible. It didn't make sense. But the blogs she'd been reading told her otherwise. She shriveled at the memory of her rage—her drive for revenge. If there was mercy in the world, that boy wouldn't find it at Grace Bible Church—or the Branscomb house. She clicked the shutter, though it felt more like betrayal than exposing a culprit. Her temples throbbed.

Luke stared too long at the spot where they were concealed. Veronica feared they were visible but dared not move. She didn't breathe until he looked away, retrieved his clothes and headed in the same direction as the boy. The dogs strained to follow, but made no noise.

Then he was gone. Veronica released her frozen muscles and Charlotte let go of Molly's nose. "Well, well. That explains a lot."

"A tormented soul." Veronica gazed at the rusty RV, its moss covered roof, its dangling siding. "Refuge for the rejected and desolate."

"Mm. And criminal." Charlotte's voice was dry. Despite the dog's protest, Charlotte turned Molly toward home.

"More a trapped and desperate animal." Veronica pulled Mortimer around to follow Charlotte back through the swamp.

"That's not what the dogs think, Roni. They smell the kid who burned the shed and threw rocks through our window."

Veronica sighed. There was never any point in disputing Charlotte's unvarnished view of humanity.

In the distance she heard an engine start, and they reached the road in time to see Luke's blue Chevy pick-up emerge from a distant fire lane. She pulled Charlotte back into the trees. The truck roared past. Luke was driving, his free fist raised, and he was yelling something at the boy, who huddled white-faced in the corner of the passenger seat.

"So what was that about, do you suppose?" Charlotte mused, watching the dusty truck top the rise and disappear.

They crossed the road and headed back to the house. "The boy won't come again? The boy will tell? Did either of them see us, do you think?"

"No. But they heard Molly—close. That's enough to scare daylights out of the kid—out of both of them." Charlotte unfastened the gate.

"Especially since their presence there makes them our firebug." Veronica unhitched Morty.

"Hardly hard evidence." Charlotte turned Molly free.

"I'll bet our local cops would buy it."

"Except they've already made up their minds it's Norris Stoner."

Veronica picked up a ball and threw it for the dogs in an effort to lift the weight that had descended on her chest at the sight of the two boys. The burnt-match scent of the boys' terror had filled her nostrils and wouldn't fade.

"Come on," Charlotte called, moving toward the house. "A drink is in order."

Veronica fed the dogs and Yin Yang while Charlotte uncorked a bottle of wine, but neither the animals nor the alcohol lifted heavy air. Charlotte lit a fire, which warmed the room and gave them something to watch as they sat, still immersed in the afternoon's revelation.

Veronica thought about the pictures she'd taken and how the boy, face blurred out, would fit in her book. And Luke ... the straight-guy vigilante attacking ... his other self. How do you take a picture of that?

"You asked me, the other day, whether I ever thought of Ellie's death as merciful—sparing her." Charlotte's voice was uncharacteristically somber.

"I should apologize for that."

"No. Today I did. Or at least I wondered how she would have fared.

What grief, shame, pain …" her voice, uncharacteristically unsure, faded out.

"No. Death of a child is the ultimate blow. I can't imagine surviving it."

"It feels that way. But it's not the only grief. I've watched you more than you know, Roni, and sometimes I've wondered what you would have been like without that weight. I never knew you then."

Veronica smiled. "I wasn't nicer, if that's any comfort." She rose and refilled their wine glasses. "I was defiant. And judgmental. I loved to hole up with the private vision my camera gave me." She returned to her chair. "My pictures were true—people weren't. They put on masks, pretended, hid …" She broke off as the image of Luke rose. "You see? I'm still judgmental."

Charlotte smiled. "And you hide your grief."

"Well, there you are. I'm a person, not a picture."

They fell silent, watching the flames.

"You know, I thought my book was going to be about harassment, but it's turning out to be about adolescence."

"That's a cauldron no one wants to dip into, Roni. Stick to harassment—which is adolescence perpetuated maybe."

"That doesn't sound like an idea that would sell, either."

"No, but maybe it's true. You do truth—brutal truth." Charlotte took a sip of wine, then another, as though hesitant to go on. "Look at Laura and David. They are still in the throes of adolescent trauma."

Veronica sat back and closed her eyes. "But they've found a shore—a place to pull themselves out of that quagmire. I can't fault that, Lotti. Church, for me, became a place of pretence and hypocrisy, but religion—that's different. There's a sense of being part of something bigger—awesome—it raises you above yourself. In church you feel that, and I wanted it. Such a marvelous relief from loneliness."

"And so dangerous." Charlotte emptied her glass.

"You never felt it? Did you ever go to church?" Veronica sat up and opened her eyes. "Or synagogue?" She amended, remembering Charlotte's rarely mentioned mixed heritage.

Charlotte shook her head. "My folks resolved their religious differences by raising us in no religion. Dad missed it, I think, but Mother had that deep-seated Jewish fear when she saw Christians in the grips of that sense of holiness—that uplift you were just describing. She wasn't religious, and she was sure if she let us go into any church we'd never come out again."

"How did your father deal with that?"

"He'd laugh and put his arms around her. 'It's just that you have this aura, Sarah, of being one of the Chosen People. Bound to cause trouble, you know.'"

"Sounds like they managed pretty well. Better than most."

Charlotte nodded. "They loved each other. And I think they knew their different backgrounds could make for trouble, so they made jokes instead—extracted the poison."

"Good for them. I tried that—with my photography—but Simon thought I was laughing at him. Making light of his feelings." Veronica sighed and rose. "And maybe I was. Who knows? Time to find us some supper."

Charlotte picked up the remote and turned on the evening news.

Chapter 16

A moment later, the room was filled with the television news. Another boat had been stolen, this one from Grafton Island, and again Norris Stoner's face filled the screen.

"Good," Charlotte stated. "He's off to some other island. Now they can't blame the next event on him."

"What next event?" Veronica slapped a pan onto the stove.

"I don't know, but there'll be one. I feel it in my bones." Charlotte punched the volume down on another shooting in Detroit.

Veronica sighed. "I know. So do I. I could use a break."

"We'll blot out the world with a lousy movie. How's that?" She switched on the guide.

"Works for me." Veronica shook off the feeling of impending explosions and reached for a cook book. "And something different for dinner."

She pulled a package of shrimp from the freezer. By the time they ate, Charlotte had found a movie to fill the rest of the day.

Veronica avoided putting the new pictures on her computer until the next morning. They weren't prizes, for sure, but when she expanded them, Luke was identifiable. The younger boy was not so clear, but if she saw that round face and red buzz cut, she'd know it, she was sure.

Charlotte came up behind her as she studied them. "Well, it's not Colin. That boy is smaller—and a redhead."

Veronica nodded. "Younger. A freshman, maybe? He looks more a child than adolescent. Barely into puberty."

"Mm. He looks scared."

"Do you think they saw us?" Veronica occupied her hands printing the pictures, but her mind conjured up the previous day's scene. "Luke acted as though he saw something—or thought he did."

"I hope not. But we did frighten them, thanks to Molly. Too bad, but I guess there's nothing we can do about it." Charlotte turned away and went back to her computer.

Veronica gazed down at the pictures in her hand. They looked like the fuzzy work of some private-eye exposing secrets to the glare of the media. She dropped them on the table and rubbed her hands on her jeans, cleansing them. Why had she printed them? She couldn't put them in her book; the faces were far too identifiable. She returned to her computer screen and backed the photos off until the faces were unidentifiable, then printed them again. They were now simply pictures of the old RV plus a couple of human figures. Useless. She needed the furtive fear of the close-up, but without the faces. "Have you ever worked with photo programs, Lotti?"

Charlotte turned. "No. Did you know that the percentage of males who admit to a homosexual experience during adolescence has dropped since the start of the movement?"

"What? You mean they're even more secretive? But that's the opposite of ..."

"What was supposed to happen. I know, but that's what this study found."

Veronica shook her head and went back to reading about photo programs. An hour later, she realized she hadn't absorbed a word she'd read, and the tension in her shoulders had increased to the point of pain. "Nuts." She rose. "I need to do something. But what?"

"I don't know." Charlotte pushed back her chair. "There's nothing we can do. Your son and daughter have warned both of us off, and I don't see what we can do about our friend Luke. We've found out what he's afraid of. That's all."

"Which gets us nowhere. Except that I feel as though we ought to protect that other boy. Without exposing Luke."

"Catching Luke as the harasser doesn't expose him—or the other boy."

"No, but ..." Veronica shook her head. "What a mess." She went back to her study of photo programs. She selected one, downloaded it, and spent the rest of the day trying to make it work.

"Patience," Charlotte urged from across the room an endless time later.

138

"I need a walk." Veronica jumped up.

"No, you don't. It's raining, and besides, your walks do nothing but get us in trouble."

Veronica stared out through the dripping eves to the yard, fenced now against all comers.

"Get back to work. Photo programs do amazing things, Roni. You just need to get the hang of it, and you'll be addicted."

"Promise?"

"Absolutely. But you can get us lunch if you want a break."

"Good idea. What are you studying so closely?" She rotated her shoulders to loosen them. Mortimer rose and shook as she headed for the kitchen.

"Homosexuality. Profiles of closet gays. Case studies."

"What are you finding out?" Veronica opened a can of soup and dumped it into a pan.

"Nothing we didn't know or suspect. Concealed sexuality is a nightmare—really screws people up. Coming out is a huge relief, but most don't manage it until they get away from home."

"Mm. Have you looked at that blog we visited the other day?" She opened the refrigerator and took out cheese, turkey and mayonnaise.

"Good idea. I will." Charlotte clicked the mouse and fell silent as Veronica made sandwiches. "Come take a look at this." Her tone commanded.

Veronica stopped stacking sandwiches and went to peer over her shoulder.

"What if you think you're being watched?" The blogger's question sprang from the screen.

"Gotta be more careful, that's what."

"Yeah, but if they're already watching you, someone's suspicious."

"Right. Then the talk starts, and you've had it."

"Tell someone. Might as well get it out in the open if there's already talk."

"Sure, if you want to commit suicide."

The words swirled from around the screen, without anchor, tainting the air.

"Do you believe in coincidence?" Charlotte asked.

"No." Veronica read on.

"What happens to your partner if you rat? Thought of that?"

"Yeah, Judas ..."

"Okay, I've had enough. Get out of there." Veronica turned away and wrapped her arms around herself to stop the chill.

"Not exactly comforting," Charlotte commented, closing the blog. She rose and looked at the sandwiches on the counter. "Takes your appetite."

"It does that. If only there was a way to tell the boy we're just a couple of old ladies who won't talk." She went into the kitchen and turned off the soup.

"Mm. Which there isn't. But maybe if talk doesn't start ..." Charlotte ladled soup into her bowl.

"I don't know. As you said, that boy looked scared." Veronica put sandwiches onto plates.

"Of talk or of Luke?" Charlotte sat down and looked at her food.

"Both." Veronica sighed and picked up her sandwich. "Why do I feel we've flicked a switch—set loose a storm that's going to sweep up everything in its path?"

"Because we have. But don't dramatize, so. It's one small island, Roni. And maybe the boy has someone he can go to—a parent even, or that counselor you talked to—without Luke knowing."

On that pallid comfort, they began to eat.

When they were done, Veronica forsook her computer and took her printed pictures to the sunroom, as though her studio would return some perspective. She arranged and rearranged them until they spoke to her of an evergreen coated island set in the Sound between the snow-clad peaks of the Cascades on one side, the Olympics on the other. A mixture of fishing boats and pleasure craft were moored in its marina and on the beach beyond, rubber-booted children dug for clams. Here and there, the black painted words on a garage door, the burnt shed, the ugly signs at the church meeting, the rusted RV, erupted like pustules through the skin of pastoral bliss.

"Lotti, I'm going out with the cameras. Do you want to come?"

"What are you in search of?" Charlotte looked up from her book. She, too, was escaping the morning's poison.

"People. Ordinary people living ordinary lives. High school kids giggling and Tweeting and being nothing but young. Medicine for our sorry souls."

Charlotte laughed. "And you think Constance is going to cure us."
She rose. "Okay, I'm game. At least the rain has stopped."

For the next hours, they wandered the island, letting Constance sniff
out a yard sale, a group at the Grange sorting Thanksgiving food dona-
tions, church signs advertising bazaars, the island kiosk with its flyers
for everything from lost cats to a play production. By the time they
reached the end of the island the November dark was upon them.

"All right," Veronica proclaimed as they returned to the car. "I'm
ready to go home."

"Let's stop at Stacey's for a beer and a hamburger. That should give
you some more local flavor."

"You're on."

When they'd settled into a booth and ordered their beer, burgers and
fries, Veronica stretched and looked around at the crowd. Families fresh
from afternoon soccer games filled the tables. Parents in Seahawk,
Husky, and Sounder sweatshirts and caps joked and laughed with their
young, some still in their shin-guards. All glowed from an afternoon in
the chill November air.

Veronica breathed in the odor of beer and fries that saturated the room.
She loved places like this—the unvarnished unraveling of a day's en-
ergy. They'd been her antidote to corporate cocktail parties. She pulled
Constance out to record the scene.

"Stop." Charlotte put a hand on her arm. "The flash will attract attention. Use your digital."

A noise, half acknowledgement, half resentment, escaped Veronica's
lips. She'd never believed it mattered whether she attracted attention or
not. She was just a lady with a camera. Who cared? She was loath to
give up that anonymity.

"The digital," Charlotte repeated, reading her mind.

"A half loaf. But I guess it'll do." She fished the camera from the
depths of her purse and scanned for a shot. It wasn't until she lowered
the camera that her gaze caught on a family rising to go. The father, in
a Seahawk jacket, was exchanging quips with the man at the next table
while the mother joined in the laugher. The children, a boy of about
sixteen and younger brother, both in soccer uniforms, pulled on their
jackets. The younger boy turned, and Veronica put a hand on Charlotte's
arm. "It's him."

Charlotte turned, and together they watched the family move toward the exit. The father and mother stopped at the booth behind them to greet its occupants, who congratulated the older boy on his play of the day. Veronica was facing the trio and watched the younger boy, who stood blank-faced and immobile, hands in pockets, his eyes roving the restaurant.

Finally, the father clapped his hand on the older boy's shoulder, and the family turned toward the door, the younger boy trailing behind.

"Whew." Charlotte took a draft of beer. "Do the parents see that boy?"

Veronica shook her head, searching memory. Had David ever looked that way? A being apart? No. David had been far more like the older boy—athletic, apple of his father's eye. And Laura? Simon's princess. Laura would have been offering her version of the play, putting herself in the middle of the conversation. "Would I have seen it if it was there? I hope so, but parents notice children who seek them—seek their approval. And if a child gives up on that, I suspect it's far too easy to fade out of sight."

"Why do I think that boy wants to be out of sight?" Charlotte waved for the waitress.

While Charlotte dealt with the details of bill paying, Veronica took pictures of the evening crowd then let the camera find more focused shots. At a table in the corner, a man helped an elderly woman to eat. His wife leaned over and wiped the dribble from the woman's mouth. At another table, one of three children was bald, telltale sign of chemotherapy. At still another, a mother cradled a child with Down's syndrome. She'd seen none of these when she'd sat basking in the glow cast by the place. She'd opened a book she could not close. Only putting it in print, acknowledging it, would give her peace.

"You're lost in thought," Charlotte commented as she started the engine.

"Which is exactly what I don't want to be." Veronica turned the camera back on and reviewed the last hour's pictures. "Now there's a wonderful Stacey's scene," she remarked, turning the display toward Charlotte. "Why can't I just stop there—with the warm, happy aura of a neighborhood pub."

Charlotte flicked a glance at the photo. "Because you're Roni. You have an insatiable need to dive deep."

"To the ugly truth, you mean. That's Constance's doing."

"Except you weren't using Constance."

Veronica laughed. "I guess I'm going to have to give this gadget a name." She went on through the pictures to the last set. "Well," she mused, looking at the family with a sick child. "Not ugly, exactly." She turned the display toward her friend again. "That's resilience."

Charlotte looked at the picture and smiled. "Neat. And I didn't say ugly. You did." She turned the car into the drive, pulled up to the garage and gave a sigh as she shut off the engine. Molly and Mortimer hailed their arrival, and the day's cloud cover parted to reveal a star spangled sky. A gentle wind hummed in the evergreens, and the air smelled of wood smoke. "It's still a wonderful place to call home."

Once inside and settled with a cup of tea, Veronica fed her pictures to the computer and studied them more carefully. She liked them. They expressed the power of community to raise people, relieve pain. Or maybe the public face that denied its darker side. Or both. With timid fingers, she began working with them, refocusing, playing with light and shadow.

"Time for the news," Charlotte commented, punching the remote.

Veronica blinked. Three hours had passed.

Charlotte laughed. "I told you it was addictive."

"Carlos Gonzales is at Grafton Island High School with the details."

They swung as one to the television screen. The correspondent's figure was set against fire.

"The Grafton fire department suspects arson in the blaze behind me, which started in a portable near the center of this row. These are the high school counselor's offices, which were empty at the time, of course. The fire chief is leaning toward some student with a gripe and is looking for possible witnesses."

"That's Ed Stein's office." Veronica swallowed her horror.

"My God. You're sure?" Charlotte's voice shot through her.

Veronica nodded, her throat dry. "Let's go." She reached down for her shoes.

"Go?"

"We need to talk to Ed Stein. If that's his office, he'll be there." She grabbed a print of the two boys and the digital camera, as she headed for the door. "Come on."

Chapter 17

By the time they drove into the high school parking lot, the flames had subsided, leaving charred wood, wet ash, and water. The smoke made their eyes sting and their throats close. Firemen kicked aside debris in search of the source, and they could see Ed Stein, hands shoved into the pockets of his pea coat, talking with the fire chief.

Deputy Hansen stopped them as they confronted the yellow tape barrier. "No further, ladies."

Charlotte, who had been lifting the tape, stopped. "Do they know what caused it?"

"Not yet. That will take a while, I'd guess. No obvious cause, so far."

"Would you tell Ed Stein ..." Veronica pointed, "... that man talking with the fire chief that we'd like to speak with him, please?"

The deputy eyed her skeptically. "Well, he's busy right now. I'll give him your names—"

"No, no, now please." Charlotte demanded. "We may be able to help."

"Veronica Lorimer and Charlotte McAllister. Tell him that," Veronica added in the same tone.

Hansen shrugged and crossed the lot toward the pair.

They saw Ed Stein listen then turn toward them. He finished what he was saying to the fireman and approached.

"Hello, again. The deputy says you think you can help with this?"

Veronica waited until she was sure the deputy was out of earshot before she spoke. "Not something for the police, but—a curious sort of hunch. You remember I'm writing about harassment—I came to talk with you."

He nodded.

She told him of their encounter with the boys in the woods. When she named Luke, his brows shot up and his mouth pursed as the implication sunk in. "When we got back to the road, they passed us in Luke's truck. The younger boy looked terrified. We wondered whether he had anyone to talk to and thought he just might have come to you." She pulled the picture from her purse. "Let's go over to the light." She led the way to one of the fire department floodlights. "Not a good picture, but do you know this boy?"

Ed Stein's face changed. "Skip—" He cut himself off.

"You know him." It wasn't a question.

The counselor nodded. "He came to see me today, but my schedule was full. I made an appointment ..." Ed broke off and ran a hand through his hair. "Damn."

Veronica alternated between gratification that Ed Stein took her hunch seriously and shock that it had been confirmed. She could find nothing to add to the counselor's "damn."

"It's not a nice thought," Charlotte added, breaking the silence, "but this could be Luke, warning him—and you—off." She waved at the ruins. "Because, you see, our shed was burned last week."

Ed Stein looked a question.

"We've been harassed of late by someone who thinks we're lesbians—and we suspect Luke is involved."

Ed Stein took a breath and let it out. "Definitely not a nice thought. I'll get hold of the boy first thing in the morning and let you know. As for Luke ..." He broke off, shaking his head. "It's hard to know how to approach that. I'll have to think about it."

Veronica handed him her card. "I suspect the one I gave you is now a cinder."

The fire chief, Captain Wilson, was approaching, and they waited, saying nothing.

"Do you recognize this, sir?" The chief held out the all-too-familiar shape of a quart jar to Stein.

"No." Stein frowned. "You found that in the debris?"

"We did. Not yours?"

Ed shook his head. "Can't imagine what I'd be doing with such a thing."

The chief shrugged. "A vase for flowers, a gift, maybe ... from someone's mother ..."

Ed gave a short laugh. "No. Thanks, but nothing like that. And it smells of gasoline."

Wilson nodded. "That it does. I'd say we've found our cause." He turned and beckoned to the deputy.

"You mean ..." Ed Stein's face was blank with shock. "... a Molotov Cocktail?"

"Looks very much like it." Wilson turned. "You're the ladies with the shed that burned."

Veronica nodded.

"The same way." Charlotte added. "Though those are common with firebugs, I imagine." She nodded to the empty jar.

"True, but two on the island in less than a week—interesting, to say the least. You ladies know anything that might suggest a connection?"

"Nothing more than we told you when our shed burned." Charlotte answered. "You know we found gasoline cans in an old RV near our house. We called the sheriff."

Wilson nodded. "We know about that."

"Deputy Hansen seemed to think our fire was the work of Norris Stoner." Charlotte looked very satisfied with the course of the conversation.

"Didn't I hear Stoner had left the island?" Chief Wilson asked Hansen.

"Yessir. We think so, but ..." He broke off, fishing for words, "... we may have to look at that again."

"Hm. Tell your boss I want to talk to him in the morning."

"Yessir."

"Meanwhile, do you know who might bear you a grudge, Counselor? Or anything that might connect with these ladies' fire?" Wilson turned his attention back to Stein.

Ed stein shook his head. "I'm the place they come to talk about their grudges, but I suppose ..." he stopped, considering. "If it's connected to this other fire, then it sounds like homophobia."

"A gay thing? Are you gay, Counselor?"

Ed blinked in surprise at the question. "No, but some of our students are, of course." He paused again, his face stark and white in the floodlight.

"How would that connect?" Wilson sounded frustrated, as though Stein was holding back on him.

Veronica's spine stiffened. She wasn't ready to name names to the authorities.

"I'll have to think about it and let you know," Ed answered.

She sighed in relief. He wasn't going to repeat their story. Not yet, anyway.

"You do that. In the morning, I'd like a list of kids who might be mad at you—might be afraid you'd tell tales—that sort of thing."

Ed's mouth twisted in distaste. "All right. But you'll have to clear that with Principal Holloway."

Wilson nodded. "Will do."

He and Hansen departed, leaving the three of them staring at the blackened hole in the middle of the Counselors' row.

"It's hard to think of your kids as arsonists," Ed said. "Even a disturbed kid."

"Believe me, I hear you," Veronica breathed, thinking of David. "But anger carries even nice kids away."

"Luke Branscomb is a mean kid." Charlotte corrected them both.

"If he's setting fires to keep the other boy from talking to me, he's scared." Ed hunched his shoulders and let them fall. "Well, I guess there's nothing more to do here." He held out a hand. "Thank you both for coming and for the information. I won't sleep easy tonight, but at least it's a path to follow. I was really at sea."

"You're welcome. At least the fire chief takes us seriously. That's a first, and I suspect he's going to have words with Sheriff Astor." Charlotte sounded well satisfied. "Come on, Roni, it's time to head for home."

Veronica nodded. "Can you salvage anything from that mess?" she asked Ed.

"I'll look in the morning, but I doubt it. Fortunately, most of it's in here …" He tapped his head. "Or on this." He pulled a thumb drive from his pocket.

"Good. You can run that and see if there are other possibilities—someone with a grudge," Charlotte said.

"Kids always have grudges … secrets … stuff they don't want their parents to know. But it's kid stuff. This …" He shook his head.

"Kid stuff is powerful. We've been reading gay blogs," Veronica told him. "It's heartbreaking—and terrifying for them."

Ed nodded. "Too true."

"But this may have nothing to do with our little tale," Veronica cautioned. "When we need answers, we grab at the first possibility ..." She broke off, fishing for words.

"The way the sheriff is grabbing the saga of Norris Stoner," Charlotte finished for her.

Ed grimaced. "I know the feeling—the need. Well, good night, ladies, and thank you again." He gave them a wave and headed back toward his blackened office.

When they got to the car, Charlotte made no move to start the engine. Instead, they gazed at the floodlit ruins as though absorbing them into their pores.

Veronica fought the need to get away and opened the car door. "Wait." She got out of the car and pulled the digital camera from her pocket as she walked back to the yellow tape. The black pock in the middle of the row of portables smelled of failure, the charred remains of file folders smelled of death. The zoom took her within touching distance. She closed her nose against the smell and clicked the shutter again and again. Deputy Hansen started toward her, and she waved and turned away.

"There's got to be a way to reach them—help them—before they do any more damage!" she exclaimed as she got back into the car.

Charlotte shook her head and turned the key. "If Ed gets hold of the younger boy, maybe he can at least pull him to safety. Luke's another story. I don't know how the man stands his job. For every kid he reaches, another crashes. It must be like trying to round up cattle headed for a cliff. All the time." She reached the road and they both took deep breaths of night air.

"The blog reaches them. Gives them a place to cry for help, join others. That must reduce the panic a little, anyway."

"Which could be enough, for a lot of them, to keep them from ..." Charlotte waved her hand in the direction of the high school.

"Amen." Veronica clicked through the pictures she'd just taken. They were good, but they didn't smell and so had only half of the impact of the scene. "This is what we do," she mused. "Blog, make words, take pictures, draw, and convert the horror into something manageable—declawed."

"But those acts also make us human. They make us pause, reflect.

Like putting mangled cars on display in high school parking lots at prom time."

Veronica smiled. "To carry adolescents into reflective adulthood?"

"Some small percentage—at least give them a chance at it."

Veronica looked at Charlotte's profile, framed in the lights of passing cars. "This must bring it all back for you, too. There are those who'd wonder how you stood *your* job."

"Mm. I can't count the number of times every day I wanted to shout, 'My God, do you ever stop to THINK?'" Charlotte turned into the drive.

The house sat in the moonlight. Only Mortimer and Molly's greeting enlivened the scene.

Charlotte turned the engine off. "And maybe that fire had nothing to do with us. Maybe the wiring went bad in that portable."

"The jar smelled of gasoline."

"Maybe someone with some other grudge."

"Maybe." Veronica got out and opened the gate, then bent over to let the dogs lick her face. "You'll turn it all back to milk and honey, won't you?" She rubbed Mortimer's ears, then followed Charlotte inside.

But once they'd turned the burner on under the teakettle and settled into their chairs, the need to stop the avalanche of events returned. Inactivity became insupportable. Veronica looked at her watch. Nine fifteen. "I'm going to call Laura."

Charlotte looked up from the evening paper and cocked an eyebrow. "Ever the optimist."

"I know. But I have to try. She can probably make Luke listen if anyone can. She or Ted." She dialed and listened to the ringing phone.

"Hello, Susan!" Her daughter's voice sang with welcome.

"Hi, Laura, it's Mom."

"Oh. Hello." Splat.

Veronica decided to forego the preliminaries. "One of the high school portables was set afire tonight."

"What?" Her voice came to life, shrill now. "Which one? How do you know?"

"It was on the news. It was Ed Stein's portable."

"Oh. That guy." Laura's tone dismissed him.

"You know him?" Dumb question. Of course she knew him.

"Not really. He's one of those liberals ..."

"Laura! So it's okay if they burned down his office? For being liberal?" Veronica heard her own voice rise and bit her tongue.

"No, no. I didn't mean … it's just that … oh, never mind."

"No, I won't never mind. You need to listen. And if you hang up, I'll come knocking on your door. Ted will let me in, if you won't." She was met with silence.

"I don't see what it has to do—"

"Maybe nothing," Veronica cut her off. "Maybe a lot. For sure one of the boys in your club is in trouble. Maybe more than one." She took a deep breath in the silence that followed.

"What are you talking about? Who?" Laura finally asked, sullen, now.

"Luke Branscomb for one, and maybe another whose name I don't know, but Ed Stein does. Here are the facts, Laura. Someone threw a rock through our window, poisoned our cat, painted 'FUCK DYKES' on our garage door, and burned our shed the same way that office was set afire. We saw Luke and another boy coming out of an old RV in the woods—half naked. They were terrified we might have seen them. I went to visit the Ed Stein to see if there are hate crimes going on—trying to get to the bottom of it. Now his office is burned."

"And you've decided Luke is at the bottom of it all—just because he was in the woods. Half of the boys on the island are in the woods on any given day. You know that. If you want to talk about harassment, look in the mirror!"

"Laura, stop! You are working to keep kids out of trouble. I know that, and I admire you and Ted for that."

Silence again.

"But you need to know that for every dozen kids you help, there's a thirteenth—one who twists your message. One who hears you saying homosexuals are damned and so helps God get rid of them. Or maybe—just maybe, Laura—one of your kids is gay and is hiding from God's wrath—or yours—by showing how much he hates them. And himself." Veronica stopped, feeling blown out and astonished that Laura had let her speech run its course.

"That's crazy." The words lacked their usual force.

"Maybe. And maybe not. Talk to Ted, because I don't know who can help those boys better than you." Veronica stared at the receiver in her hand, then returned it to its cradle.

"So there!" Charlotte breathed in admiration. "Did she hear you?"

Veronica stared at her friend. "You know, I think maybe she did. Enough to tell Ted, anyway."

"Is that good?"

"I think so. I think Ted sails on a more even keel—not so eaten up by anger at me, anyway. I'm not his mother." Veronica returned to her chair and her tea, her need to act spent. "We'll see what tomorrow brings."

Chapter 18

The phone rang the next morning as they sat over coffee, trying to talk the night's events into something explicable. Veronica stared at the instrument, her feeble attempts at rationality scattering in the jangling waves of sound. She picked it up. "Hello, this is Veronica."

Ed Stein dismissed preliminaries. "The younger boy—he's a freshman—didn't come home last night." They heard a chair scrape in the silence that followed. "He'd made an appointment to see me."

Veronica sat back with a thump. "Repeat that." She switched the phone to speaker.

"The boy is missing." His voice filled the room. "His parents reported it to the police."

"Dear, God," Charlotte breathed. "What now?"

Veronica could only stare.

"I don't know." The counselor's words broke the silence and spoke for all of them.

"Maybe he'll show up," Charlotte offered without conviction.

"Let's hope." Veronica pressed a hand to her forehead as though to force her brain into action. "He may be hiding out. Scared of Luke."

"Right." Ed Stein's single word stamped worry with certainty.

The room fell silent again.

Charlotte stood and refilled her coffee cup. "Have you made that list Captain Wilson asked for—of students who may be angry at you?"

"Yes. And I've talked with Holloway. I'll add both boys names, but not for publication."

"Good." Charlotte had gone into lawyer mode. "And add a note at the bottom that the missing boy had asked for an appointment—you don't know what about."

"Right." He sounded tired. "Of course, that won't mean much to them without ..."

"Our story," Veronica finished for him.

"If he doesn't show up," Charlotte stated, "we'll have to tell it ... to Wilson, Hansen ... both."

"Oh, Lord, I don't want to do that," Veronica breathed. The idea of exposing the boys' activities in the RV to their parents and the news media turned her stomach.

"We've no choice." Charlotte's tone was flat. "It's gone beyond harassment, now. Particularly if that boy doesn't show up."

"We'll hope it doesn't come to that." Ed Stein's voice was calm. "Meanwhile, I'll add the note, and we'll keep our fingers crossed."

"All right. Thanks for letting us know, Ed. And do call us if he appears." Veronica turned off the phone and sat looking at her friend.

"I know what you're thinking." Charlotte put down her cup. "Okay, get your coat." She rose heavily. "Molly! Morty! Walk time."

They put on boots and slickers against the blackening sky. Veronica picked up Constance and put the digital in her pocket on her way out.

The evergreen laden air had acquired the raw edge of winter, and Veronica could think of nothing to say that would disperse the damp chill of the woods.

It was raining by the time they reached the clearing where the battered RV hunched against the elements. They stopped at the edge of the woods, searching for signs of life, then Veronica folded her arms across her chest, took a deep breath and plunged forward.

The door gave with a squawk, and the fetid air that washed over them seemed colder than the out of doors. The grey light was dimmed further by the dirt coating the windows, so they could do little but stand in the doorway letting their eyes adjust. The gas cans now sat on the floor inside the door. A heap of tangled blankets on the bed and a half-full soda bottle sitting on the floor were the only occupants.

Veronica felt the tension bleed out of her limbs, whether from relief or disappointment, she couldn't tell. Then she saw the table lamp lying on the floor and a broken plate next to it.

Charlotte crossed the room to the couch. "Look."

Only when she was standing next to her friend did Veronica see the streaks and splatters of blood on the blankets, the stain on the bare mattress.

"That wasn't there before." Charlotte's tone was certain.

Veronica turned her attention to the floor. "Or there." She pointed to fresh smears, leading to the door. When she turned, examining the room more carefully, she spied a jacket in the corner by the bed.

"Don't touch it." Charlotte's voice stopped her as she reached to pick it up.

She straightened and spied a soggy towel in the sink. It, too, was bloody.

Charlotte was dialing her cell phone. "Deputy Hansen, please."

Far off in the woods, an eagle called. Pine trees murmured in the breeze. But inside the desolate room there was nothing but the rancid chill. It ate into their bones, but they seemed incapable of moving.

"Yes," Charlotte burst at last. "This is Mrs. McAllister. We're at that old RV where we found the gas cans after our fire. I think you need to come. There's been a struggle here—there's blood. And someone's jacket."

Her face tightened in exasperation as she listened to his response. "Yes, I know you're investigating a missing boy. That's precisely why I'm calling you. I think he may have been here." She closed her eyes. "Yes. Thank you. We'll wait." She shut her phone and blew a noisy puff of air. "Let's get out of here." She headed for the door.

"He's coming?"

"Reluctantly, but yes."

Veronica started to follow then hesitated. Time to put the cameras to work. As always, she let Constance choose the shots, simply moving it about until something arrested her hands. Then she took out the digital and clicked identical shots. "Now we'll see if you're really up to the job," she told it as she slid it back into her coat.

Charlotte, hands jammed into her pockets, stood breathing fresh air.

Veronica joined her and studied the ground around the RV. "No footprints, I'm afraid." She put up the hood of her slicker.

"I can't even make out ours." Charlotte wrapped her arms around herself as she gazed at the wall of trees. "Tell me again why we live in the woods."

Veronica smiled. "To be surrounded only by the murmur of the trees, the call of woodpeckers, the sound of a pine cone dropping on dead leaves."

154

"Ah, yes. Serenity. Thank you."

"Well, we'd best go stand in the serenity, or we'll be soaked." Veronica crossed the clearing.

Fifteen minutes later, the sheriff's car came down the grass lane, and Deputy Hansen emerged. "Good morning, ladies."

"Good morning." Charlotte led the way to the trailer without further greeting.

Deputy Hansen stood in the doorway, surveying the scene. Then he crossed the room and looked down at the smears of blood on the blankets. "Looks like a struggle, all right." He took in the tipped lamp and broken crockery.

Veronica pointed out the towel in the sink.

"And you think it has something to do with the Johansen boy, do you? How do you figure that?"

"That's his name? The missing boy?" Charlotte glanced at Veronica.

"Mmhm. Steven Johansen, but they call him 'Skipper.'"

"Ah. Well, we've had two arsons in a week, and there are the gas cans—except they've been moved. They were on the counter after our shed fire." Charlotte's voice again carried the authority of a lawyer. "Secondly, we saw a pair of boys—not Norris Stoner—at this RV, and now one of those boys is missing."

"I suggest you see if that jacket belongs to him." Veronica pointed.

"You sure it's the same boy?"

"We think so. The jacket should tell for sure. And I suspect that's his blood." Charlotte bit her words.

"And who was he with, do you know?"

"Yes. Luke Branscomb." Veronica watched him write down the name. "Who we think has been harassing us and burned our shed."

"With this Johansen boy?"

"I don't know, but Skipper was going to talk to Ed Stein. Now there's another fire, he's missing, and we have this." Charlotte waved her hand around. "Bears looking into."

Deputy Hansen nodded. "Well, the woods are full of kids, but we'll get a forensic crew in here and check it out." He pulled on gloves then picked up the jacket. It was a high school football jacket—blue with yellow stripes and well worn. "And see if the Johansens recognize this." He pulled his radio from his belt. "Get me Sheriff Astor." As he waited, he turned to them. "Thank you, ladies. I'll let you know what we find out."

They nodded at the dismissal and hurried for the warmth of home.

Fifteen minutes later, they settled at the table. "I think maybe he listened, this time." Charlotte warmed her hands on a mug of hot chocolate.

Veronica nodded. "If that jacket is Skipper's, what does it mean? That he was there? That he knew about the high school fire, and Luke beat him up to keep him from talking?" Veronica knelt to pull the corn popper from the cupboard.

"What are you doing?"

"Popping corn."

Charlotte raised her brows. "He didn't need to know about the fire. If Luke knew he was going to tell Stein about their relationship that would be enough to set him off."

"But why would Skip agree to meet Luke at the RV? Wouldn't he be terrified of him?"

"Probably. But he doesn't know Luke's on to him."

"Are we sure there is a relationship?" Veronica thought back over the events as she poured kernels into the popper. "We only have a half-naked boy buttoning his jeans."

"In November. And a half-naked Luke."

"Mm. So, do we think Johansen was also one of our harassers?" In her mind she saw the white-faced terror of the boy in the truck beside Luke. "I don't, for some reason."

"I'm with you. I think Luke Branscomb is living a double life—gay in the woods, good Christian in public. Activist Christian."

"With Conrad's boy. Colin." The popping corn took over the conversation for the next minutes. By the time Veronica had salted, buttered, and served two bowls, the theoretical sequence of events had settled in. The pieces fit.

Veronica sank back in her chair. "So Luke beat him up, either before or after he set fire to the portable. And then what? Where did Skipper go?"

Charlotte eyed her. "You're assuming Luke didn't kill him."

"Dear God, Charlotte ..." Veronica put her cup down. "Don't say that." She got up and crossed the room to her laptop, taking the digital from her slicker pocket as she went. Three minutes later, she was looking at the disheveled room. A murder scene? With Charlotte looking over her shoulder, she flicked from wide angle to close-up and back again. "There isn't enough blood ... is there?"

"I don't know." Charlotte leaned closer. "Back up." Veronica brought the distance shot back. "That window shade. Was it ripped before?"

"I can't remember, but we can see." She retrieved the earlier pictures. "No. It's ragged, but not torn. Meaning?"

"Someone grabbed for it? Who knows? And that overturned lamp and broken crockery could be from dragging a body out."

Veronica closed her eyes, blocking out the new and grisly perception of the scene. "Let's not go there, yet. Okay?"

"Okay. But where did they go?" Charlotte sat warming her hands on her cup, gazing at the screen.

Veronica shook her head. The new vision of the scene had knocked out all other possibilities.

"Is Skipper a member of Laura's Bible Study Group, did she say?" Her friend shifted her gaze from the screen to Veronica.

"I didn't have a name—just said 'another boy.' But she was defensive—angry."

Charlotte sighed, then went to the kitchen and put the fire on under the cocoa. "Do we know whether Luke is missing from school, also?"

"No." Veronica stared at Charlotte, standing silent and stoop-shouldered at the stove. "You're thinking they might go to David's camp." Her voice was flat.

Charlotte nodded. "Exactly. But the boy—Skipper—is too young to drive. Luke would have to take him."

Veronica leaned back and closed her eyes again, willing the whole tangle of events to evaporate. She fought to stop the spinning of her brain, but once the tentacles of possibility reached out, they couldn't be called back. She heard Charlotte dialing the phone, asking for Ed Stein.

"Hello, Ed. ... Good. What have they found out? ... He hasn't shown up, then? ... Well, we'll hope they're right. Ed, could you find out whether Luke Branscomb is in school today? ... I don't know. We're just playing with hunches. And while you're at it, Colin Stevenson, too. ... Thanks. We'll hope it all boils down to nothing."

Veronica opened her eyes as Charlotte put down the phone. "Do we have to keep charging down the road? I want to stop … take up knitting like a proper old lady. Plant flowers."

"Right. And in fifteen minutes you'll be heading out with your camera, stirring it all up again. Eat your popcorn."

Veronica stared at her dish.

"We have to know, Roni." Charlotte's voice was soft.

Veronica sighed, nodded, put a single kernel in her mouth and chewed.

Less than five minutes later, the phone rang. Colin Stevenson was in school. Luke Branscomb was not.

"So Luke and Skipper are together." Veronica put her hands on either side of her pounding head. "And if Deputy Hansen took us seriously, he'll find that out very soon. What then?"

"I expect he'll go see Jeanine Manning, who probably hasn't a clue where Luke is."

"I suppose. Which might be David's camp. But if Eagle's Rest is connected to the religious group, why would Luke take the boy there, Lotti?"

"Can you think of a better way for Luke to keep him from talking? Particularly if Skipper is a member of the church group."

"And how would they explain their presence up there on a school day, Lotti? I don't think the camp is even open during the week in the winter. There won't be anyone there."

"Precisely. Except maybe that caretaker—Mike, was it?. Might David be there, do you think?"

Veronica lifted her shoulders and let them fall.

"Well, if he is, Luke will probably make up a story. About being persecuted, I'd wager—blamed for the fire, or something. He'll have to explain Skipper's being beat up."

"We're spinning tales, Lotti. We don't know any of this. For all we know, Skipper beat up Luke!"

"True. But we have to go see, anyway, don't we?" Charlotte plopped into her chair and put her hands on her knees.

Veronica sighed and looked at her watch. "It's an hour until the next ferry." She gave Constance a long look—had an image of herself walking into Eagle's Rest with the camera hung over her shoulder—and winced. "I think you'd better stay home, this time." She reached for her coat and felt in the pocket. "Your little sister will take care of it."

Chapter 19

As the ferry plowed the grey waters toward the mainland, Veronica stood on the open foredeck. The Pacific wind whipped through the Straits of Juan de Fuca and plastered her coat to her body.

"Veronica, for God's sake come inside!"

For several long minutes, she ignored her friend as the cold washed away her dread of what she was about to face—Luke and David side by side united in their condemnation. When the foreboding was numbed into cold determination, she turned, pulled open the door, and went inside to the warmth of Charlotte's presence.

"Masochism is out of date," Charlotte commented as she took her seat.

"Call it preparation, then." She reached for her purse. "I'm getting coffee. Want some?"

"No, thanks."

The coffee line was short, the coffee hot, and the steady throb of engines beneath her feet reassuring. Soon, she was back in her seat, warming her hands around the cup.

Charlotte watched. "You'd be far better off angry. Call your son the blockhead he is and get on with it. You're just too damn much ... a mother."

Veronica laughed. "An incurable condition, as you know full well. Anyway, it's his father I want to be mad at, and it's difficult to be properly mad at the dead."

"Too true. Though I used to be pretty good at being angry at Ellie for dying."

"That's different. A stage of grief. This never changes. For twenty years it's gone on ..."

Charlotte gazed out of the window. "It's not normal, you know, for your kids to bear a grudge that long."

"Yes, but it's not a grudge anymore. Or so they'd tell you. It's just a way of being—where I don't exist. If I hadn't ruined it by knocking at their doors ..."

"Roni, cut it out! When you talk like that I want to ..."

"All right, all right." Veronica held up a hand. "They're closed-minded zealots, building barricades against what they don't want to deal with. Is that better?"

"Getting there." The loudspeaker directed drivers to return to their vehicles, and Charlotte gathered her coat and purse.

"Just so David doesn't know what Luke's up to." She followed Charlotte down the stairs. "His attacks, that is, not his sexual preferences."

"Let's hope he doesn't know the latter—for Luke's sake."

The ferry bumped the dock as they closed the car doors. While they waited to unload, Charlotte turned to look at her friend. "Besides, we're probably on a wild-goose chase. The camp will be closed up tight and empty."

"Which will leave us exactly where we are, answering nothing. I'm all right, Charlotte, really. I'm ready. If Luke and Skipper are there, well, I've had enough of my son's hatred masquerading as religion." She realized she'd just answered her own question. David's hatred had contributed to Luke's attacks, whether David knew about them or not.

Ahead of them, engines started up and the line began to move. "Okay, then." Charlotte turned the key. "Here we go."

The sun broke through as they rolled off the boat and stayed with them through the long interstate drive to Everett, but once they turned East across the farmlands, they drove into deep clouds piled up against the foothills. Charlotte slowed the car as they approached the entrance to the camp. They drove by slowly. The parking lot was empty.

"Stop." Veronica twisted in her seat. "That's David's SUV. Behind the lodge."

"You sure?" Charlotte drove a block further and turned into a dirt lane.

"Yes. I am."

They went back to the lot. Charlotte let her take the lead as they mounted the steps to the door and knocked.

The door opened. "Yes?"

The face was David's. The voice was that of a homeowner dealing with a solicitor of magazines, windows, or roofing. Veronica rocked back on her heels, speechless despite all of her preparations.

"We're looking for Luke Branscomb and Skipper Johansen." Charlotte's voice filled in the empty space.

"Oh? And why would you look here?"

"Because they're campers of yours." Veronica's newly-found voice was louder than she intended. "And because someone set fire to a counselor's portable at the high school ..."

"And the two of them haven't been seen since." Charlotte, who usually let Veronica deal with her children alone, finished the sentence with a flourish.

Veronica spied a flicker of motion behind David. "Hello, Luke."

Her gamble paid off. Startled, David turned then shifted his position to block her view. "Go away. This is none of your business."

"Come off it, David." She recognized her tone as that of a mother fed up with a child's lies. "Their parents are frantic."

"Their parents know they are safe." David folded his arms across his chest.

"But not where they are," Charlotte surmised.

"Exactly. They're here because they were attacked by a bunch of hippies out to harass Christian kids."

"Really. They told you that?" Veronica gaped then realized that's precisely what Charlotte had predicted.

"Like it or not, Mama. Hippies can be vicious."

His tone chilled her, but hardened her determination to get into the house. She eyed the distance between his shoulder and the door jamb.

"I don't know where you got that fire story," he went on. "It sounds like a set-up to me."

"Ask Luke and Skipper if they know," Charlotte retorted.

He turned to Charlotte to respond, and in that second, Veronica slipped past him. Well, slipped wasn't quite the word, more like brushed—or pushed.

"Hey!"

Luke Branscomb stood in the kitchen doorway, his face immobile.

"Are you hurt, Luke?"

"None of your business!" David grabbed her arm from behind. "You can't bust in here as though …"

She jerked her arm away and walked across to an open door at the far end. A large knotty-pine desk faced her, but to her left was a couch covered in a Native American blanket, and under it was a boy with a bandaged head, facing the wall. Automatically, her camera came out of her pocket and recorded the scene.

"Hello, Skipper." She stepped forward, ignoring the commotion behind her, and rolled him toward her. The dark circles beneath his eyes accentuated a defiance that failed to conceal his terror, and his lips were blue. Gently she unwrapped the gauze to reveal a two inch gash and a rapidly growing lump on his forehead. She replaced the bandage, and he turned his head away as she continued her exam. His arms were scratched and bruised, and he cried out when she touched his ribcage.

"This boy needs a doctor." She turned to face her son who stood in the doorway behind Charlotte's outstretched arm. However much David might loath her friend, he apparently wasn't prepared to manhandle her. Veronica felt a moment of satisfaction that she'd drilled at least that much civility into him.

"I can take care of him." He sounded defensive now, but made no move to get Charlotte out of his way.

"He needs stitches, and he's in shock. I suspect he has a broken rib. Those aren't things you can take care of, David." She tempered her voice, hoping to carry them past confrontation into a more reasonable state. Then she turned back to the boy without waiting for his answer. "Who did this to you?"

He rolled over to face the wall again.

"Was it Luke?"

He didn't move.

"You need to give us a chance to help, Skipper. Was it hippies or Luke?"

Still no reaction.

Veronica gave it up and headed for the door. "Let's ask Luke, shall we?" Charlotte dropped her arm, and David stepped back, but the room beyond him was empty. Luke was gone.

David crossed to the stairs. "Luke?" He took the steps two at a time and disappeared down the hall. "Luke? Answer me!"

But he returned to the head of the stairs alone. "You've scared him off."

"I daresay. He was afraid that boy would talk."

Beside her, Charlotte was punching numbers into her cell phone. "Deputy Hansen, please."

David clattered down the stairs. "You cut that out! You can't just barge in here ..."

"David, stop!" Veronica stepped between his charging form and Charlotte. "For once in your life listen to me!"

Something in her voice, some familiar tone from the past, made him pause. "You do great things for kids who haven't had much chance, but even you can get hold of a bad apple, once in a while."

"There are no bad apples, only bad parents."

Charlotte started talking into her cell phone as she headed for the kitchen, out of hearing range.

"You may be right, but Luke beat up Skipper to keep him from talking." Her eyes held him as they had long ago. The forgotten skills of motherhood.

"Talking about what?"

"Nothing!" The cry of protest from the office startled them all.

David raised his head, perplexed. Veronica looked at Charlotte, then grabbed David's arm and pulled him, bringing another echo of the past, out to the porch and closed the door. "Luke and Skipper are good Christian boys. They both—maybe especially Luke—need that ... need you. But they are also gay."

He jerked and turned away. "That's absurd." He stared into the trees. "Ridiculous. Don't ask me to listen to that guff!" He started for the door.

She stepped in front of him. "You'll listen because I say so, and it's high time you did!"

His eyes widened, as though with a faint memory of another time she'd yelled at him like that, the cause lost in time.

"Because if you don't, you're condemning those boys to hell. Not your Christian Hell—living hell right here and now."

"I don't believe you! You've got that stuff on the brain." He shifted his gaze away from her again.

"No, you do, David. And it's high time you got over it."

"We're taking Skipper to the hospital." Charlotte spoke from the doorway, turning them both toward her. "Monroe's the closest. Hansen's calling his parents. The jacket we found in the RV, by the way, is his."

"Good. Let's go." Veronica headed into the house, glad to stop while she was at least even. She'd laid the egg; now let it incubate.

In the office, Charlotte laid a hand on Skipper's shoulder, turning him toward them.

"I'm not going anywhere!" The words were more bellicose than the voice.

"You need to get stitches in that forehead and someone to see to that rib," Veronica told him. "And your parents are frantic. They need to know you're okay."

"I'm not going! I'm not talking to anybody!"

"You don't have to talk. You have to mend your head. Okay?" Charlotte put a hand in his armpit, Veronica did likewise and they heaved him to his feet. "There. Are you dizzy?"

He shook his head and winced. "Just some," he mumbled.

"Well, let's get you to the car, and you can lie down again." Veronica took a step and felt the fight go out of him. They moved across the living room. Skipper kept his head down, not looking at David, who watched without speaking.

At the door, Veronica stopped and turned her head. "Luke will probably be back. It's up to you, now."

He didn't answer, and she turned to resume their journey without clarifying what she meant. She wasn't sure she knew.

Despite their care, Skipper cried out in pain as they helped him into the back seat and again as they helped him lay down.

"Luke did a good job on him," Charlotte mumbled after they'd closed the door.

Veronica's head was light, almost woozy, as they pulled out of the parking lot,. She put it against the headrest and identified the cause. Relief. They'd found Skipper—alive. More than that. Luke was the culprit. They were right. More than that. She'd unloaded at her son. Really unloaded. High time. Yes, indeed. High and hell time.

She opened her eyes on that note and chuckled aloud, gazing at the passing woodlands.

"Charlotte, stop!" She craned her head to look again. "Back up a little. There. Down that track. Isn't that the back of Luke's truck?"

Charlotte leaned over. "I can't make out the color."

"It's blue. Which means he's still around." She pulled out her camera and shot a picture.

"Interesting. But why would he hide it?" Charlotte put the car in gear and moved off.

"I don't know. In case someone came looking, I guess."

The rest of the drive through the fading light was uneventful and short. An occasional groan from the back seat was the only accompaniment to their thoughts.

"Aha …" Charlotte said, bringing Veronica out of her daze. "There's the 'H.' Welcome sight." She turned the car as directed and a quarter mile later pulled up at the hospital's emergency entrance. "Get a wheelchair," she directed, turning off the engine.

But before Veronica could pull a chair out of the vestibule, a uniformed deputy approached. "Mrs. McAllister?"

"Mrs. Lorimer. That's Mrs. McAllister." She pointed.

He nodded. "Good. You have the Johansen boy? We've been waiting for you."

"Do you need a gurney?" An attendant in scrubs had come up.

"Yes, please. Far better than a chair. He's in pain." She pushed the chair back to the wall.

From then on, they had only to watch as the medical forces lifted Skipper Johansen into their care. When they'd wheeled the boy away into an examining room, the deputy turned to them. "His parents are coming, so you ladies don't have to wait, but I'd like to ask you a few questions before you go, if I may."

They nodded mutely and followed him into an office.

"How did you happen to find the boy?" he asked.

Veronica and Charlotte exchanged a look. How much were they going to tell? Where did this story start, and what did he need to know?

"He's a member of a church group on Grafton Island—he and Luke Branscomb, the other boy who's missing. A fellowship group that's connected with Eagle's Rest camp," Veronica started. "The camp is run by my son, you see, so we knew they'd been campers there. When they disappeared, we thought maybe they came up here—to the camp." She watched him write, hoping that would be enough.

"And the other boy? Luke? Was he there?"

"Yes," Charlotte took over. "But he ran off when he saw us, I'm afraid."

Again they watched him record the information.

"Do you think he'll go back there?"

"I'd bet on it." Charlotte sat back, as though relaxing. "I think his truck is still parked down a track a quarter mile east of the camp entrance. Blue."

"Hm. We'll have a look." He made another note. "Do you know these boys? Know why they might have run away?"

"Not really, I'm afraid," Veronica hastened before Charlotte could speak. "We just know them through my daughter who runs the youth group at the church. And through my son."

"Good. We'll keep an eye on the camp to see if the Branscomb boy comes back. I'm sure the parents will be in touch to thank you." He rose and shook their hands.

Once back in the car, Charlotte cast her an evil glance. "So we're now good members of Grace Bible Church."

"Sometimes it's useful to be a little grey-haired lady."

"Little?"

"It worked."

"Hmph." Charlotte turned on the headlights, backed the car out, and headed for the highway. "So as far as the Monroe authorities know, it's just a case of a pair of runaway kids. I guess that's good."

Chapter 20

Veronica felt her muscles release the tension of the past hours. She was hungry. "Let's stop for a bite to eat." She looked at her watch. It was an hour and a half drive to the ferry, and they'd missed the four thirty. There wasn't another until eight. "We have time."

"All right. We never had lunch, did we?" Charlotte turned the car toward the business district.

"Popcorn, as I remember." Veronica scanned the stores as they passed.

"I hope you left your dish on the counter."

"I don't remember. Why?"

"Well, if not, I daresay Molly and Mort enjoyed their feast."

Veronica snorted. "The least of my worries. Slow down! There's a café."

Charlotte braked and craned her neck to see. "It looks okay. A bit quaint, but it'll do."

It was a Scandinavian café, scalloped wood and blue and white checkered clothes. The air smelled of muffins. When they'd settled into a booth, Veronica scanned the menu—meatloaf, pork chops, pot roast—and felt her hunger depart.

"Coffee for both of us," Charlotte told the waitress who appeared at the table. "And I'll have the Swedish meatballs, please."

"A bowl of your chowder and a salad," Veronica ordered, "and one of those wonderful muffins I smell." She smiled to make up for her meager order, then turned to meet Charlotte's frown. "I'm fine," she insisted, "just tired." She leaned back and looked through the lace curtains into the glare of the unfamiliar street. Her head pounded. "Very, very tired." She closed her eyes. When had this day started, anyway? The chill damp of the RV, with its tangle of blankets and blood-smeared carpet tumbled with her son's angry face and the weight of the boy dragging at her shoulder. She could feel Charlotte studying her but didn't open her eyes until she heard the rattle of coffee cups.

"Drink up," Charlotte ordered. "You look downright pasty."

Veronica winced at the word, but did as she was told and followed the scalding liquid with a long drink of water.

"How are you doing?"

Veronica gazed into her friend's concerned face and thought about it. "I don't know. Happy that I yelled at David."

Charlotte smiled. "Good. You were great."

"Scared of just about everything else. Luke …?"

Charlotte nodded. "They need to catch that boy."

"Tell me, Charlotte, did you know Luke before? When he was younger—living with his mom?"

"Not really. I interviewed them—the children—when Social Services brought the case, and I've been trying to remember. They seemed almost indifferent to the whole process. But kids get that way when they've lived too long without decent care. Withdrawn. Adults aren't to be trusted. They deal with things alone. I got the impression the brothers were close, though. Joseph looked out for Luke."

"But Joe was killed. How old would Luke have been then? Thirteen?"

Charlotte nodded as their food arrived. "That must have been rough."

"Is he beyond help, do you think?" The soup smelled good, and she began to eat.

"Well, he ran to David. That suggests some kind of a relationship."

Veronica put her spoon down. "Which we—I—have now screwed up."

"How so? If David can't cope with Luke being gay, the relationship is screwed anyway." Charlotte dug into her food with relish. "This smells wonderful."

But she had blown Luke's cover. Veronica stared at her soup, remembering David's rigid face.

"Roni, eat! You absolutely can't take this on yourself."

Veronica ate a bite of muffin, then another, then stopped. "Luke doesn't know I told David. What if we're wrong? What if Luke isn't gay?"

Charlotte looked at her, then down at her food. "Well, Luke will surely go back. If he denies it, David won't have any trouble thinking you're spreading false tales." She glanced up, her eyes softening the words. "Will he?"

Veronica took a deep breath and let it out. "I suppose not. I'll just become twice the ogre I am now." She picked up her spoon and looked at it, then clenched it as tears, unstoppable, rolled down her cheeks.

Charlotte reached out a hand and laid it over hers.

For a long time they sat like that.

"Your meatballs are getting cold," Veronica said at last, mopping her face with her napkin.

"There is a possibility, you know, that it could go the other way. That David could make his peace with homosexuality." She picked up her fork and speared a meatball.

Veronica blinked as the words sank in. "And with me, too?" She laughed and took another bite of muffin. "What a thought."

"Isn't it?"

Veronica felt the possibility of a future warming her veins. Her chowder, though barely warm now, was full of clams and tasty. When the waitress appeared, and asked them if they wanted dessert, she ordered chocolate cake.

Charlotte looked at her watch. "Take it with you, Roni. We need to move if we're going to catch that ferry."

Once they were out of town, Veronica leaned back and watched the road spin out of the darkness into their headlights, thankful that this day was over. The cake, in its cardboard container, lay forgotten in her lap.

She turned on the radio and closed her eyes, fully intending to doze her way out of the mountains, and so was half asleep when the squeal of tires and a sound from Charlotte woke her in time to see the flash of blue before the car pitched … trees spun …the shriek of metal split her ears. … Then nothing.

* * *

Moving forms took shape, sounds became voices, shafts of light pierced through the haze then faded. The screech of metal brought her back, but searing pain from her legs sent her out again. Cold air woke her again and with it, dim memory. "Charlotte …"

No answer. A face appeared, helmeted, eyes clothed in goggles.

"Charlotte …" she shouted, but the word came out as formless noise.

"Take it easy. We've got you."

Her legs came free, and she heard her own howl before it all went black again.Rocking motion, shouted directions, blinding light. She was being carried. Pulled up a hillside. The fog closed in.

The scream of sirens brought her back. A face above her. "Charlotte …"

"We have her." A hand on her arm. "It's okay."Veronica opened her eyes to white light that, after a long moment, became ceiling tiles. Her body floated somewhere she couldn't reach. She raised an arm and looked at it. Turned her head. A metal pole, another bed. White sheeted. A metal table. A hospital room.

A face appeared. In a cap. A nurse. "You're awake! How are you feeling?"

Veronica frowned. "I don't know." She was relieved that she heard words. The nurse smiled and gave her a pat.

"Where am I?"

"In the hospital. Harborview. They flew you in last night after the accident. For surgery."

"What? How?" Then some locked room in her brain sprung open and terror flooded every cell. "Where's Charlotte … Mrs. McAllister?"

"I'll find out. Now, you just rest …"

"No!" She grabbed the woman's arm. "Is she all right? Tell me!"

The nurse looked down at her for a long moment. "She's still in surgery, dear. I really don't know more than that." Her hands busied themselves with Veronica's blankets.

"She's alive, then …" Veronica collapsed with relief.

She didn't hear the nurse's response, if she made one. Light streamed in a large window. Her legs were on fire. She looked down, but the glare of sunlight off white blankets blinded her, and she sank back. When she could summon the energy again, she turned her head. The bed next to her was empty. She could hear dim voices. Far away. No one was here, and she was sinking into a sea of pain. In the moment before panic set in, she found the buzzer.

A nurse appeared, and she closed her eyes in relief. Then she opened them and read her name badge. "Wanda. Where's Charlotte?"

"Charlotte?" Wanda frowned. "Oh, you mean the lady who was with you?"

Veronica nodded.

"She's in Intensive Care, I believe."

Veronica's eyes popped open in alarm. "What? Why?"

"No, no." The nurse reached out and laid a reassuring hand on her arm. "Don't get upset. I'll have the doctor come talk with you. Okay?"

"Please. And soon." Veronica closed her eyes.

"I'll tell them … but now I'm going to dial up your pain meds. "When she woke again it was dark beyond the window, and a single light burned at the head of her bed. Her mind would not clear, and she faded out again.

The clatter of metal brought her into another day. A golden-skinned attendant in blue brought her a tray—a girl whose long black tresses were gathered into a hairnet and whose dark eyes smiled with the certainty of those untouched, as yet, by life. "What … is this for me? Are you sure?"

The girl blinked, then drew a slip from her pocket. "You are Veronica Lorimer?" She checked the name plate at the end of the bed. "Yes. This is yours." She beamed then turned and left.

Veronica lifted the lid and peered at the pallid grey soup she supposed was oatmeal. She took a sip of tea, then worked up her courage to try a bite. Nausea overtook her and she gave the tray a shove as she laid back, her head spinning. After a few minutes, she lifted the covers and looked down at the Velcro and Styrofoam contraptions that encased her legs. Dizzy nausea overtook her again.She woke to a hand on her forehead and opened her eyes to see a white-coated woman standing over her. A nurse stood at a distance behind her. "Good morning. I'm Doctor Burke."

"Charlotte … McAllister. How is she?" The words blurred into each other

"We're optimistic. She came through surgery well, but her injuries are serious. She fractured her skull as well as two vertebrae and several ribs, plus she sustained substantial internal injuries …" The doctor stopped and took Veronica's hand. "But she's stable now, and in another twenty-four hours she should be out of danger."

"Is she paralyzed …?" Veronica's voice came through reed-thin and squeaky.

"It's too soon to tell. We don't think so."

Unconscious, Veronica thought.

"Let's see how you're doing, shall we?" The doctor lifted the covers off her legs and began loosening straps.

"What ...what's broken?" Veronica managed.

"Just the tibia in your left leg. That's a simple fracture, but both the tibia and fibula of your right leg are another story. There was splintering ..." She bent over to examine a bandage, then stood and started closing the straps again. "You have quite a bit of metal in that one." She smiled. "But they seem to be doing well. How's the pain?" She put a hand on Veronica's forehead.

Veronica flinched.

"Sorry." She shifted her hand. "Those bruises are from the airbag. They won't last long. How about the pain in your legs?"

"Making me dizzy," Veronica mumbled.

"Mm. We can change your meds. I'll take care of that." She wrote on the chart.

"Doctor," Veronica called as the woman turned for the door. "What happened? Don't remember ..."

"I'm afraid I can't tell you much, except that your car left the road and rolled, then hit a tree." She came back to the bed. "Your friend Ms. McAllister was driving, I gather. Actually the police have been waiting for you to tell them what you remember."

Veronica shook her head. "Nothing ..."

"Most of it will probably come back. But not now. Our systems are very good at protecting us in a crisis." The doctor patted her hand.

Veronica closed her eyes as the fog encroached. "The dogs ..."

"Your daughter's taking care of them." The nurse spoke for the first time. "She's been here ..."

"She ... has?" The last word was half-formed, but she let it float away. The next time she woke, Laura was sitting beside her bed. She let the flood of warmth close her eyes again, convinced that this was a dream. When she opened them the next time, Laura was still there.

She started when she saw that Veronica's eyes were open. "Mama?" Laura got up and put a hand on her mother's where it lay outside the covers. "I'm here."

Veronica felt tears come in spite of herself. "So I see." She stopped to get the frog out of her throat. "Thank you, Laura."

172

She nodded. "How are you feeling?"

"Don't ask." Veronica tried for a smile, but it was all she could do to string two words together. "Better. Dopey."

"That's the pain medicine. We're staying at your house to feed the animals. Ted said we should."

"Thank him ..." She was awake enough now to examine her daughter's face, which looked somehow crumpled. Soft. She fished for the right word. Drawn. That was it. "Glass of water ...?"

Laura obliged and stood watching as she drank. "What happened, Mama? Do you remember?" She was near tears.

For the first time Veronica was conscious enough to focus her mind. "We went up to David's ..."

"But why?" Fear and bewilderment heightened Laura's voice.

Veronica reached for her daughter's hand but it was out of reach. "To find Luke and Skipper." The scene at the camp flowed back. "They were there." She saw protest in her daughter's eyes then was diverted by motion at the door. Ted.

"You're awake." He came forward and smiled. "That's good. We were worried about you."

Again she was dizzy with incredulity and could find no words. "How long ... been here?"

"Off and on for ..." he broke off and shrugged. "A day and a half, I guess." He shrugged and smiled.

"That long ..." She closed her eyes and let it sink in. "Thank you ... and for animals ... that, too." Her voice ran out.

He nodded. "We're just glad you're better. Hoping you can tell us what happened."

"Told Laura ..." She looked at her daughter whose face gave meaning to the words *suspended animation.* "... too tired now ..."

He nodded. "Later."

"They went to Eagle's Rest," Laura said, outrage tingeing her voice. "Luke and Skipper were there. That's all she said."

Veronica lay back and closed her eyes, concentrating on the scene rather than on their anxious faces. What was it they were afraid she'd say? "David ... angry ..."

"He said you were chasing ..." Laura's voice broke off as Ted put a restraining hand on her arm.

Veronica felt the words in the pit of her stomach. "Did he?" She swallowed hard. "Skipper was hurt. Took him to hospital." The blurred words were incomprehensible to her ears, but there was no surprise in their listening faces. They already knew this much. "Luke ran away."

Laura moistened her lips with the tip of her tongue. "He—" Again her husband cut her off, this time with a jerk on her arm. She pulled away from him. "David says ... you told him they were gay." The words tumbled out, and her face accused.

Veronica closed her eyes. "I did." She was tired. So tired. "Luke beat him up ... Skipper." She stopped a moment as another thought hit her. "How's he?"

"All right," Ted answered. "His folks took him home."

She closed her eyes and returned to the scene. "We started home ..." She put a hand to her head. "Don't know ... Charlotte cried ... how ...?"

"She's still unconscious, but they say she's doing all right." Ted lifted his shoulders and let them fall. "Stable. That's all they'll say."

Veronica closed her eyes, frustrated by the void where answers should be.

"You're tired," Laura said. "We'll come tomorrow, okay?"

She managed a nod then she was alone.

174

Chapter 21

Anger shot through her. Rage whose cause she couldn't name. Her mind produced a jumble of images and sounds ... the screech of tires ... a flash of light ... flying ...Charlotte's cry. " Damn!" No sense connected them.

A murmur of voices at the door interrupted her struggle, and she opened her eyes to see a state trooper entering the room.

"Mrs. Lorimer? I'm sorry to interrupt, but they said you were awake. I'd like to ask you a few questions."

Veronica stared, her brain struggling out of confusion.

"My name's Carson." He proffered a hand and Veronica raised hers in a limp wave. "I wonder if you could tell us what happened."

Veronica repeated the story as far as she could remember. "The rest is a blur," she finished, putting a hand to her head.

"Do you remember whether there was another car?"

She frowned. "I remember a screech of tires. Charlotte crying out ... Yes! Blue ... coming up ..." She closed her eyes, struggling to bring it out of the murk.

"Was he passing you?"

"Passing ... yes, but too close ... Coming at us!" She clenched her hands as terror seized her. The unmistakable sensation of being attacked. "Luke?" She opened her eyes. She was unaware she'd said the name aloud, but the trooper's brows had shot up.

"You knew him? The other driver?"

"So it was Luke?" She closed her eyes. "Yes. No. Not really." She gave a puff of exasperation at her own confusion. "It's a long story ..." She heard her voice trail off in exhaustion. "Only second-hand, but he was angry ... Did someone see it? Did you catch him?"

The trooper shook his head. "Looks like the driver lost control. His truck went off the road a hundred yards beyond yours."

"And … it *was* Luke?" She asked again. "How …?"

"A Luke Branscomb. He didn't make it."

The words hit her midsection and drove the air from her lungs. Her heartbeat stuttered and her limbs turned to ice. A cry was stuck in her throat without air to force it out.

"I'll need that story, Mrs. Lorimer."

His face was a blur. "Not now," she managed to whisper. The last weeks had spun themselves into a ball and crashed, sending splinters. "Call Sheriff Astor," she muttered, "Grafton Island …"

She heard him clear his throat. "Was Mrs. McAllister racing him, Mrs. Lorimer?"

A hoarse noise escaped her. "You're not serious. Go away. Please." She clamped her eyes closed until she heard the soft shush of a closing door. He didn't believe her. It wasn't possible … couldn't be true. Charlotte near death, and they … Her thoughts broke away and scattered in pieces into the void. *Someone forced us off the road! Damn it, listen!* But there was nothing. A circle of silence, impenetrable. An uncrossable moat of air.

"Mrs. Lorimer?"

She opened her eyes and met warm concern in the dark eyes of the nurse's aide.

"Bless you …" She read the name tag pinned to her chest … "Angela." She gave a chuckle of appreciation. Perfect.

"Are you all right? Do you need more pain meds? You look so white."

"Something to knock me out. Yes, that would be wonderful, dear." When she woke again, the early dark of a November afternoon was falling beyond her window. A heavy pulse beat against her skull as memory returned. Luke dead. Driven to a mad act by their … she cut herself off. She'd been about to say persecution when memory of the crash cut off the word. She reached for the glass of water and took a long sip, but it did little to quiet her thumping heart. Some things can't be undone. How lightly she'd used that phrase. Just a way of putting aside something she couldn't change. Not the death of a boy. Never. And Charlotte? What if she …?

Angela appeared with her dinner tray, cutting short the thought, and for a split second, Veronica saw an image of Charlotte as a young girl. She choked and closed her eyes.

"Mrs. Lorimer, are you all right?" For the second time, the girl sounded frightened.

She took a deep breath and let it out, opening her eyes. "Yes. Just a jolt of … thank you, I'm fine."

The girl put the tray in front of her.

"Angela, could you ask at the front desk how my friend Charlotte is? She's in Intensive Care."

"Sure." She started for the door then hesitated. "They said to tell you that you need to eat. Or try. So they don't have to feed you intravenously." Angela smiled her apology for the threat.

"All right." Veronica smiled back. "I'll tell them you relayed the message."

Then the moment of relief was gone, and the unformed thought behind her panic flooded in. What if they were wrong? About the whole thing. What if they were right, but they'd threatened, even destroyed Luke's path to survival? Ibsen's *Wild Duck*, a play that had penetrated deep into her young soul, came back. In destroying an old man's wild duck, the self-righteous protagonist had taken the man's only hold on life.

At the depth of her gloom, Wanda appeared, carrying a pot of gold chrysanthemums.

"Who …?" Veronica mumbled.

"There's a card … here." Wanda handed it to her.

"Just found out. Asking questions. The best, Ed."

The pot and note fought gloom that had threatened to bury her.

The old man's duck harmed no one—didn't throw rocks through windows and beat up kids, didn't set fires. Luke's secret drove him to destroy. But to kill? Her mind bolted at that. Ibsen's play had ridden on her shoulders ever since those college days, whispering, as she focused her camera, that the images she froze in time were her truth. Naming her camera Constance was only a ruse to make light of the responsibility. Her pictures weren't The Truth, despite Charlotte's compliments. The play lived on to remind her that truth-telling in the wrong hands can be a weapon. Surely Reverend Strathmore's Truth had to be fought. She gazed at the pot of gold and smiled. "Thank you, Ed."

"Mrs. Lorimer?"

Veronica struggled awake. Dr. Burke stood by her bed. "Yes?"

"I just stopped by to let you know your friend, Mrs. McAllister, has improved. If all goes well, we'll bring her out of Intensive Care tomorrow."

"Thank God." Veronica closed her eyes then opened them. "Thank you." She struggled to find more words but could only repeat her thank you.

"And now you need to eat."

She nodded obediently and took the cover off her now-cold dinner. "Dr. Burke," she called as the doctor headed for the door. "Do you know what happened to my things? My purse?" Her digital was in her purse, wasn't it? Where was Constance? At home. She remembered now.

"I'll ask at the front desk."

As soon as Dr Burke responded, she realized her belongings were hardly the concern of the doctor and was grateful she had responded with courtesy.

She had managed to make a respectable dent in her mashed potatoes and applesauce by the time the stout, gray-haired night nurse appeared. "Dr. Burke says you were asking after your things. They're right here." She headed for a locker in the corner of the room. "What's left of them." She pulled a purse from the shelf and crossed the room. "They cut your clothes off of you, you know, so there's not much left of those."

Veronica pushed the table away and opened the purse. She tumbled through the contents. No camera. "Was there a camera in my coat, do you know? Or in the car?"

The nurse drew a plastic bag from the floor of the locker and brought it to the bed. "It might be in here."

Veronica opened the bag and gazed at the tangle—dog leashes, car registration, CDs, tissues, lip-balm, sunglasses, maps—the interior life of her dead car. She reached a hand into the mess and gave a gasp of relief as it closed around the camera. When she drew it out and examined it, she saw it was encrusted with dirt and dented. Had it fallen out of the car as they rolled? Where had it been? Dimly she remembered pulling it out of her coat pocket at the lodge. Taking a picture of Skipper as he lay bandaged on the bed. Somehow it had managed to get from her coat pocket to the dirt.

She turned the camera on, but got no response.

"I'd say you're going to have to buy a new camera," the nurse commented, watching her, "but the card should be all right."

"Hope so." Veronica opened the battery compartment and drew it out. "Would you like to test it in my camera? I have it in my purse."

"Thank you ..." She read the name tag "... Catherine ... but not right now." She smiled. One whole part of her hoped the images—the boy with the bandaged head, the bloody RV with its tangled blankets and gas cans—were gone—wiped out, never to return. Fond hope. Those pictures were already on her computer. And deleting them could never erase their ... persecution. There, she'd said the word, and it was still wrong.

"Are you through with these, then?" Catherine waved at the scattered belongings.

"Yes, do put them away, thank you. And you can take the tray, too." Veronica put the card into the drawer of her bedside table and asked the nurse to put her purse in the cabinet below.

Catherine gathered the detritus and returned it to the plastic bag. She examined the half-eaten food. "The attendants will collect this—which will give you time to eat a bit more." She smiled and returned Veronica's possessions to the locker.

Veronica stroked the battered digital. "And you never even had a name." She watched the nurse depart and closed her eyes in exhaustion.She was running through trees under a sky tinged red. Black trunks sprang up in her path, and she tripped, regained her feet, bumped into another, but went on, scratched and bruised. Ahead was a cougar. She was chasing it. Her legs burned. Hands reached out to stop her, but she escaped and ran on, tripping, falling. The cougar vanished. Too late she saw the cliff's edge. Her foot struck nothing ...

Veronica woke gripping the bedrails, a scream stuck in her throat. She couldn't draw a breath. The ceiling tiles took shape and gradually the muscles of her throat relaxed. She lay gasping for air. Only the burning legs were real. Her head throbbed; her throat was parched; she needed to pee. Desperate to see another human face, she pushed the button for the nurse.

No one came.

Veronica reached for her glass and drank warm, stale water. Then punched the button again. Harder.

No one.

She yelled.

A stranger in a nurse's cap appeared. "Stop that! We have sick patients on this ward."

Veronica closed her eyes. "I punched that … twice."

"Well, we do have to take breaks, you know. Now, what is it?"

"Bedpan." She put as much anger into the word as her dry throat would allow.

By the time Veronica had finished that contorted operation, she relented a bit. The dim light accentuated the hollows under the woman's eyes, the long deep lines alongside her mouth. She was looking at burnout. Anger had dissipated the terror of the dream, and she felt a little ashamed of her spite. "Thank you," she managed in apology.

"That's all right." The nurse plumped her pillow. "It's been one of those nights, is all." She replaced the pillow and brought fresh water. "There. Think you can sleep, now?"

"If I had pain medicine to knock me out …"

"I'll check your orders and be right back."

When she returned a few minutes later, the nurse's voice was that of a caretaker once again. She twisted the dial on the medication rig. "There you are."

"Thank you." She smiled. "And I'm sorry I yelled that way. I had a dream …"

"That's okay. Someone should have seen the light, but we're short-handed tonight, and we've had three emergencies." She straightened the covers.

"I'm fine now. Thank you."

"Sleep tight."

When she'd departed, Veronica lay listening to the cough of a patient in the next room, the distant rattle of bed frames, the murmur of voices, a cry of pain—the night sounds of the sick. She thought of Charlotte, lying in a room filled with machines that clicked and whirred, sustaining the rhythm of life for her battered body. And Luke. What to think of Luke. How to feel …

Medicine-induced fog relieved her of further thought and dropped her deep into blackness. Jolted awake, she reached for Charlotte.

Faded back into oblivion.

Came up screaming. She stared at the ceiling. Where was she? A nurse's face appeared. A hand on her forehead.

Sank back into sleep.

A wall of black-coated figures in front of her, coming for her ... faces ... Laura's face among them.

"No!" The white ceiling again. She wanted to turn over to escape it. Couldn't.

Chapter 22

The clatter of trays brought Veronica out of a sea of screams flashing orange and purple into daylight. She lay gasping in relief.

Angela appeared with her tray, and her smile was genuine.

Veronica smiled in return. "You look lovely this morning."

The girl smiled broadly.

Veronica lifted the lid covering the plate. "Far better than the presents you bring." She lay back, exhausted by the effort at sociability.

"Try the toast," Angela advised. "It's not too bad."

Veronica smiled and picked up a piece. Indeed, it wasn't so bad. And they'd given her coffee. A sign of improvement, maybe?

An hour later, the rumble of a gurney roused her from a daze induced by her morning medications, and she opened her eyes to see them wheeling Charlotte into the room.

"Ahhhhh ... thank God. Charlotte?" She saw her friend lift a hand before the attendant blocked her sight. A rush of tears followed.

Wanda came in to read Charlotte's chart and take her vital signs, followed by a doctor Veronica didn't recognize, and another nurse. Then an attendant. Veronica caught only glimpses of the bandaged head, a neck brace, and a long form also encased in Velcro-straps. Then the procession finally came to an end. They were alone.

"Charlotte? Can you hear me?" She choked back tears of relief.

"Roni? That you?" Charlotte's voice was low and rusty, a dim imitation of her self-assured tones. "Can't turn ..." the words became a garbled buzz.

"I'm here. And thanking God you are. At last."

"Wha ... happen ...?" Her voice faded away.

Luke. Did she know he was dead? Well, this wasn't the time to tell her. "I'll tell you later. You rest, now. I'm just going to lie here and look at you."

Charlotte mumbled an assent that sounded like "gla youeer…" and fell silent.

The clock above the television ticked away the hours. Sun poured in the window. Veronica lay listening to her friend breathe.She was awakened by the rattle of trays in the corridor. Some motion out of the corner of her eye turned her head. Charlotte. She closed her eyes as tears began to flow again. The raw fear she'd only half-acknowledged released its grip and vanished. She looked at the clock. Eleven fifteen. Lunch. She'd slept the morning away. "Charlotte?"

"Mmm …"

"You're awake. Can you talk?"

An attendant Veronica didn't recognize arrived with their lunch before Charlotte answered. She put a tray on each overbed table, smiled and left without a word.

"Can you eat that?" Veronica asked in surprise. The attendant hadn't even raised the head of their beds. Charlotte mumbled something she couldn't make out. The warm smell of soup wafted from the covered dish on her friend's tray, and Veronica realized she was hungry. Actually hungry. She punched the button to raise her head and then the one for the nurse. The small acts renewed her sense of control.

Wanda arrived, pursed her lips at the attendant's neglect, and then raised the head of Charlotte's bed. "There now," she said, uncovering Charlotte's soup. "Can you manage this?"

Charlotte felt for the spoon on the tray that was beyond her sight range. "Don't know … there." She felt for the bowl with her other hand then sank back exhausted. "Later."

"Can't you feed her, Wanda? She can't even see the bowl."

Wanda picked up a cracker and put it in Charlotte's hand. "Try this."

Charlotte raised her hand, looked at the square, and took a bite, then put it down and waved the nurse away. "Later."

"Try a little soup," Wanda urged, putting a spoonful to her mouth.

Charlotte dutifully took three spoonfuls and a couple more bites of cracker. "Enough." She closed her eyes.

"Okay. That was good." Wanda turned to Veronica. "See if you can get her to try a few more bites after she rests."

Veronica nodded and sized up her own tray. She raised the cover and stared at the soft white bread filled with something that looked like chicken salad. She needed food too much to argue and picked it up. What her eyes and nose had disdained, her stomach actually welcomed, and it was several minutes before she turned to Charlotte. "Are you awake over there?"

She was answered with a groan.

"Good. Then eat." Veronica had learned long ago that ordering Charlotte around was fatal, but there she was, obediently reaching for the spoon. Such submissiveness wouldn't go on long, she was sure. She might as well enjoy it.

On the other bed, her friend managed to find the bowl and take a spoonful of the liquid. Then another. She felt around for the crackers.

"They didn't tell me much, Lotti. What's broken?"

"My neck. That's the worst of it." Charlotte gave up the effort and closed her eyes. "But I can move … a miracle they say."

"Amen to that," Veronica breathed.

"But my left side … doesn't work. Busted skull, rib, arm …"

"They say we spun and rolled, then hit a tree on your side," Veronica explained.

"Must have been a mess …"

"They said you had internal injuries."

"A general pummeling … they told me … don't remember what …" Charlotte's voice faded out.

Veronica watched her friend sink into semi-consciousness, exhausted by talk.

"What about you?" The words came with a last burst of energy.

"Broken legs—one bad, the other not so bad, I gather. That's it. You caught the brunt of it."

"Good. You can do the thinking ..." Charlotte's words were slurred as she faded from consciousness once again.

More a curse than a gift, Veronica thought, as she watched her friend sleep.

For the next hours, Charlotte's breathing, even and steady in the bed next to her, righted the ship, anchoring Veronica in a safe harbor. Wanda appeared to check their vital signs, Angela brought dinner, Catherine appeared, passing out the evening medicine. Veronica sank into the rhythm without protest. In the middle of the evening, as visitors plied the corridor, she asked Wanda to test her camera's memory card.

The nurse went out and reappeared with her camera. She slipped the card in, turned it on, switched the camera to display mode—then gasped.

Veronica reached out her hand and a moment later was viewing the bandaged boy. She looked up into the questioning eyes of the nurse.

"It's okay, Wanda. We took him to the hospital in Monroe."

The nurse waited for her to continue, and Veronica was tempted to pour out the whole story, but she refrained. It was too long, and she was in no mood to condemn Luke, a boy who could no longer defend himself. She looked down at the picture. "This boy got beat up, but he's home with his folks now." She flicked through the rest of the pictures. "Thank you for this." She held up the camera. "The card's okay, and it puts my mind at rest." An out-and-out lie, she thought. The pictures did nothing but bring back the whole mess.

She flipped into camera mode and took a picture of Charlotte's inert form, then handed the camera to Wanda and asked her to take a picture of the two of them. Wanda obliged, though her face expressed her mystification at the whole business. Then she opened the camera, removed the card and handed it to Veronica.

***

"Mrs. Lorimer?" The voice roused Veronica from a doze, and she was looking into the face of the state trooper again. Yes?" She forced a calm she didn't feel.

"They said you were feeling better, and I'd like to ask you a few more questions, if I may." His voice was polite, but his eyes were flat—not friendly.

She nodded as she tried to clear the fuzz from her head and remember his last visit.

"Do you recall any more about what happened?"

Veronica closed her eyes. "Charlotte cried out. A blue truck swerving into us. Then nothing … a scream from somewhere …"

"Roni?" Charlotte's voice startled them both.

"I'm here."

Charlotte rolled her eyes toward Veronica's bed and made a futile effort to turn toward her.

The trooper stepped into her line of vision. "Hello, Mrs. McAllister. I'm State Trooper Carson. We're trying to find out what happened."

Charlotte groaned and closed her eyes. "… wish to God I knew …"

"I understand you had quite a bump on the head, but I'd appreciate anything you can tell me." His tone was rote, expressing none of the sympathy his words conveyed. His pen waited, poised above his notepad.

"I remember the hospital … Monroe … and heading home." She closed her eyes. "That's all … just haze…" She lifted a hand and let it fall.

"You were driving, is that right?"

"Yes … see the road … but nothing …"

"You don't remember a car passing you? Mrs. Lorimer says it was blue."

"A truck," Veronica corrected.

"Blue truck … Luke? …" Fear and confusion fought for dominance in Charlotte's voice. "Roni? What did you see?" Fear cleared her blur from her words.

"A flash of blue coming up beside us, then swerving." The recollection became more certain with every telling. "Coming at us."

"Well, we don't know that. If you didn't see him before he tried to pass, that might have startled you." The deputy wrote in his book. "All that's certain is that you both lost control."

"Both? What happened? Roni?"

Veronica closed her eyes then opened them. "Luke lost control, too, Charlotte. He's dead."

"Oh, my God …" Charlotte's eyes closed, and air seemed to escape from her already inert body.

"Did you talk with Deputy Hansen?" Veronica broke in, deflecting his attention to give Charlotte a chance to absorb the news.

"Yes'm." He turned toward her. "He said you'd been having some trouble on the island, and you were convinced this boy had something to do with it." His tone made it clear that Hansen questioned their state of mind far more than Luke's guilt. "I'm wondering, you see. If Mrs. McAllister recognized him …" He flicked Charlotte a glance, "It's possible she swerved into him."

"WHAT?" Veronica's shout turned the head of an attendant passing in the hall. In the bed opposite, Charlotte's eyes widened.

"Well, you knew his truck." Carson's tone was reasonable. Simply stating the evidence. "And the boy's foster parents say Mrs. McAllister has had dealings with him before."

"Dealings." The word came from Charlotte. "I'm a lawyer. Had nothing against the boy ... doing my job."

"They say you were instrumental in taking the boy away from his mother." The trooper's tones were flat and certain.

"So the boy had something against Charlotte!" Veronica's voice rose in helpless frustration with the man's thinking. "And so do the Mannings!"

"The Mannings say you both came calling, accusing the boy of harassing you."

"Right." Veronica's certainty was accompanied by a groan from Charlotte.

"So there was bad blood between you." The trooper's words tone left no room for doubt. "Your son, Mr. Lorimer, says you came to the camp chasing after him."

The blow flattened Veronica's chest. The scream of denial that rose in her throat had no air. She could only lie silent as the words and their implication sunk in. *David! Dear God ... you didn't ... tell me that's not true ...*

"You think ... I'm at fault ..." Charlotte's voice was barely above a whisper.

"Well, we're leaving the case open, for the moment, until we can get more information." He closed his notebook, muttering something that sounded like "... does look like it." He put the book into his breast pocket and drew out business cards. "I'm going to leave these with you, ladies, in case you remember anything more."

His departure left incredulous silence behind. Veronica looked over and read terror on her friend's face.

"Lotti, he's crazy. You didn't swerve."

"But I don't remember. I can't ... I don't remember." Her voice was hoarse.

"Well, I do. He came at us, Lotti." Veronica cursed the weights that held her legs and kept her from going to her friend.

Charlotte closed her eyes. "All right ..." But nothing in her tone carried relief or conviction.

"Lotti, look at me!"

"I can't ..."

"Come off it! Come back from wherever you are. You're a lawyer! You know better than to believe his logic. You're Charlotte, for heaven's sake."

"Am I? Don't feel much like it." Charlotte raised a hand to her head. "If I could only remember ..."

"You see that pot of chrysanthemums over there?"

Charlotte made an effort to look, then shook her head.

"Well, it's there. And it came from Ed." She groaned as she reached for the drawer of her nightstand, but found the note and read it aloud. "*'Just found out. Asking questions. The best, Ed.'*" She looked up. "So fight, Charlotte! Yell!" She lay back exhausted. "I need you," she went on more quietly, "to damn David to the skies. Tell me to fight. Tell me to turn against my son now ... and for good ..." Her voice broke on the words.

Charlotte's eyes changed. "What son? No son would do that." The words came on a burst of strength, then she closed her eyes and went limp.

Veronica lay back exhausted. She'd heard the words she needed. The twin lumps of longing and hope that had long since become a part of her broke, dissolved, and drained off into her bloodstream, leaving her vacant, without energy or purpose. Her eye sockets were parched, her lips dry, and she didn't bother to lick them. A faint echo told her to be angry, but she didn't respond.

"Veronica!"

She was vaguely aware that it was the second or third time she'd heard her name and that the shout belonged to Charlotte. "I'm here." She managed.

"Talk to me." Concern and need mixed in Charlotte's voice.

Veronica stared up at the blank face of the ceiling tiles. "I just found out," she started slowly, letting the words flow as they formed, "how you felt when Ellie died."

Chapter 23

An attendant with an elaborate bouquet of fall flowers and leaves broke the suffocating silence that had fallen over them. "These came for you while you were in the ICU," she told Charlotte. "They've been at the nurses' station. Where shall I put them?"

Charlotte waved an indifferent hand. "Yes, they told me ..."

The attendant looked around bemused, chose a table across the room, deposited them and left.

The new splash of color lifted the weight from Veronica's chest. "Who're they from?"

"Jonathan. They say he came while I was out cold." Charlotte's voice was empty of both surprise and pleasure at this show of concern from her brother. The trooper's visit or pain medication or both had wiped out all else.

"Nice of him."

"Mm."

Veronica could think of nothing to say that would lift the pall. Let her rest, she decided, and so let the silence fall. A few minutes later, even breathing told her Charlotte had dozed off. She gazed at the twin spots of color across the room and searched her mind for that bit of light—some unnoticed bit that would break apart the implacable certainty of Trooper Carson and Deputy Hansen. And take away her own uncertainty in the bargain. A witness. Had no one stopped? They hadn't asked, but surely someone had seen the accident. She cast her mind back to the mountain road. Not much traffic. Then who had reported it? How long had their cars lain there before someone came along? Her brain, unleashed by shock, flooded with questions that demanded answers.

Their dinner trays arrived, waking Charlotte, and this time Veronica reminded the attendant to raise the head of Charlotte's bed. "You have to eat," she told her friend when the aide had departed. "Because we're going to fight. Because Ed Stein's out there helping us. We'll find someone who saw the accident or … I don't know what. You know these things better than I do, so eat up, because we're not taking the blame for this."

Charlotte smiled. The first smile Veronica had seen on her friend's face since the accident. "Sounds like you have the bit in your teeth." With her good hand, she took the lid off her supper and gazed at the unidentifiable brown and white lumps. "What is it?"

Veronica lifted her own lid. "Meat loaf, I think. And mashed potatoes."

Charlotte groaned, then found her fork and began on the white mound.

Veronica managed to cajole her into half her dinner before the attendant arrived to clear their trays. She turned on the television to fill the silence, but could find nothing but the evening news—bodies from Iraq, civilian casualties in Afghanistan, early snowstorms crippling Boston. She flipped it off. "Do you remember how much traffic there was on that road, Lotti?"

"No. Not much anytime on that road."

Deflated, Veronica could do nothing but let silence take over once again.

A burst of voices in the hallway drew their attention, and she watched a visiting family pass. Then a couple, then a pair of chattering women. The working world had arrived to visit their relatives and friends.

"Where's Laura?" Charlotte barked out of the blue. "Or your sister?"

"Laura and Ted were here," Veronica assured her. "Right after I woke up." She hadn't asked after David, Veronica noted.

"They haven't been back?" Charlotte's gaze circled the room, looking for evidence—a plant, a flower, a stuffed animal. "And Dorothy?"

"No. Haven't seen her. Which is not surprising."

"Yes, it is, Veronica. Your family should be here regardless of squabbles. That's what families do."

As though on cue, the doorway darkened and a tall portly man with silvering hair, dressed in a gray pin-striped business suit entered. "Hello, Charlotte." He approached the bed. "Glad to see you've made it out of danger."

"Into I don't know what state you call this, but thank you Jon." Charlotte's voice was friendly but guarded.

This was Jonathan then, the brother Veronica had only heard about.

"Better than Intensive Care. That's a spooky place." His voice was hearty, crisp, and sure. "Do you remember what happened?"

"No, but the police seem to have decided that it was my fault."

"Which is bullshit," Veronica broke in, turning the man's attention to her for the first time.

"You're Veronica?" His tone was well-starched.

"Yes. And Luke's truck forced us off the road." She was determined to fling some passion at the man to break his guarded politeness.

He stared at her for a moment, then without responding, turned back to Charlotte. "It's bad, you know, Charlotte. There was a fatality. That always changes things. I'm afraid you're going to need a lawyer."

"I am a lawyer." Charlotte sounded tired.

"Well, I know that. And you know it isn't a good idea to represent yourself. I can recommend someone if you like."

Charlotte closed her eyes. "Thank you, Jon, but I do still have lawyer friends. I'll be all right."

An awkward pause followed. The man hunched his shoulders then put them down again. "Ahh …" He rubbed his chin. "Philip says you talked to him. That he gave you information about that camp." The words came in a rush.

Charlotte rolled her eyes in his direction, as though trying to read his face. "Yes," she said after a long moment. "Thank him for me. It was helpful."

"Well, I don't want him involved in this, Charlotte. You do understand." Jonathan no longer sounded unsure. His voice carried the authority of a man used to being obeyed.

Charlotte's eyes turned flat. "Does Philip know you're asking that?"

"No. He doesn't, and I'm not asking; I'm telling you. Leave him out of it."

Charlotte closed her eyes, then opened them. "I really hadn't thought to put him in it, Jon, and if I find I need to, I'll surely consult him first." She spoke through clenched teeth.

"I would expect you to consult me first, as his father."

"Good-bye, Jonathan."

Veronica watched the man turn and leave without another word. Mission accomplished. "Your brother is a self-centered stuffed shirt. Now tell me again why I should want to see my sister."

Charlotte gave a laugh that made her wince. "All right, I take it back."

But where was Laura? They said they'd be back. How long ago? Veronica tried to sort the days, but they were too fuzzy, marked by periods of wakefulness and sleep rather than night and day. Still, their absence increased the sense of isolation Jonathan had breathed into the room as he hastened away.

"Older siblings never change. He never got over being left to take care of me." Charlotte's voice showed signs of recovery. "We'd go off to find his friends with me tagging along, an unwanted tail."

"Mm. Sounds familiar. And I can still hear it in his voice."

"No," Charlotte added after a minute. "What you hear is fear that we'll upset his life. We used to love doing just that, my best friend, Betty, and I. We'd put toothpaste on the seats of chairs for his girlfriends to sit on or squeeze lemon into their sodas. Things like that. But we never could break that ... that impenetrable sense of himself. He was the perfect son, the perfect husband—though Janet divorced him long ago—and the perfect father. Then, incomprehensibly, Philip ran wild. That's what you hear in his voice."

Veronica laughed. "Afraid you'll screw with his son's now perfect life."

"Mm. Fragile is more like it—having nothing to do with the fact he and Janet have been fighting over custody since Philip was six. Philip *has* been fine for a good five years now; it's time Jonathan treated him as the adult he is."

"You seemed on good enough terms with Philip when you called him."

"I like Philip. He used to spend a lot of time with Ellie when she was sick. He was like a little brother to her. They'd play computer games. In fact they invented one—a fantasy game that sounded vaguely like Peter Pan. A place—sort of a hole in time with meadows, trees, and brooks, where everyone was their age and they had magic potions that cured everything and kept grown-ups out ..." Charlotte's voice faded out.

Veronica let her friend remember in silence.

"Jonathan could never figure out why Philip wanted to spend so much time at our house. He made it clear he found it difficult to be around sick people. I told him about the game. 'The boy's got a future in electronics,' he said."

"Just didn't get it."

Charlotte grunted her assent. "When Ellie got too sick to play, Philip'd sit there and tell her what was happening in the story—for hours."

Veronica lay visualizing the scene. "Ellie was lucky to have such a friend."

"He misses her badly. Sobbed at her funeral, to his father's embarrassment."

"I think he probably misses you, too."

Charlotte, lost in thought, didn't answer for a moment. "He used to come over and sit with that game, playing as though she was still there." Her voice was uneven. "I drew a lot of comfort from that, odd as that may sound. As though we were both continuing her life until we could absorb her loss a little. Jonathan put a stop to it—drew the line. Jonathan is fond of drawing lines. Said it was morbid." Charlotte's voice curdled on the last words.

"Yuk. That's what I heard in his voice. Fear of—anything he finds strange." *So family for both of us exists only on the other side of a chasm.* They had appeared, after the accident, and vanished back into their safe worlds. No, that wasn't true ... not anymore. Laura, standing beside her bed, had been the girl she remembered. Just for a minute—but there, still.

"And how are you ladies doing?" Catherine, the night nurse was starting her shift with good cheer and energy. "Time for pain meds to start the night?"

"Please," Charlotte begged.

"Oblivion sounds good," Veronica agreed.

***

The next day, Trooper Carson appeared and charged Charlotte with vehicular homicide.

Charlotte stared at him, wordless as he read her her rights, but no longer passive. Her jaw muscles showed, as though she was wishing she could spring at him.

"You can't be doing this," Veronica exclaimed. "What possible evidence do you have? He came at us."

Carson held up a hand to stop her. "This doesn't involve you."

"Then tell *me*," Charlotte barked. The exchange seemed to have cleared her brain of the last remnants of fog.

"We have evidence from Mr. and Mrs. Manning, as well as the pastor of Grace Bible Church that you were after this boy."

"Oh? No tire marks then? If someone swerved into me, I would surely brake, wouldn't I? Wouldn't you?" She closed her eyes. "I did brake," she mumbled as though a flash of memory had returned.

"Tire marks indicated Mr. Branscomb braked as he tried to regain control after he was hit."

Charlotte stared at him. "And how, exactly, do you tell the difference between hitting and being hit—unless there was a witness, of course. "

Carson shook his head. "No witness, unfortunately."

"Then I wish to speak to my lawyer."

Carson nodded. "That's all right." He handed Charlotte a legal paper. "We'll be posting a guard outside your door, but you can ask him to leave when your attorney comes. You're entitled to keep your consultation confidential." He flicked a glance at Veronica. "Mrs. Lorimer may have to leave ..."

"That won't be necessary," Charlotte shot.

Carson took his leave, and Charlotte lay staring at the ceiling, her hands clasped over the legal paper that lay on her chest. "I've interviewed people who thought they were set up, but I never properly appreciated their bewilderment—trying to believe someone would do that at the same time they were trying to convince me. They stuttered with frustration. Now I know why."

"I'm beyond ... outrage! I want to wring their necks." Veronica pressed her hands on either side of her head to ease the pain of engorged blood vessels.

"The Mannings? It's what parents do."

"Oh, come on, Charlotte. Not all parents. The Mannings were paranoid about you from the get-go."

"Paranoid about the legal system." Charlotte gave a rough laugh. "At the moment I can see why." She cast her eyes toward the corridor where a brown uniform was barely visible beside the door.

"Roni, do we have a phone book?"

Veronica frowned, opening the drawer on her night stand. "No. Not here." She scanned the room, then pushed the button for the nurse.

Wanda appeared, and through the glass Veronica saw her startled look as she encountered the guard. "Excuse me," she muttered, passing him as she entered. Her expression as she regarded them was uncertain, reflecting the chasm the guard had created. "Yes?"

"I need a Seattle phone directory, if you would, Wanda." Veronica said. "And bring Charlotte the telephone, please."

Wanda did so then hurried away.

Charlotte watched her go. "It's as if we're surrounded by crime tape, all of a sudden."

"Flies caught in a web that might ensnare others if they get too close."

Wanda, still stiffened by the presence of the guard, returned, placed the book in Veronica's outstretched hands and hurried away.

"Look up Jacob Strathmore, will you?"

"Because he has an intimidating name, or do you know him?"

Charlotte laughed. "I went through law school with him. We teased him unmercifully—told him his name chose his profession for him. What else could he be?"

"A governor. Definitely a name for a governor." Veronica found the number. "Give me the phone, and I'll dial. Can you reach?"

She could. The length of the phone filled the space between them. Veronica dialed and handed it back.

"Jake? Lotti McAllister here." She smiled at his response. "No kidding. Are you still in Seattle?" She listened. "Ah. Well Kirkland will do. Still specializing in auto stuff?" She listened and relaxed. "Good. I need you."

Charlotte summarized her situation thoroughly but succinctly. Veronica was relieved that Charlotte's lawyer's brain seemed fully revived.

Then Charlotte listened to Jacob for what seemed like a long time, giving monosyllabic answers about time place, brands of autos and such. "Thank you," she finished, finally. "It will be good to see you again. Oh, and Jake? Stop on your way—well, it's not on your way, but go up to Cougar Gap before you come, and have them show you the accident site. I think I braked, but I don't remember enough. If I did, it's evidence he was coming at me." She smiled, listening to his response. "Sorry. It's an old habit, as you know. See you soon." She clicked off the phone. "He'll be here tomorrow afternoon."

"What's an old habit?"

"Telling him his business."

"Ah."

The act of eliciting an ally lifted them both out of shock. Veronica lay watching the street lights come on beyond the window. How little the rotation of the sun seemed to mean these days, but out there the engine of justice was rolling on and on. "Tomorrow, we need get our memories together, Lotti," Veronica began, but was stopped by Charlotte's raised hand. She pointed to the door, and Veronica realized the guard would be listening to every word they exchanged. She gave a huff of annoyance. "Pencil and paper, then."

Chapter 24

Jacob Strathmore arrived the next afternoon. A tall, angular, lantern-jawed man with a tangle of salt and pepper hair, scuffed loafers, and a loosened tie, he bore none of the polish his name suggested. The room lit with his energy as he dismissed the officer at their door, but his face registered shock when he saw Charlotte.

"My God, what did he do to you?" He strode to the bed and gazed down at her.

"Damned near killed her, that's what."

Jake turned at her voice. "You must be Veronica." He held out his hand. "How long ... when did this all happen?" He turned back to Charlotte. "You might have told me, but I missed it."

"We're both a bit fuzzy on that," Veronica offered, "but according to the nurse, we've been here a week ... which makes the accident ..." She struggled to remember a date.

"It doesn't matter, Jake," Charlotte intervened. "It will be on the police report."

He looked down at her for a long moment, as though fishing for words.

"It's not as bad as it looks. I'm not paralyzed, and everything else will heal."

Jake looked a question at Veronica.

She nodded in agreement. "With God's will. She spent most of the week in Intensive Care, however. How anyone could think she'd do that to herself deliberately is beyond me."

Jake looked around the room, then went to get the only chair and pulled it up between the beds. "So. Tell me how all of this started. From the beginning."

Veronica reached for the sheaf of notes they'd spent the morning writing. "Here. This will save you time and us energy."

They watched him in silence as he read. Either he didn't have a lawyer's poker-face, or he didn't put it on for them. He frowned, pursed his lips, grimaced, and ran his hand through his hair. Then, in conclusion, he leaned back, lips compressed and thought about it. "Your belief these incidents were the work of Luke Branscomb came from the Stoner boy?"

"I'm afraid so," Veronica answered. "Not a sterling witness, I admit. Except that it fits with everything that happened after that—the minister's defensiveness, my son ..." She broke off.

"Does anyone know of your encounter with Stoner? He's not exactly an available witness. As far as I know he's still a fugitive."

"No one." Charlotte spoke this time. "We were already being discounted. We didn't want to make ourselves laughing stocks."

"So the boy could have simply been deflecting the blame." It wasn't a question.

"He wasn't." Charlotte sounded positive. "My nose for liars isn't totally gone, Jake. His whole demeanor—that the world doesn't give a damn about people like us—delinquent children, lesbians and other freaks—was genuine."

"Plus it fits with his history. He's never—or at least at that point he hadn't—broken into occupied houses, and he knew who we were and where we lived." Veronica felt certainty return.

Jake nodded. "But you didn't report him." He raised his shoulders and let them drop. "I mean, he's a celebrated outlaw."

"Thanks to the media. He's a neighborhood vagrant—a lost boy, really—blown large by the media." Charlotte's voice carried her chronic anger at sensationalism.

"Granted, but ..."

"You need more to go on, or we'll be laughed out of court. I know." Charlotte conceded.

"Is there any other reason someone would target you? Have you had any quarrels with the neighbors? Merchants? Friends?"

"Nothing. We're just a pair of old ladies. At least we thought we were." Charlotte sounded tired.

"Except for Constance ..." Veronica mused aloud. "My camera," she explained as the lawyer raised his brows. "I'm a photographer, and it has, on occasion, created problems."

"Oh? And what do you take pictures of?"

"Anything that catches my eye. Which isn't necessarily flattering to the subject." She sighed. "I just published a new book, and according to Deputy Hansen of Grafton Island, some of the pictures upset some people. Other than that, I haven't caused any trouble on the island that I know of—until this."

"I'll need to see those pictures," Strathmore mused.

"And he needs to see the pictures you've taken since this started." Charlotte's spoke with a renewed surge of energy. "They're at the house."

"As is the book. All of my books, in fact." Veronica added. "My God …" She closed her eyes as realization struck. "Ted and Laura are there taking care of the animals."

"They are? Oh, shit …"

Jake looked from one to the other.

"My daughter and son-in-law," Veronica explained. "They're members of the same church as Luke. In fact they run the youth group Luke and his friends are a part of."

"Ah. Yes." He waved the notes. "So you said." He frowned. "Please don't take this wrong, but I have to ask. Is it possible …" He cleared his throat. "… this whole thing …" He waved the notes, "… is a family quarrel?"

He was greeted with silence. He had managed to put into words the silent center of the storm.

Charlotte spoke, finally. "After all this time without contact, they start throwing rocks? I don't think so, Jake. That doesn't make sense. Actually, there's more evidence Luke was angry at me for taking him away from his mother."

"Thank you, Charlotte, but let's face it. It could be." Veronica raised her hands and let them fall. "You need some history." In short sentences, she told the story. The words, bitter in her mouth, came out like hammer strokes. Her head pounded. Jake was eyeing her quizzically, and she realized that she was proving Charlotte wrong. The past can erupt with pain untempered by the years. She stopped again, her energy drained.

"Unfortunately, before Veronica could convince the children she was not abandoning them, her husband—drunk and with her son in the car—drove off a cliff in the mountains. He died, David was badly injured, and the children blamed Veronica for his drunkenness, the accident, and everything else that was wrong. Then they ended up in the hands of her sister, Dorothy, who was more than eager to mother them correctly." Charlotte finished for her.

Veronica heaved a sigh of gratitude to Charlotte for saving her this part of the telling. "Who to this day, believes I deserted my husband and children for a lesbian relationship," she added. "So you see ..." She stopped. *So you see what?* "I don't know what they've told Luke, but he was in Laura and Ted's church group, and Luke did go to David's camp."

"So they could be behind Luke's attacks on you?" Jake nudged the subject to its conclusion.

"We don't know," Charlotte responded, relieving Veronica of the burden once again. "I suspect Luke and his friends acted on their own. The acts had the smell of adolescent pranks—at least at first. But Luke may have gotten the family story from Laura or David, and for some reason it merged with his own troubles."

Jake nodded. "Right. So ..." he thought for a minute. "You think Laura might destroy the pictures. But why?"

"They tell a story of harassment and its connection to their church group. The church is their life."

"That depends on how they interpret them, Roni," Charlotte objected. "There's no direct evidence ..."

"The boys coming out of the RV," Veronica interrupted.

"Oh." The words silenced her friend for a moment. "I'm not sure they're identifiable ... unless you know them ..."

"Which Ted and Laura do. Go get those pictures, Jake." Veronica's tone was urgent.

"Right." He sat thinking. "Well, we'll see what we can do, Lotti, but ..."

"It doesn't look good. I know."

"Did you look at the scene ... the tire tracks?" Veronica asked, remembering Charlotte's request.

"Yes. It's clear Luke braked to regain control as he went off the road. And there's a lot of rubber at what must have been the point of impact. It's mostly in the traffic lane, so I'd say it's from your car, but there are other skid marks that confuse things. I expect they'll argue that you tried to avoid collision at the last moment. Had a change of heart or something."

"But they don't swerve out of my lane?" Charlotte's voice was sharp.

"Not that I can see, but of course accelerating wouldn't have left a trail of rubber."

"No, but if I swerved then braked, the rubber would be out of my lane, wouldn't it?"

"That's what I'll argue." He stood up.

"I just want to know for me, Jake. I can't remember ..." Charlotte sounded exhausted.

"Oh." He patted her shoulder. "I saw no evidence that you swerved into him. There was rubber in his lane, and I'll argue that he swerved into you, then braked too late to save himself."

"Trying to force us off the road, not hit us," Charlotte finished for him." But we can't prove his intention. I understand. Thank you, Jake." Charlotte visibly relaxed in relief, whether at the news she hadn't swerved or simply the unloading onto Jake's shoulders, Veronica couldn't tell.

"Okay. Well, I'll be off to talk to some of these people." He waved the sheaf, then turned to Veronica. "Can you give me directions to your house? That sounds like my first stop."

Veronica obliged then added, "They may not be there during the day, though. Laura works and Ted is job hunting."

"That's all right. I'll need to prowl around and familiarize myself with the place."

"Don't be surprised if Molly and Morty raise hell. They probably won't let you into the yard." Charlotte's voice was faint with fatigue, but humor, released from the weight of guilt, had returned.

"I'll remember to take treats. I have a way with dogs."

"Do you? I don't remember that about you." Her lighthearted quip was almost smothered by the effort it took to utter it.

"I have a pair of Newfies that worship me."

Veronica smiled and watched him amble toward the door. "Don't forget to talk to Ed Stein," she called after him. "His number is lying on the kitchen counter, if Laura hasn't destroyed it. In any case, you'll find him at the high school."

"Right. He's top of the list after the pictures." He waved and disappeared down the corridor.

"So much for dogs resembling their owners. I like him."

"Mm. Because he doesn't look like a lawyer, right?"

"Probably."

Their dinner arrived along with the return of their custodial officer. Angela frowned as she came in. "What's he doing here?"

"Guarding me," Charlotte snapped.

"To be sure she doesn't escape," Veronica finished.

Angela broke out laughing. "No kidding!" She set their trays down then eyed the officer, clearly waiting for further explanation.

"They say Charlotte drove her car into the boy who was passing us." Veronica let her voice carry all of the disdain she felt, and was pleased when Angela's brows rose in incredulity.

"Why on earth would she do that?"

"I haven't a clue, unless she's suicidal."

Angela looked at Charlotte and shook her head. "I don't think so."

"Thank you," Charlotte muttered.

"Would you tell the gentleman at the door that he should be feeling very silly?" Veronica smiled.

"I will!" Angela seemed delighted with the task and marched out with purpose.

"Never mind," the officer grumbled. "I heard her."

Angela departed, trailing a ribbon of laughter behind her. But when it faded, the air in their room escaped, exposing the ugly bones of their predicament.

"If it wasn't Luke, the harassment will go on." Veronica's voice pushed against the weight that seemed to increase by the minute.

"So if it stops ... which it will ... but that's not going to be enough, Roni." Charlotte's voice sagged and dropped off.

A few minutes later, Charlotte's breathing told Veronica that her friend slept. She looked at Charlotte's untouched dinner, then at her own. The chicken stuck in her throat. The applesauce dissolved the lumps but left a sweet coating on her tongue. She sought refuge in the tea, then lay back exhausted, and gave in to the weight.

She was dimly aware of Angela collecting their trays, but that was all. When Veronica awoke, the sunlight was glaring off her white spread. Wanda was placing a folded paper on sleeping Charlotte's nightstand.

"What's that?" Veronica whispered.

"Someone left it at the desk for her." Wanda turned, holding it up. A newspaper.

"Local Woman Charged in Fatal Accident."

The headline took Veronica's breath. "Let me see." Her tone was harsher than she intended, and Wanda frowned. "Please," she added, then gasped in pain as she twisted her body reaching for it.

Wanda handed it to her.

It was the weekly *Grafton Island Press*, and center front was a picture of Grace Bible church, its steps strewn with flowers and candles in memory of Luke Branscomb. At the top of the steps, Reverend Starkweather in clerical robes raised his hands in blessing. Ted and Laura stood near, surrounded by members of their youth group. The story, though couched in "may haves," alleged that Charlotte had swerved into the boy's car, causing him to lose control. There was no evidence of alcohol or drugs, but the accident was under further investigation as Mrs. McAllister was reported to have had hostile encounters with the boy on other occasions.

"I need to know who left this, Wanda." Her whisper was harsh this time.

"I'll ask, but I doubt if they know." The nurse came forward and looked at it. "Is it important?"

"Yes. Sending it to Charlotte was plain nasty. This," she said, pointing, "is a false account of the accident based on no evidence. Charlotte isn't to see it. In fact, she isn't to know about the paper. Okay?"

Wanda took the paper and scanned the article. "Oh, dear." She looked up. "Is it true? Did they charge her? Is that why there's a police officer outside your door?"

Veronica nodded, glancing at the sleeping Charlotte. "But there is no evidence she swerved into the boy's truck. In fact, he swerved into us."

"But why would they print such a thing, then?" Wanda handed the paper back.

"I don't know. Somebody is angry at us—or several somebodies. That's why I want to know who left it. See what you can find out, would you please?" Veronica tried to soften her tone so she sounded less peremptory, though she was consumed with anger at the gratuitous meanness of the act.

"All right. I'm sorry if I ... I didn't even look at it. I thought it was some friend ..."

"I know. It's okay, Wanda. I'm angry at the sender, not you."

Wanda returned a few minutes later to report that the desk staff remembered only that it had been a woman.

Veronica let out her breath in a hiss. "Thank you." Probably Janine Manning, then. Luke's aunt and foster-mother.

Wanda went out, and Veronica was left to stare at the picture, fear freezing solid in her veins. The island would never be home again. Not after this. *Nonsense,* another voice in her head shot back. *You act as though all the island attends Grace Bible Church. Fight back.*

Anger melted the ice but didn't dissolve the certainty the earth had shifted beneath them, leaving their lives changed. She reached over to hide the paper in her bedside cupboard and cried out in pain again.

In the bed opposite, Charlotte groaned and mumbled.

Veronica looked at her and cursed. Would she walk again? Drive? Spend the rest of her life fighting a body that only half-worked? She looked down at her own legs. Hardly fit to run about caring for an invalid. Would they end up in a nursing home and become the old ladies the rest of the world deemed their proper station in life, anyway?

With a shake, she folded the paper and tried again to hide it in the cabinet. Pain shot from her legs up her back into her head, forcing her to pull back.

"Let me do that, for Heaven's sake!" Wanda ran from the door and took the paper from her.

"Put it in my locker, will you?" Veronica mumbled, laying back exhausted.

Wanda did as she was told, then returned to the bed to read Veronica and Charlotte's vital signs. Charlotte stirred but didn't waken.

"I'll see if I can up your pain meds. Maybe you can sleep."

When Wanda left, Veronica fought with herself, finally giving in to the need to know, and turned on the television. She reduced the volume and kept a close eye on her friend to be sure she didn't waken. An early snowstorm in the mountains and a murder in Tacoma took priority over Grafton Island, but just as she believed they had escaped, the memorial scene for the fallen boy appeared in living color—church member, graduating senior, senselessly mowed down too soon. The other driver, a local woman, has been arrested and charged with vehicular homicide. One memorial participant after another testified to Luke's warm and loving nature. Janine Manning sobbed into the microphone, and her husband took it from her. "We want justice."

Wanda, who had returned to adjust Veronica's pain medication, gazed at the screen, biting her lip.

Veronica snapped off the set and lay back in anticipation of the promised oblivion "Don't worry, dear," Wanda assured her. "People forget the news about as soon as they watch it."

"Thank you. I wish I could say the same thing about the island."

"Is that your church?" Wanda straightened her covers then turned to take Charlotte's vital signs.

"No, thank goodness. I'm afraid Charlotte and I aren't churchgoers, which probably makes us ripe for suspicion in any case."

Wanda chuckled. "Only for some. Me, I go to church, but I'm always the one to shoot my mouth off when that sort of thing gets going— which it does."

"What sort of thing?"

"Ganging up that way." She gestured at the television. "Rousing the devil, I call it."

"I like that. And they certainly have been stirring him up. Thank you, Wanda." Veronica felt a smile on her face as she closed her eyes and waited for oblivion.

But sleep didn't come. Her head buzzed with possible senders of the newspaper. Janine Manning still topped the list. The deputy had said he talked to her. Or Luke's mother, Marybelle Branscomb. Devastated by Luke's death, they would surely have been enraged when they heard Charlotte was the driver of the other car. Charging her would bring some sense of justice to what must seem—and was—a senseless death. Justice? Charlotte could probably tell many tales of vengeful acts committed in the name of justice by grief-crazed parents—tales that would only increase Veronica's fear. The story was being fed to the island, to Grace Bible Church's angry congregation, to her daughter who already disliked Charlotte—all of it creating a tornado of emotions with Charlotte at the vortex. Veronica flung out an arm to ward off the picture in her mind.

The medication finally began to work, making her unable to focus on thought. She was shut behind an impenetrable barrier.

Charlotte groaned then cried out in some nightmare of her own.

Chapter 25

Nurses and attendants came and went. They brought food and took away trays, took vital signs, adjusted medication. Doctors arrived, trailing interns, checked charts, spoke encouraging words and departed. A physical therapist visited to exercise available limbs. The perpetual motion of the hospital failed to cover their isolation. They lived in absence. Family and friends of other patients walked past their room going elsewhere.

Beyond their windows, days settled into a steady mist that bordered on rain, as only a Northwest November could do. The uniform at their door kept all but the necessary attendants away and made the voices of those who had to enter wary. Idle talk with Angela, Catherine and Wanda evaporated in his aura. One afternoon, nurses and attendants distributing Thanksgiving decorations hesitated at the door of their room and moved on.

Jacob Strathmore strode through this implacable barrier, scattering its weight, and Veronica felt air fill her lungs for the first time in days—until she looked more closely at his grim face.

"I'm afraid I haven't much good news to report," he said, after the barest of greeting. "I'm facing the blank face of belief everywhere. Totally unsupported by fact, but ..." He shrugged and pulled up a chair.

Charlotte frowned. "How about the tire tracks?"

"Don't mean a thing to them."

"Who is 'them'?" Veronica used the trapeze above her head to pull herself up.

"Well, law enforcement, to start with—either on the island or at the accident site. They say there are too many possible explanations."

Charlotte let out a sigh. "And who else?"

"The Mannings, Marybelle Branscomb, Reverend Starkweather ..."

"David Lorimer?" Veronica's voice cracked.

"He wouldn't talk to me."

She sank back. Well, she'd had to ask, hadn't she? Never could manage to hold her tongue. "And … my daughter?" Might as well hear it all.

"I don't know. They don't talk much, either. The pictures were still there—at the house—by the way, and you're right. They tell a story. I'm sure Ted and Laura had looked at them, because when I asked her about them, she burst into tears. But she won't talk, so I don't know what to make of it."

Veronica sighed. "I suppose tears are better than outright blame."

"Maybe." Jake ran a hand through his hair. "You have one ally. Ed Stein. He's asking a lot of questions of a lot of kids—especially that boy, Skipper Johansen. Maybe he'll break something loose. I hope so, because I'm sure not having any luck."

"Don't blame yourself, Jake," Charlotte protested. "I can only imagine …" Her voice faded.

"I watched the memorial service," Veronica began, noted Charlotte's startled glance but continued, "the media glorification of the wounded community …" She closed her eyes. "I didn't recognize the place … the island I live on—but it must have been there all the time, ready to burst forth …" She ran out of words.

"I watched it too. There's nothing you can do to stop that snowballing when the media is driving it," Strathmore agreed. "It just has to burn itself out."

"Or be fed red meat," Charlotte muttered.

"No, no, don't talk like that, Lotti," Jake chided. "If worse comes to worst, and it goes to trial, those tire marks and the lack of any evidence will count, whether the police discount them or not. I just don't want it to go that far. I want the charges dropped."

"Amen," Veronica breathed. "Well, maybe Ed will succeed. But what can he do if someone does talk, Jake? Isn't he bound by confidentiality the way you are?"

Jake nodded. "He is. All he can do is get the boy to talk to me or the sheriff."

"That's a lot to ask, given the attitude of that community on homosexuality."

Veronica glanced at the doorway to be sure the deputy was absent.

"Charlotte, what was that blog you were checking where we thought Skipper was writing?"

"Aha. Yes. You need to look at that, Jake." Charlotte closed her eyes in concentration. "I can't remember the name of it, but try 'Gay Life.' If that doesn't work, try 'gay blogs.' The entries we thought were Skipper's were around the first of the month, and the topic was the high school scene. There's a blog from a kid who's afraid someone knows and will tell or hurt him. They advise him to tell his parents, and he really gets upset—says that would be worse. We think that might be Skipper. You'll also see entries from "Nicky" and "Chuck"—that's us, saying we just moved to town and are looking for support groups."

"It's grim stuff," Veronica warned. "And it feels like we're going after a kid who's already scared to death, but I'm not willing to let Charlotte go to trial to save him."

"You bet. I'll take a look, though it's tough to identify blog authors."

"By IP addresses, maybe?" Charlotte asked.

"I'll have to find that out. The police can, probably, but not civilians like me." Jake closed his notebook and stood up. "Thanks for the lead, anyway, and let's hope something breaks in our favor for a change."

"Thank you for coming in any case," Veronica offered, though she was already feeling the weight that would drop at his departure.

"Sorry to be bearer of grim tidings—or lack of any tidings at all."

"Not your fault," Charlotte insisted.

But he took the air with him when he left, and the blue uniformed officer looked refreshed by his break. His presence shriveled the conversation between them to topics like bed controls and hospital diet.

"Those flowers look as though they'll come through anything," Veronica remarked, looking at Ed's card. She was desperate to hang on to the single hope the day had brought.

"That they do," Charlotte replied. "And they're still fresh—full of energy."

"Indeed." Veronica smiled, delighted that her friend had perceived her code.

"Is it still raining?" Charlotte asked.

"Yes, but sooner or later light will break through," Veronica persisted.

"And we'll have Thanksgiving."

"On hospital trays, but Thanksgiving nonetheless."

Having completed their benediction, they fell silent, resting in its comfort. Veronica nodded off and dreamed she was running with Mortimer on the beach. Exhausted, she stopped and let him run ahead. She raised her camera as he dashed into the surf; then, just as she clicked the shutter he raised his head, a dead fish clutched in his jaws. A spatter of shots blew the dream apart, and she woke to the clatter of dinner trays. She made a rude noise.

"You snore," Charlotte commented.

"Be happy I don't talk." Veronica raised the cover. Meatloaf again. She glanced over to see whether Charlotte had fared any better. She hadn't. "Would you believe I was once proud of my meatloaf recipe?"

"Is that what it is?" Charlotte raised her good hand and picked up her fork, giving the mound a couple of jabs. "Not turkey, then."

"Not today. But the days march." Veronica watched Charlotte lay down her fork. "Eat," she ordered. "Otherwise you'll never get out of here. You're getting weak as it is—we both are. No one will recognize us."

"Which may be a blessing." Charlotte picked up her fork and raised a bite, viewing it with disgust before popping it into her mouth.

"We'll be sylphs. Totally transformed by the experience."

Charlotte took a bite of boiled potatoes. "Now that's what I call a half-truth."

They finished the meal in silence. Angela appeared to take their trays, treating them each to a shy smile.

"Thank you," Charlotte murmured, then lay back and closed her eyes.

Veronica picked up the television control and flipped through the channels, trying to find something not too unbearably trivial. She was distracted by a rustle at the door.

Ted Reilly stood there, as though looking for courage to enter.

"Hello, Ted," Veronica managed.

He looked from her to Charlotte as he stepped into the room. "Hello." He turned and put his hands on the rail at the foot of Veronica's bed. "I had to come."

They waited as he visibly gathered himself to speak.

"You see, I believe you. I had to tell you that." His face was stripped of its usual bland polish; he looked haggard.

"Believe what, Ted?" Veronica tried to make her voice gentle.

"About Luke. I'd wondered a couple of times. Saw him go into the bathroom at church with Skipper. I followed him once, in fact, and ... well ... he acted funny when he saw me—froze up, like." Ted's hands beat a tattoo on the bedrail. He seemed at a loss on how to go on.

"Bless you, Ted." Charlotte's voice was quiet but emphatic.

"I didn't tell anyone. Even Laura. But after the accident, she kept having bad dreams. Screaming 'NO!' Then waking up, insisting it was just an accident—your accident, I mean—no more. And when we looked at your pictures ... she ran away. Literally. Into the woods. I decided something she knew was tearing her apart, so I told her what I was thinking—about Luke." He stopped, out of breath from the rush of words.

"And?" Veronica urged.

"She started to cry. In relief, I think, that I'd said what she, too, suspected. But when I told her I was coming here, she went white. She thinks the church will turn on us, you see. They'll think we're turning the blame on them to protect you ... and Charlotte."

Veronica saw a wry smile on her friend's face at his late addition. Charlotte, they would have tossed to the wolves. True? She took a deep breath to chase the thought away. "And will they? Turn against you, that is?"

"I don't know ..." Ted rubbed his hands down his face. "Yes, probably. They're in a fierce mood, because of Luke's death. Which is another reason I had to come. I don't like it." He turned and went to the window. They could see his reflection pale against the dark glass. "I've never been a part of anything like ... like this ..."

"A lynch mob?" Charlotte offered.

"Exactly." He turned, relieved. "A lynch mob."

"Have you told anyone about this besides Laura?" Veronica asked, glancing at their guard, who seemed either deaf or unaware of the significance of Ted's confession.

Ted shook his head.

"You need to go to Deputy Carson. In Cougar Gap. And to our lawyer, Jacob Strathmore." Charlotte's voice carried authority again, the lawyer returning from a long absence.

Ted stared at her and nodded bleakly, but said nothing.

"Laura doesn't want you to?" Veronica guessed.

"She's terrified. The church has been our home, you see. But she knows I have to."

"Good." Veronica felt a surge of relief at this measure of acceptance from Laura. "Because you do. Then I suggest you go talk with Ed Stein, the counselor at the high school," Veronica continued. "He's an ally, Ted. Together maybe you can get Skipper to talk."

"Skipper." His toned made clear he'd forgotten the other boy. "Oh, no. His family ..."

"Need not know," Charlotte finished for him. "We don't think Skipper was one of the harassers, Ted. We think, like you, that he was a partner. But I suspect he knows who the harassers are ... were."

"No one but the police need know where you got the information. Or Skipper's sexual preferences."

"No one need know Luke's, for that matter," Veronica added. She watched as he thought it through, his lips clamped tight over his unsavory task, his eyes closed, his hands once more clasping the bedrail. "You know, Ted," she said when he didn't respond, "there is one thing you can do to help Skipper talk." She waited for him to raise his head, which he did after a long silence. "You and Laura can convince the boy that God accepts him and Luke as they are. That when He says all creatures are equal in the eyes of the Almighty, He means it."

Ted frowned at the heretical suggestion, but something changed in his blue eyes. A deepening. She'd struck a chord, somewhere.

"Of course, first you have to convince Laura." She smiled.

His face relaxed and he almost smiled back. "I've tried, you know. Even before all of this. I've never agreed with her that you and Charlotte are ... anything but friends."

"Really!" Charlotte exclaimed.

Ted looked at her. "Really. Yes." He raised his shoulders and let them fall. "I fancy I'm pretty good at picking up clues, and ... well ... I don't. That's all. But Laura ..." His voice faded.

"Is angry," Veronica finished for him.

He nodded. "Her brother has a powerful influence on her." He turned his gaze to her. "Someday you'll have to tell me why David is so angry."

Veronica closed her eyes. Exhaustion fell on her like a weight. The words, "because he loved his father," came to her, but she hadn't the strength to utter them. "Someday ..." she murmured instead.

"Right." He lifted his hands from the rail. "Well … I guess I'd better get to it."

"Wait," she called after him as he went out. She reached for the drawer of her nightstand. "Here's our lawyer's card. You'll like him. And thank you for coming, Ted. It means more than you can know."

He took the card and raised a hand in acknowledgement.

She closed her eyes to hold the image of the man who'd just left, the man she'd seen emerging in the past weeks—now full blown. The Ted that corporate America had submerged. She thought back to the tall, blond, far too polished man Laura had introduced as her fiancé—the glitter of white teeth as he shook her hand, the high-end polo shirt and pressed chinos. She'd been put off, but had suspected another man lay under the façade. Her attraction to Simon back in their college days had been much the same as Laura's, she guessed—that aura of knowing how to deal with the world. With a deep ache, she suspected Laura saw, in Ted, an image of her father in his successful days.

But Laura had been more fortunate. Stripping the mask had revealed a man of substance. Or had Laura seen that man all along?

"What are you thinking, Roni?"

Charlotte's voice brought her back. "I'm rethinking."

"Mm. Right. Is Ted going to do it, do you think?"

"Go to Carson? Yes, I'd bet on it." The consequences of her own words sank in. A break. No hard evidence of Luke's intentions, but a crack in the implacable block of belief.

"What time is it? Too late to call Jake?"

"Nine fifteen."

"Call him."

Chapter 26

Veronica reached for the pad where she'd jotted Strathmore's number and dialed, but got only his answering service. "Jake, this is Veronica. We've had a break. Call us," she finished. "As soon as you can," she added and left the number of the room phone.

Charlotte was gazing after Ted, though the hallway was empty. "You know, Roni, if he does manage to persuade the boy to talk, with or without Laura's cooperation, it puts him on a collision path with Reverend Starkweather."

"And the congregation." She sighed. "It's a real crisis for him."

"Mm. But the best break we've had in a long while."

They fell silent.

"I'm sleepy." Charlotte sounded surprised.

Veronica realized she was, too. "Must be the collapse of tension."

"Mmm. More like a house dropping on me."

Angela arrived to take the evening vital signs. They greeted her with broad smiles, and she gave an uncertain one in return.

"Angela, don't look so scared," Charlotte chided, as the nurse put the blood pressure cuff in place. "You thought the whole thing was a silly joke, before. Remember? What's happened to your humor?"

Angela flushed. "I don't know, I …" She ducked her head, and her voice faded as she turned away to read her watch.

"You saw the television coverage, didn't you?" Veronica guessed. "Of the funeral."

Angela looked up and met her gaze, then nodded, embarrassed.

"That's okay," Veronica assured her. "I understand. We're upset about Luke's death, too."

Angela rubbed her hands together. "Our priest talked about it … the accident … in his sermon …" Her voice broke off, misery clear on her face. "He said it was an example of the dangers Christians face from …" Her shoulders went up then down again.

"Lesbians?" Charlotte provided the end of the sentence.

Angela nodded. "I told my sister you seemed like ordinary nice women to me, and she … well, she started screaming at me to stay away." She met Charlotte's gaze then and broke into a sudden smile. "That's ridiculous, isn't it?"

"The whole thing," Veronica agreed. "Loony Tunes."

"But you never know," Charlotte quipped. "It might be in the air. You might catch it."

Angela laughed. "My sister is very devout," she explained. "And sweet, but …" Her voice faded. "You two have a good sleep."

They turned on the television to bring on the recommended oblivion and watched Dr. Phil, then two make-overs of women far too young to need refurbishing, and finally the rescue of a moldy basement, before flicking the set off.

The following afternoon was fading before Jake arrived, but he was smiling, his eyes bright in anticipation. He stopped at the door. "This is a confidential lawyer-client visit," he told the guard.

The officer nodded, rose and stretched, then ambled off down the hall. Jake closed the door. "I've spoken with your son-in-law." He pulled up a chair. "And he's talked with Ed Stein. They're going to meet with Skipper together."

"At his house?" Charlotte frowned.

"No, no. At Ed's office—temporary office, that is."

Charlotte relaxed. "Good. He'd never talk at home. When?"

Jake consulted his watch. "In about five minutes. As soon as basketball practice is over."

Veronica took a deep breath as tension stiffened her spine. "I wish we were flies on the wall."

"You will be." Jake beamed and drew his cell phone from his pocket. He punched in a number. "Hi, Ed?" He listened to the response. "Right. Just tell me when." He held the phone to his ear and turned to them as he waited. "Ed is going to leave his phone open and on record. I'm putting this one on speaker."

Charlotte looked impressed. "But without Skipper's knowledge?

That's not legal."

"No," he agreed, "but I figure you two have a right to hear it. We won't use it. We can't. They have to convince him to go to the sheriff."

Veronica bit her lip. "It seems like entrapment—of a minor, no less."

"Trust me. If he won't go to the authorities, it will end right here. We'll zap the recording."

They waited. The clock ticked. They waited some more.

The phone rang. Jake punched the receive button, then the speaker.

Ed Stein's voice filled the room. "Hi Skipper. Thanks for coming."

"Yeah." The boy's response was soft, trying for offhand and failing. Then he made an indecipherable sound between surprise and fear.

"Hi, Skipper." This time it was Ted's voice. "Ed said I should be here. You see, we both need your help."

"Yeah? What about?"

"Sit down, why don't you?" Ted urged. "There's nothing to be afraid of. Promise."

There was a pause and the sound of a chair on linoleum.

"It's about the accident," Ed resumed.

"I wasn't even there!"

"True. We know," Ed assured him. "But Ted and I are trying to find out what happened."

"We just want to be sure, Skipper, that we—that everyone—has it right. We don't want innocent people going to jail."

"What's that have to do … with me?" Skipper tried to sound belligerent, but the words came out as a stutter.

"We know you were a friend of Luke's," Ted began, "so we were wondering whether you might also know Mrs. Lorimer or Mrs. McAllister."

"Or know whether Luke knew them," Ed added.

"Knew who they were, that's all," the boy mumbled.

"Did Luke know them?"

"Dunno … I guess …"

There was a long silence. Ed and Ted waited.

"He didn't like them—those ladies who were in the car wreck." The words tumbled as though into a hole.

"Why not?" Ed's voice was almost inaudible.

"Said they were dykes." The chair screeched. They could almost see the boy squirming. "And snoops."

"When was this?" Ed asked.

"Dunno," he muttered.

"Skipper, you made an appointment to come see me."

"What?" The word shot out. "No, I didn't!"

"Just before my office burned." Ed paused, waiting for a response that didn't come. "Skipper, you need to talk to someone. We're your friends."

"It's not got anything to do with the accident!"

"Maybe not, but you see, Mrs. Lorimer and Mrs. McAllister say someone was harassing them. We need to find out whether that's true." Ted's voice insisted quietly.

"We aren't accusing you of doing anything, Skipper, but we think you know whether Luke did anything. You say he didn't like them."

Again the phone was silent.

"He said he'd fix them so they wouldn't tell." The boy sounded close to tears.

"Tell what?"

Another silence.

"Luke and me were in the woods." The boy stopped. "In the old RV. He said they saw us and they were snoops, but he'd fix them so they wouldn't tell." Again the words came in a rush.

"Thank you, Skipper. That's a help." Ed's tone was warm.

They could almost hear the men exhale with relief.

"Had Luke done anything to the women before that, do you know?" Ted asked.

"I don't know … I guess … He said David—up at camp—told him Mrs. Lorimer was his mom. She did something bad—ran off and left him—for a lover or something. He said he was just getting back for David."

"Ah. Anything else?"

Silence.

"It can't hurt Luke now, Skipper."

"Well … the other one—Mrs. McAllister—had taken Luke away from his mother. Luke said he and Colin had fixed them—don't know how. He said it was a secret."

Veronica winced. "Our handyman's son," she whispered to Strathmore.

216

"Colin …" Ted paused. "Colin from the youth group? Colin Stevenson?"

The chair scraped. "Are you going to tell him I told?"

"No. But the sheriff will need to talk to him." There was a pause. "You see that, don't you?" Ed asked.

"Skipper … what was it Luke was afraid the women would tell? What was it they saw?" Ted's question came as a surprise to Veronica and clearly to Charlotte and Jake, too. It seemed unnecessary to press the boy further.

"Nothin! We just weren't supposed to be there! That's all."

"All right." Ted seemed to let it go. "But I want you to know God loves you, Skipper, and Luke, too, no matter what you were doing."

"We were just … messing around is all."

"And if I—or Laura or Reverend Starkweather—have said anything to make you think otherwise, I apologize," Ted continued as though Skipper hadn't spoken.

Suddenly Veronica realized this was for Ted's sake. He was haunted by the possibility that the church group had contributed to the attacks.

"God hates perverts." The flat certainty of the boy's voice startled them all.

"Did Luke tell you that?"

"And David. We all know that, though. Everyone."

Veronica had the vision of a boy curled up like a bug behind the shield of his words.

"Well, they're wrong," Ted said firmly.

"The Reverend, too? Are you saying Reverend Starkweather is wrong?" Skipper's voice mixed incredulity with derision.

"Skipper," Ed cut in, "was Luke a homosexual?"

In the hospital room the silence was strung so tightly that they dared not look at each other.

"What?" The word was only a breath.

"You don't need to answer, and whatever you were doing in that old RV is your business. It's just that you look very scared, and if that's what you're scared of, you needn't be."

"Luke hated homos! He just liked to mess around, that's all."

"Okay. We understand." Ed's voice closed the subject.

"Thank you for all of this, Skipper. And we'll make sure you aren't in any trouble."

"But if Luke was harassing Mrs. Lorimer and Mrs. McAllister, you need to tell the sheriff," Ed repeated.

Again there was no response.

"You can't let Mrs. McAllister go to jail for something she didn't do, Skipper." Ed was firm.

"You can do it," Ted assured him. "Let's pray together, shall we?" A chair scraped again. "Come on, stand up and take my hand. Maybe Mr. Stein will join us?"

"Sure."

Veronica visualized the prayer circle like the one she and Charlotte had watched through the church window. She prayed that it would indeed relieve the boy's sense of isolation.

"Dear Lord, walk with us. Give us strength to be who we are and do what we know is right. Take our fear and show us the path, we pray. Amen."

"Will you come with me?" The voice was a child's.

"Of course."

"Do my parents have to know?"

"Know what? About the messing around? No," Ed answered. "About Luke's getting back? Maybe. The police may need your parents' permission to question you. But no one else needs to know where the information came from."

"Promise?"

"Promise. Ready to go?"

The phone clicked off, and Jake pushed the disconnect button. They sat silent in the echo of the scene. Veronica felt tears rolling down her cheeks and did nothing to stop them.

Charlotte was the first to speak. "I hope there is a God, and He gives that boy his due."

Jake grunted his assent. "He already has one reward—two allies. Two men who know his secret and don't condemn him. That's huge."

"Let's hope the sheriff doesn't press him too hard."

"About the messing around? Right. It's not relevant, anyway. Strictly. They only need to know Luke was getting back—the harassment is partly that in any case. Which is the truth."

"If not the whole truth," Charlotte muttered.

"In this case, the missing part changes nothing—only makes it worse—a hate crime. So we're letting Luke off easy." Jake rose and stretched as the sound of voices beyond the closed door took their attention. The cart loaded with dinner trays stopped at their door. "I'd better get out of your way."

"I don't know how to thank you," Charlotte told him.

"No need. But remember, you don't know any of this. Right?"

Veronica laughed. "That's going to take a performance worthy of Helen Mirren."

Jake grinned. "I have every confidence." He waved toward Charlotte. "I've seen this lady in court." He opened the door. "I'll be back tomorrow when we see how this all plays out." The buzz of dinner hour swallowed his last word.

"Who was that guy?" Angela wanted to know as she brought their trays. "He looks like Abe Lincoln."

Charlotte laughed. "I'll tell him that. He's our lawyer."

"Ah." Angela set a tray on each of their tables. "That explains it."

"Explains what?" Veronica asked.

"He looked very pleased with himself."

Veronica grinned. "They are a smug lot, aren't they?" She uncovered her tray to examine the day's climax. Fish.

Angela waved and left them to their dinner.

"One of these days," Charlotte warned, "I'm going to pay you back."

"Oh?"

"You bet. I have a boatload of stereotypes about artists." She poked at her plate and raised a forkful of fish to eye level so she could see what she was about to eat.

"Photography isn't an art. Hadn't you heard?"

"The temperament is the same." She popped the fish into her mouth. "Yuck."

Their levity faded as they ate, and their minds returned to the scene just overheard.

"I'm sorry it was Colin." Charlotte sighed. "Sorrier for his dad. Conrad seems like a good father." She gave up on food and lay back.

"And not one to buy into mob think," Veronica agreed. But her mind was on David, a man in position of power who had fed Luke's hatred. Her son. Would he ever understand what he'd done? That his need for vengeance had landed, in the end, on Luke? Would she ever get her mind around the depth of his passion—his need for a target?

"You're thinking of David," Charlotte guessed from her silence.

"Trying to. I'm trying to put myself into the shoes of a boy watching his father drink himself into oblivion."

"Needing a target. Something to explain it all. But he's not a boy any longer, Roni."

Veronica looked from her friend's encased limbs to her own. "Indeed."

They fell silent.

"He was always intense about anything he was doing. But it was Erector sets, fort-building—boy things. And his camera—he loved following me around taking pictures. I thought it was a gift." Veronica heard her voice break.

"It is, turned in the right direction, Lotti. Like your photography, when you have a camera in your hands or are fixed on an image you're working on."

Veronica groaned. "And I was even proud he got it from me."

"You should be. It can make for greatness—that power of concentration." Charlotte reached out a hand, as though to grab Veronica's.

"Unless it gets twisted."

Charlotte didn't answer. No response was needed.

"Maybe your son-in-law can unscramble him," Charlotte offered, after a time.

"I wonder. He certainly shone in that interview. I hope at least Laura listens to him."

Her musings were interrupted by Catherine, bustling in the door. "Well, ladies, how was your day?" She headed for Charlotte with her blood pressure cuff.

"Eventful," Charlotte told her.

Veronica forced her mind to return to the event—Skipper's confession, Charlotte's reprieve—to feel the elation evident in Charlotte's voice.

"I guess it must have been good," Catherine exclaimed, reading the dial. "Your blood pressure's wonderful tonight."

And blood pressure doesn't lie, Veronica thought. The condemnation of David was Charlotte's release. For some reason, her mother's face rose in her mind, drawn, its lines hardened by the years, standing at

220

the sink after her husband's death. "Truth is always Janus-faced," she'd said. "It never pays to forget that."

Sometime during the night, Veronica wakened and noticed that the guard was gone from their door.

Chapter 27

With the morning sun streaming in the window at his back, Strathmore told them all charges had been dropped.

They raised a cheer that made passing nurses turn.

"And Luke?" Veronica asked in the silence that followed.

Strathmore shook his head. "The accident has been ruled that—an accident. If Luke were alive …" Strathmore shrugged, "they would probably pursue it, but …" He spread his hands.

"There's not a lot of point now," Charlotte finished for him. "That's all right. The transcript will make it pretty clear."

Strathmore nodded. "It does that. So!" He clapped his hands and waved toward the window. "Welcome to the new day, ladies!"

They lay back, beaming. "And I'll expect your bill, Jacob," Charlotte added.

They spent the next few minutes listening to the legal details, but Veronica's brain was fogged with euphoria. When he left, they lay without speaking, the sun bouncing off their white spreads.

Wanda came in and crossed the room to close the blinds.

"Don't," Charlotte ordered. "We want to bask." She laid back and closed her eyes, lifting her face to the blazing light.

Wanda turned, her eyes wide.

"To just lie here and breathe it in," Veronica assured her. The sun, a relentless spotlight, penetrated her elation. *All of this started with you.* She closed her eyes, shaking it off and fell in with Charlotte's exultation.

"Something good happen? I noticed there is no guard at the door."

"Ah." Charlotte stretched. "Yes, it seems we are no longer dangerous felons."

"Or flight risks," Veronica added.

They all laughed.

"Well, just let me know if you change your minds. That sun is right in your eyes." She proceeded with her morning routine, taking their blood pressure and temperature. "You're looking good, both of you." She dropped the thermometer back onto the cart. "What was it, if you don't mind my asking?"

"The tide has turned. The sea is running the other way," Charlotte murmured.

"That's all we can say, really," Veronica explained. "But we've gone from being perpetrators to victims."

"Really? Oh, the staff will be happy. That guard was confusing them."

"You mean we don't look like dangers to society?" Charlotte asked.

Wanda laughed. "Something like that." She took the pillow from behind Charlotte's head, smacked it to life and replaced it. "I'll tell them they can talk again."

"Talk about what? What dark secrets were they hiding?" Veronica lifted her head so Wanda could give her pillow like treatment.

"Who knows, but they all complained they felt gagged."

"Amazing isn't it, what a uniform will do to the atmosphere." Charlotte pressed the button to raise the head of her bed. "By the way, where's breakfast?"

Wanda grinned. "Soon."

The rattle of trays filled the hallway not long after the nurse left, and the smell of coffee replaced the antiseptic smell of the ward, however briefly. Even lukewarm oatmeal couldn't dampen their spirits.

They engaged in physical therapy with an energy that bewildered the therapist.

"Life's a state of mind." Charlotte grinned at her, repeating the therapist's favorite aphorism.

"Amen," Veronica added. Her sense of being the root of the whole mess faded a little, replaced by Charlotte's exuberance and a faint, newly formed sense of entitlement. Maybe she did deserve this moment of redemption.

"You sound better today," Charlotte remarked after the therapist had left. "Is it real?"

Veronica laughed. "Some of the time. You're infectious."

"Good. But don't buy into your son's paranoia."

"Simon's paranoia. David breathed it in, an emotional carbon monoxide. But I can't help wondering what I could have done differently, back when Laura and David were ten and thirteen. When Simon began to change—started resenting me."

"It frightened you. I remember. Like standing on the brink of a gaping hole where you thought there was solid ground."

"And made me angry, too. Don't sugarcoat it, Lotti. I ran from it. Went to a conference I hadn't really planned on attending. I remember standing on a cliff above the sea—La Jolla, I think it was, feeling the lift of the air, the freedom."

Charlotte flipped a hand. "So who doesn't feel that sometimes, in the best of marriages? You don't think I felt that when my only freedom was driving from some nerve-racking client to an invalid's bedside?"

"All right, all right. But David and Laura must have been frightened, too, by the change. Simon became unpredictable. And I left them with him." Veronica drove the words out. She would unearth the worst or die trying.

"Mm. You did not. He took them. That's very different." Charlotte's tone expressed the depth of her distaste. "Stop thinking your way into a hole."

They were silent for a while, then Charlotte spoke again. "You know, there was a time when I thought—when it seemed possible—that Ellie's illness ... the shock of her diagnosis ... set off Henry's Parkinson's. And that I could have done something ... said something ... to help. I even asked the doctor about it. He told me not to obsess about things beyond my control."

"Did that help?"

"Some. At least it made me admit some things *are* beyond my control."

Veronica smiled. "A needed lesson."

"Then Ellie asked me if she made Daddy sick." Charlotte's voice broke. "It took my breath away. I couldn't do anything but pick her up and hug her and tell her never to think such thoughts."

Veronica looked over and saw tears running from beneath the lids of Charlotte's closed eyes.

"Which is truly a stupid thing to tell anyone," Charlotte resumed after a minute. "At that moment I really wanted a God to blame it all on. But

I just couldn't conjure Him up. So I collected the scattered pieces of myself and told her that none of us has the power to make such things happen, or unhappen. We can only take care of each other." Charlotte reached for the box of tissues on the bedside table.

Veronica picked up the out-of-reach box and tossed it onto her friend's chest.

"Thanks." Charlotte put a tissue to her eyes. After a long time, she spoke again. "Then I realized what I'd said was true. Something shifted in my core. I wasn't tormented anymore by what I'd done or not done to make it all happen. And the anger died—that helpless rage. I could just take care of them. It was all right."

Charlotte's words sank in like an answer long sought. "Yes," Veronica breathed, "that's what was wrong. I couldn't take care of their pain. Laura's and David's. At the breakup. They wouldn't let me get close."

"And it's still wrong. I think that must be the sort of frustration that never dies. There's no closure." Charlotte's voice was soft with understanding.

"And for them? No answers. No wonder their grief turned rancid."

Doctor's rounds interrupted their conversation, and for the rest of the morning, the renewed chatter of attendants dissolved the weight of the past into the air. Neither was reluctant to let their mood lighten or their attention be absorbed by lunch and the afternoon soaps.

It wasn't until after dinner that the interlude was brought to a halt.

Laura and Ted appeared at the door.

Veronica caught her breath then bit her lip at her daughter's pallor. The shiny patina of politeness was gone. "Hello."

"Hello." Laura came half-way across the room and then stopped, as though her motor had failed.

Ted raised his hand in greeting but said nothing.

"I didn't … I'm sorry about ..." Laura took a breath and started again. "Ted says it was Luke who … I didn't see how …"

"I know that, Laura."

The tension went out of her daughter.

"I didn't … I couldn't imagine one of our kids doing that stuff, Mother. But Ted says it's true. Skipper told the police, and Ted was there. He heard it."

Veronica nodded. "Luke thought hating us was a good thing."

Laura bit her lip. "That isn't what we teach, Mother. Believe me." Her voice bordered on a whine. She stopped, took a breath, and straightened. "But I've come to apologize." She turned to Charlotte. "And to you, too. I'm sorry. He almost killed you, and I ..." She broke off and shook her head. "I don't know what else to say. It was wrong. That's all. And Ted says we were a part of it ..." The words faded off into misery.

Veronica held out her arms. "Come here."

And her daughter came, burrowed her head in her mother's breast, and then burst into tears. Veronica stroked the dark hair and said nothing.

Ted, hands in pockets, stared at the floor, separating himself from the scene.

"Thank you, Ted. You're a good man," Charlotte whispered.

He raised his head and smiled.

Laura stood up and took the tissue Charlotte offered.

Then Veronica caught her hands before she could back away. "Look at me."

Laura looked, then bit her lip again as fresh tears threatened.

"I love you, Laura. And you need to let me love you."

Laura frowned.

"You and your brother have carried your anger—your father's anger—far too long. It has infected everyone you and David touched. Luke thought he was carrying out the vengeance of God ..."

"We didn't mean that!"

"I know. But you couldn't know how Luke had been twisted by his own unhappy life or what would get mixed with your words to produce ..." She gave a wave.

Ted stepped forward and laid his hands on Laura's shoulders. "Your mother forgives you, Laura. But she says you need to face it square. And we'll make it right. We'll talk to Colin."

"And it wouldn't hurt to tell this story to Reverend Starkweather, also." Charlotte added. "He needs to know the effect of his sermons about who God loves—and hates."

"Oh, he wouldn't condone ..."

"He shares the blame." Charlotte interrupted. "And there are youngsters in his flock—in your group, in fact—who are homosexual and think God hates them. You need to fix that."

Laura turned and buried her face in Ted's jacket. He put his hands on her shoulders and pushed her back until he could look down into her face. "We'll do that—fix it. Right?"

She stared at him without answering for a long minute then turned around to her mother. "I don't know. I have to say this. You have to know ... Dad called us into his study and his face ... it was as though he was going to tell us you were dead." She broke off and rubbed her hands over her face. "I stopped breathing I was so scared. Then he said. 'I have to tell you. Your mother is a lesbian.'" The last word came out on a rising pitch, and she cut it off. "Like he'd just said you were a murderer or something ... I don't know, but I can't get my mind beyond it ... the shock. I didn't even know that the word meant!" She wrapped her arms around herself. "David told me ... told me it meant pervert ... a woman who has sex with women ... and I didn't ... I barely knew what that meant except it was awful ..." Laura twisted around and went to the window where she clutched the sill.

The clock ticked. No one spoke.

"I can't get past it, Mother. I've tried, but ..." She flung her hands up.

"Well, I don't think Reverend Starkweather's sermons helped," Veronica tried to keep the anger out of her voice and failed.

"I suppose not, but ... I need to know, Mother, whether you are ... or not."

"No, you don't, Laura. You need to know it was your father's aversion you've been breathing in. Your father's anger at me. And you need to know God loves—loved—Luke as much as he loves you, and that it was up to us to help that boy and others like him—and we all failed because we caught the nasty bug called hatred from others—your father and Reverend Starkweather."

Laura stared at her mother.

"And when you know that, I'll tell you, because then it won't make any difference."

Laura turned her bewildered face to her husband, as though for clarification. He smiled. "It's time to go."

"No." Laura turned to Charlotte for the first time. "I've been rude. I'm sorry for that, even if ..." Words failed her, "... anyway," she finished lamely

"Come here," Veronica breathed in gratitude.

With the automatic response of an obedient child, Laura came.

Veronica took her in her arms. "I love you. That's all that matters. The rest is just the nonsense you have to get past to learn that."

With what sounded like a mix of anger and tears, Laura grasped her mother for a long moment before pulling away. "Goodbye ... for now."

A long silence filled the room after the pair's departure. "Thank God." Charlotte breathed.

Veronica didn't answer. Silence returned. "Amen," she said finally. "Do you think she'll get through it?"

"Yes. You broke through to that shock she's never dealt with."

"Damn him."

"Indeed. But maybe, with Laura changed you'll even get to the last step—forgiving Simon."

"Not today."

Chapter 28

"Charlotte's coming home today," Veronica told Molly, who wagged her tail in response. Just saying it was enough to make the loneliness of the last month roll from her shoulders. "See?" she pointed to the porch where the racing January clouds parted, splashing the room with sunlight.

Mortimer jumped up, expecting a run in the woods or some other treat.

"Later," she told him. "First, we make sure everything is ready." She continued her chatter as she moved around. Talking with Yin Yang and the dogs had kept the towering cedars from closing over the little clearing and maintained the illusion of company.

She checked the hospital bed on the sun-porch and relived her amazement at its arrival—a gift from the congregation of Grace Bible Church. "Down," she told Morty, who had jumped up on it. "Not yours. Just stand still for a moment, and let it sink in."

Veronica smoothed Charlotte's quilt and plumped the pillow, driving away the ever-present question. Would this bed be Charlotte's permanent home? Charlotte, of course, swore not, and that determination would have to do. She turned to the new gas-log stove which she prayed would keep the glassed-in room warm. When she flicked it on, both dogs immediately joined Yin Yang in its glow.

She gave them each a rub, then walked to the other end of the porch and touched the folio on harassment that lay ready for the publisher. She leafed through the images whose impact was already fading and smiled at the memory of evenings spent with Ed Stein, writing the text. For other books, she'd always written the text herself, but Ed, as it turned out, had an unrealized love of photography, and words flowed as he ran through the pictures. Words she knew instantly she had to capture. She flipped quickly past the picture Ed had taken of their wrecked car—that one she could not yet study with dispassion—and stopped for a long while on the concluding images. On the left, Luke's gravestone and the lily she had placed on the grass before it. On the right, the same image, now with four lilies from unknown mourners. "From each of us who failed you," she murmured, reading the caption.

She closed the book and moved on, checking the equipment from the local pharmacy—bedside table, portable potty, walker—then went to the kitchen, which she had stocked with tortillas, enchilada sauce, jalapenos, and salsa for their reunion feast. The room was beginning to smell of the slow-cooking beef she'd put in the oven an hour ago. Molly nudged her leg, and she looked down at four large brown eyes. "Not yet. But it will be good, I promise you."

In the living room, she gazed at the new recliner, designed to give the occupant a boost when rising. "Charlotte's going to hate that," she confided to the dogs. "It's exactly the sort of rig she sneers at." She picked up an afghan and laid it across the arm. "There. That completes the picture, don't you think?" They wagged their tails.

Above the chair, on the bookcase that flanked the fireplace, sat a father-daughter picture of Henry and Ellie McAllister. They had always sat there, on the left, emphasizing the absence of pictures on the right. Veronica had made an effort to fix that one long afternoon, while the dogs and cat slept and the trees dripped. Next to the fireplace was now a picture of her sister, Dorothy, accompanied by a get-well card. Veronica had blinked in amazement when Laura brought it to her. "She doesn't think she had anything to do with it, Mom. She doesn't remember any of the things she said. She just flicks her hand and tells me to stop brooding about the past."

"Then why this?" Veronica had asked, fingering the card.

Laura had smiled, an imp of a smile Veronica remembered well from the toddler she'd loved. "I quote: 'I only tried to do what was right, you know. I never wished her any harm.' I think the card puts it right with herself."

"I'm sure that's it." And she'd set the card on the mantle next to a picture of Dorothy Veronica had taken after her sister had won a place on the high school honor roll. The good-girl smirk was perfect.